THE SOUTH

MY YEAR OF CASUAL ACQUAINTANCES

A Novel

Ruth F. Stevens

Black Rose Writing | Texas

The author grants the final approval for this literary material.

First printing

ISBN: 978-1-68513-484-6
LIBRARY OF CONGRESS CONTROL NUMBER: 2024935854
PUBLISHED BY BLACK ROSE WRITING
www.blackrosewriting.com

Printed in the United States of America
Suggested Retail Price (SRP) $23.95

My Year of Casual Acquaintances is printed in Book Antiqua

*As a planet-friendly publisher, Black Rose Writing does its best to eliminate unnecessary waste to reduce paper usage and energy costs, while never compromising the reading experience. As a result, the final word count vs. page count may not meet common expectations.

Cover art by Jamie Ponchak

For my husband, David . . .
and all those folks at the gym

PRAISE FOR
MY YEAR OF CASUAL ACQUAINTANCES

"*My Year of Casual Acquaintances* is a fun, entertaining novel that doesn't disappoint. Stevens has created multiple characters that are all well drawn, realistic and a delight to get to know. From the very beginning of the story, I fell in love with the protagonist, Margaret, who was impossible not to root for. Her struggles are reminiscent of many women in midlife, many women I know. She has flaws and makes mistakes but does her best to learn from them, and the reader gets to go along for the ride. I read the book quickly, as I needed to know how Margaret's life would turn out. There's also a love story that's beautifully developed and expertly woven into the plot. I can't imagine there's anyone who wouldn't enjoy this novel as much as I did. I can't wait to read the sequel."
–Leslie A. Rasmussen, award-winning author of *After Happily Ever After* and *The Stories We Cannot Tell*

"Ruth F. Stevens chronicles a woman's messy yet heartwarming journey to find the way out of her old life and into something new. What should she keep? What needs repair? Can she be brave enough to open her heart again? Stevens writes with humor, compassion, and wisdom about how to move past loss and the power of meaningful connections along the way."
–Joani Elliott, WFWA Star Award-winning author of *The Audacity of Sara Grayson*

"I found myself tearing through this book because the writing is so strong, the characters so relatable, and the prose very often so funny. And one of the main messages is a favorite of mine: When it comes to relationships, timing is everything. An entertaining read for anyone who's had to start over."
–S.M. Stevens, author of *Beautiful and Terrible Things*

"Stevens crafts an endearing cast of characters that draw you in, tug at your heart and leave you wanting more. With a witty, touching story that any woman can relate to on some level, Stevens entertains you while serving you some of life's hard truths, pure joys, and ultimately a journey of healing, forgiveness, and the message it's never too late to start again."
–Andrea Couture, author of *Embracing What Remains*

"An absorbing and satisfying read that had me hooked right from the prologue. Stevens' prose is taut and witty, and her characters are so well drawn they feel utterly genuine. Lively, romantic, and often heart-wrenching, *Casual Acquaintances* is jam-packed with laugh-out-loud passages followed by moments of true tenderness."
–Erica Karlin, co-author of *The Sipping Sisterhood Series* and contributor to *Shakespeare & Company, Paris*

"Ever wonder what it'd be like to start over in a new life? Recently divorced, Margaret is a middle-aged woman who is attempting just that. She's smart, sensitive, and not afraid to try new things. From yoga to hip-hop, she takes on new gym classes with aplomb. She has a slightly harder time trying to find new friends, deal with her son, and figure out if she's ready for new love. *My Year of Casual Acquaintances* is a feel-good book with a main character worth rooting for. I love how this book illustrates a second chance at life. We need more stories like this! The characters are so real, you'll feel like you go to the gym with them. It's the type of book you look forward to reading, and I honestly was sad when it ended."
–Julee Balko, author of *The Me List*

"I laughed... I cried. This story will resonate with anyone who has imagined a do-over or has had to push the restart button on life. The main character, Mar, is smart and insightful. The friends and acquaintances who travel in and out of Mar's life are an endearing and eclectic group. I loved every storyline. Stevens has created an interwoven plot that comes full circle and lands with a most satisfying ending."
–Julie Mayerson Brown, author of the *Clearwater Series*

"Ruth F. Stevens has written a coming-of-age novel about a woman in middle-age. In *My Year of Casual Acquaintances,* we keep intimate company with Mar, forced by divorce to come out of her complacent shell. Skillfully told from Mar's point of view, we laugh out loud at the comic scenes (goat yoga!) but also feel her vulnerability as with each encounter with a new acquaintance, she's slowly but surely propelled into deeper waters with family and friends.
–Amy Gordon, award-winning author and poet

"When a woman disappointed with her life sets out to construct a new self, we accompany her on an absorbing year-long journey to discover the person she's meant to be."
–Marsha Jacobson, author of *The Wrong Calamity*

MY YEAR OF CASUAL ACQUAINTANCES

PROLOGUE

I pull out into the intersection as soon as the traffic light turns green, but I don't see the black SUV bearing down on me until it's too late. The mammoth vehicle smashes into the driver's side of my little Prius, propelling my car across the wide road in what feels like slow motion.

They say your whole life flashes before you when you're facing the possibility of death. But for me, it isn't my full history on replay, it's only my *reinvented* life – the one that began eight months ago. The faces of all the new people who've come and gone in this short time flash by in rapid sequence, their expressions solemn and detached. *Whitney. Judith. Sunny. Nic. Connor. Cheryl. Audrey. Jax. Charlie.*

Charlie. Charlie. Charlie.

The car stops spinning. My knees knock against each other with violent force. My back spasms. I groan and survey the damage around me. The windshield has disintegrated into a thousand tiny green pebbles that occupy my lap, the front seat, the floor, the pavement. Why didn't the airbag deploy? You count on something – or someone – to protect you, but then when you need it most, it's not there. Just like the people who paraded through my consciousness at the moment of impact.

I can't worry about them now. All I can do is contemplate the wreck that is my car, the wreck that is my life.

EIGHT MONTHS EARLIER
PART ONE: JANUARY
WHITNEY

1.

It's not yet five o'clock when the Lyft driver drops me off at the waterfront Manhattan Beach bar where I'm scheduled to meet Whitney for happy hour. Though I'm a few minutes early, she is already standing at the entrance awaiting my arrival. Upon spotting me in the growing dimness of the mild California January evening, she grins and waves one arm wildly. Her eager body language might be better suited to someone reuniting with a twin separated at birth.

Whitney and I are not long-lost relatives - in fact, we're not even friends, having known each other for a grand total of two days. She is an acquaintance from my new gym, which is a convenient ten-minute walk from the ocean view apartment I leased for the year in King Harbor, in Los Angeles's South Bay area. I know little about this woman except that she is blond and pretty, with shiny white teeth that glisten within the arc of a perpetual scarlet smile. Whitney's demeanor is carefree, cheery, undemanding. She doesn't carry much baggage or wield much intellectual heft. In short, she is exactly the kind of person I want to associate with as I embark on my new life, in the first month of my first year of full—if involuntary— independence.

"Mar," Whitney says, still beckoning as if desperate to capture my attention, though I am now three feet away. She leans in and gives me a brief hug, then steps back to admire my aqua-blue leggings, plush ankle boots, and dove-gray cashmere sweater. "You clean up nicely," she tells me with a wink. This is something gym rats like to say when they meet any place outside of the gym. I'm pleased she's noticed my spiffed-up wardrobe.

"So do you," I say, a reciprocal compliment being the expected response. Two weeks into my membership at Seaside Fitness, and I've nailed the etiquette.

We go inside and grab a high table near the bar. A glass of California chard for me, a dirty martini for Whitney. We clink our icy glasses in a merry toast as I stifle the impulse to complain that my chardonnay has arrived overchilled. I don't want to spoil this lovely moment of camaraderie with my newfound acquaintance. I check my cellphone before tucking it inside my purse, but not before Whitney glimpses the screenshot of a towheaded toddler.

"Who's that little cutie?" she asks.

"My grandson Benny."

Her jaw drops. "Get *out.* How can you have a grandson? We're, like, the same age, right?"

"Not unless you're fifty," I say, a hint of braggadocio in my voice. On the first week of January, I celebrated my fiftieth birthday quietly and alone by preference. People always think I'm at least ten years younger than my age. It's in the genes. "Our family is like Dick Clark's. We all look insanely youthful for decades, then we drop dead."

She gives me a blank stare. "Who's Dick Clark?"

Seriously? I know this woman is many years younger than me, but isn't Clark still revered as an icon of American pop culture? I give her the benefit of the doubt and briefly explain *American Bandstand.* Whitney pretends to listen, but I can tell she's still hung up on the grandma revelation. Is my new buddy already backing off from our relationship out of misplaced ageism?

But I've misread the situation. "Wow, you look amazing," she says. "You remind me of someone."

"A famous actress?" I ask hopefully.

She studies my face. "No, I don't think so. It's someone else. So . . . where did you find the fountain of youth? I'm thirty-five, and I'd like to know how I can look as good as you in fifteen years."

Ah. She is trolling for beauty secrets. I wish I could offer some pearls of wisdom on personal maintenance, like "get a lot of sleep and drink plenty of water." But the truth is, I'm not much of a sleeper and I drink more wine than water. I assure her it's a mix of favorable genetics and dumb luck.

"So . . . are you married?" Whitney asks.

"Divorced. But it's all good. No hard feelings between Henry and me."

"Oh, cool. I'm not married either, never have been. Maybe someday, but I don't know . . . I like having fun, fun, fun, not being tied down to anything, you know?"

Oh, I know. At least, I'm trying to know. Fun, fun, fun, with no commitments—that's what I want my life to be now.

"So . . . how long were you married to . . . what's his name again?"

"Henry. Like Henry Kissinger."

Her eyes glaze over in another blank stare. Not to be unkind, but last week they had a question about Kissinger on an episode of teen *Jeopardy!* and the high school kids got it right. Has this woman been exposed to nothing but the inside of a martini glass? I push this uncharitable thought from my mind, along with my mild irritation over the way she begins every other sentence with an elongated "so . . ."

"Let's not talk about Henry and me. It's a boring story." What I don't tell her is that Henry and I were married for twenty-eight years. There are indeed hard feelings, at least on my side. And divorce is seldom boring.

Over the first round of drinks, we discuss a variety of safe if vacuous topics: hair, clothes, restaurants. Then she tells me about her favorite exercise classes, which I find instructional, being a newbie to the gym. Whitney reps a line of women's sportswear and athletic apparel, which she sells through trunk shows at boutique hotels and health clubs.

"I'm editor of an engineering publication based in New York, but they let me work from my home," I say.

She shows little interest in this. That's fine. I'm not into talking about my life nowadays.

The server cruises by with a "last call" announcement, urging us to capitalize on the rock-bottom happy hour prices by placing our food and drink orders in the next five minutes. After minimal discussion, Whitney and I agree to share the Margherita pizza and a side of roasted Brussels sprouts with our next round of drinks. This time I switch to a glass of Malbec that is warm to the touch as if the wineglass had been yanked from a steaming industrial dishwasher. To my mind, any restaurant that serves its white wines too cold and its reds too warm might as well hang out a sign that says, *Mediocrity rules here,* or maybe even, *we don't know what the fuck we're doing, but we do it with a smile.* Because the service, I have to concede, is indefatigably cheerful, even by Southern California beach restaurant standards.

"So . . . you live in King Harbor?" Whitney asks, struggling to get her lips around her first slice of pizza, which is topped with stringy browned cheese that sticks to the plate.

I stab my fork into a Brussels sprout and pop it into my mouth, biting down with caution. It is smothered in an overaggressive basting sauce, a sticky blend of balsamic and maple syrup. Bacon bits and chopped candied nuts have been tossed into the mix. Somewhere I believe there is a roasted vegetable in this sorry mess, but I can't taste it.

"Yes, I'm renting a little apartment," I say to Whitney. "They call it a two-bedroom, but the rooms are all tiny. Still, it's a nice building, and the views are great. It has everything I need." Everything and *more,* I reflect. Every nook and cranny of the place is piled with unpacked boxes of possessions I dragged over from my sprawling suburban house up on Peninsula Hill, a mere four miles from here. Why I saved all that stuff, I can't imagine.

I don't say this, but the best thing about my new apartment is that I can't picture Henry there. When I rattled around alone in our big family home for ten months after he left, I would descend to the kitchen every morning half expecting to find him downing a mug of black coffee like he used to do before heading to the office. Or I'd walk into the den we had repurposed into a man cave for Henry five years ago – I guess I'd have to call it a *manless* cave now – and be surprised, all over again, that the seventy-inch wall-mounted TV was all mine to watch. Goodbye, golf and football. Hello, cable news networks and History Channel.

"You're so lucky to have a place on the water," Whitney says, and I know it's true. "All I can afford is a little studio about three miles inland. It's so hot there in the summer."

"At least you can escape to the club when you need an ocean breeze," I point out. Seaside Fitness, as the name implies, is right on the waterfront. Though the floors are scratched from years of use, the cardio machines are dated, and the workout spaces cramped, you can't beat the views or the sensation of well-being that results from those wonderful negative ions generated by the constant motion of the sea.

"I love Seaside Fitness," Whitney says, smiling. "It's so friendly."

"Until this year, I belonged to a gym on Peninsula Hill." I tell her the name of my previous health club, but she shakes her head. "It's that big uber-modern building north of the mall," I explain. "The facility is beautiful and everything is state of the art, but it's not a friendly place. I didn't know how much I disliked it until I moved down off the hill and resigned to join Seaside."

Whitney looks pleased by this revelation, as though I have just signed up for her team. "Are you coming to the power sculpt class tomorrow? Ten-thirty?" she asks.

"I haven't been to that class."

"You should totally try it. Donna's the instructor. She's the best."

I nod and tell her I'll be there.

"And when the weather's nice, bring your grandson to swim. The kiddie pool is great for the young ones," she says.

Another thing I don't say is that I see little of Benny and his parents – my son, Michael, and my daughter-in-law, Heather. I miss them, especially the little guy. But I find it too uncomfortable to be around them knowing they're all in cahoots with Henry and . . . with *her*. Alice.

Alice, the woman Henry left me for. She's been employed at his company for a couple of years now, in an inside sales position. Although Henry has suggested it might be a good idea for the two of us to meet – *"For what possible reason?"* is my answer – I've never laid eyes on her. All I know about Alice is the way she speaks.

When I called the office one day around six months ago to check with Henry on a missing bill payment, she answered the phone in a soft, melodious voice resembling that of a trained singer or professional announcer. "Alice Hanley. How can I help you?" she crooned, rather than spoke, into the phone.

How should I respond, I wondered at the time. Perhaps I should answer, "This is Margaret, Henry's ex. You can best help me by disintegrating into thin air, since your non-existence might allow me to reclaim my former life." Not wanting to say this, I hung up.

I imagine Alice Hanley to be in her thirties, dishy and self-confident, a blonde or a redhead. But this is all conjecture. I have dug in my heels and refused to meet this Alice or learn anything about the mystery woman with whom my ex-husband has cohabited for almost a year. Even our friends have become *their* friends - Henry and Alice's. This was a bitter lesson learned during those first weeks of the separation, when I tried to socialize with our old pals and discovered that couples want to be friends with other couples, not with an abandoned wife. I more or less went into hiding at that point until finally emerging from my shell to make the short but significant move down to King Harbor.

Whitney interrupts my thoughts. "Your grandson. I was saying you should bring him to the kiddie pool."

"Great idea. Benny would love that." I force a smile.

• • •

I enjoyed my two hours of baggage-free banter with Whitney, or that's what I tell myself. It was the perfect prelude to an evening of hard work. I'm back at my apartment before seven-thirty when I settle down with a glass of wine in my little office, which is occupied by a workstation and a futon stacked with file folders I haven't gotten around to organizing. I'm ready to dive into tonight's assignments, reviewing staff-written articles and columns for the next issue of *Powder World,* the magazine I edit.

In common industries from food to pharmaceutical, countless powdered substances must be mixed, blended, conveyed, captured, packaged, stored, and manufactured into final form. It is the job of *Powder World* magazine to tell readers how to approach these daunting tasks with efficiency and accuracy. Granted, the average citizen doesn't give a rat's ass about any of this. But for our audience of engineers, plant managers, and equipment suppliers, these are life and death topics.

I take a sip of chardonnay and smack my lips. Unlike the happy hour wine, this one is chilled to the perfect temperature, and the taste on my palate is more crisp than creamy. My editorial work takes on a pleasant aura when it's fueled by a steady flow of good quality vino. I think I average around five times the recommended consumption limit for a woman my age – that is, if you listen to the so-called health experts. Having learned a thing or two about engineering during my editing career, I've also become adept at reverse engineering. I begin at the end – stating a premise, then selecting the facts that support my foregone conclusion. For example . . . alcohol is good for me. Wine reduces my anxiety, improves my verbal skills, sharpens my editing, curbs my appetite, facilitates my sleep, and even raises my good cholesterol.

Perhaps there is something hard-wired into my genes that gives me such a high—no pun intended—tolerance to alcohol while producing such sanguine physical and mental results. Perhaps I'm burning off the booze with my two or three hours of daily exercise. But drinking agrees with me. Besides, I confine my consumption to topnotch products from the best-regarded California vintners. There's no question it is healthier for me to imbibe than not to. The cherry-picked facts are indisputable.

I scroll through my inbox. The first message is from my boss, Robert Carlson. This afternoon, I forwarded him an article submitted by one of our big advertisers, Camfield Corporation. In my accompanying email, I wrote:

Sorry to report, Camfield is playing fast and loose with the editorial guidelines. They've sprinkled some blatant sales messages through the copy. How do you want to handle?

I skim through Robert's reply.

Let's discuss. Working late tonight. You can call my cell up until 11 P.M. Eastern.

I double-check the time before placing the call.

"Margaret, hi."

I bristle a little at his greeting. "Hello, Robert."

"About the article . . . I only took a quick glance. Is it fixable from your end?"

"Yes. If I delete the product plugs and the other self-serving stuff, it will be fine," I say. "Camfield won't like it though. I wanted you in the loop before I piss off a big advertiser."

"Understood. Make the changes, send it back to them with your usual reminder about our strict editorial rules, and copy me."

"Do you want to review the changes first?"

"Nah. I know you'll get it right. You can fudge in the email and tell them I've already approved the revisions. If they come whining to me, I've got your back."

"Sounds good."

"All right, then. G'night, Margaret."

"Uh—remember what we discussed? It's 'Mar' now." I'd told him weeks ago that I wanted to be called "Mar" going forward.

"But why?" he asked when I first made the request.

"Margaret sounds too much like an old schoolmarm. I'm going for a younger, hipper vibe," I said.

The truth is, I changed my name along with everything else in my life to escape the painful reality of Henry's defection. But for whatever reason, Robert has trouble remembering to use the new name. I'm not sure why this bothers me so much. "I'll try to be better about calling you that, I promise," he says. "But it's not easy to change after all these years."

You can say that again.

As I sip my chardonnay, admiring the subtle aromas of citrus and pear, I tackle the Camfield article first, making the agreed-upon edits. My next assignment is a piece called "Doctor Dave's Dust Diagnostics." The author, David Silverman, has a Ph.D. in engineering and writes this popular alliterative monthly column in which he troubleshoots readers' questions. As usual, Doctor Dave's answers are spot-on from a technical standpoint but are delivered in execrable prose. Don't they teach the basics of grammar in engineering school? He either writes in endless run-on sentences or short, choppy ones that aren't sentences at all, littered with misspellings that clog the path to comprehension, the way flotsam and jetsam might block a riverboat's course down a narrow canal. Fortunately, I learned years ago how to translate "Doctor-Dave-speak," so the editing proceeds without a hitch. Within forty-five minutes, I've whipped an unintelligible draft into a succinct, informative Q&A column that is sure to snag a high readership score as always.

I unwrap a one-ounce portion of dark chocolate to munch on as I settle back to work, this time to review an article written by my young associate editor. This girl knows her stuff. I make a handful of minor edits and compose an email to compliment her on the work. After such a productive evening, I think I've earned a final glass of wine to enjoy while I catch the evening news. I'll give these articles another read-through in the morning before sending them off. As I refill my wine glass and retire to the living room, I reflect on how work is the only part of my life that's going well right now. I'm fortunate to have Robert as a boss. He's flexible, he's supportive, and he even allows me to moonlight, as long as my freelance clients don't represent a conflict with *Powder World*. My one quarrel with him these days is his failure to use my preferred name. He can't bring himself to embrace the new "Mar."

I wonder if anyone anywhere will ever embrace the new Mar.

But why would I even want that? The people I used to hold close to me have done nothing but disappoint. Much better, much safer, to keep others at arm's length, free of the yoke of any suffocating connections.

2.

At ten-thirty the next morning, I am in the main fitness studio, where the power sculpt class with Donna gets off to an unpromising start. After a brief warmup, she directs us to do a hundred lunges and a hundred pushups right out of the gate – not all at once, thank you very much, but in alternating sets of twenty-five reps each, which is distasteful enough.

"Who wants to do a hundred of anything?" I grumble *sotto voce* to Whitney. My chest and quads will be screaming tomorrow.

"Oh, don't worry. It gets better after this," she reassures me, flashing me her signature crimson smile. Whitney doesn't skimp on the cosmetics, even at the gym. I marvel at her ability to remain fresh no matter how long she works out, her heavy layer of black eyeliner and mascara still intact. If I tried to duplicate that look, in twenty minutes I'd resemble some sad-ass clown with dripping dark rings around both eyes, the sort of clown you see in those cheesy paintings.

Is Henry's beloved Alice a whiz with a makeup brush? No doubt her skills rival Whitney's.

After the pushup-lunge circuit consumes the longest twelve minutes of my life, we continue to alternate between upper and lower body drills. There's one contortionist move where we rotate back and forth into a side plank position while flinging our upper legs into the air and aiming our feet about thirty degrees backward.

"Am I doing this right?" I ask Whitney, squinting hard from the exertion. She somehow manages to shrug even as she executes the moving side planks with consummate skill.

"Okay, everyone, grab two sets of dumbbells for our weightlifting," says Donna. "We'll do two different exercises for each of the remaining muscle groups: biceps, triceps, shoulders, back."

We tackle the bicep curls first, and my forearms ache with the strain as I maneuver the twelve-pound dumbbells up and down. Maybe I should have used eight-pounders instead. We heft our weights while seated on big inflatable balls. "Ladies, you won't believe how well the balance ball works your core. And the best part is, you can't even feel it," says Donna.

"I'm feeling it plenty," I inform Whitney in my same kvetchy voice. By the time we reach the final cooldown and stretch, the room has grown warm and malodorous. Strands of sweaty hair cling to my forehead and to the hot, sticky blue mat on which I stretch my legs. I wrinkle my nose at Whitney, who gives me a puzzled frown that says she doesn't understand my latest complaint.

As the instructor turns off the music, she says, "If you liked the class, my name is Donna. If you didn't like it, my name is Debbie."

A few scattered chuckles follow this announcement, but nobody is busting a gut over Donna's tired old joke. As we exit the studio together, I groan and tell Whitney, "They used the same line at my last gym. There must be some book of *Feeble Fitness Jokes* where all the instructors get their material."

Whitney looks more distracted than amused. She says, "I still can't figure out who you remind me of. It's driving me crazy. I guess it'll come to me."

Afterward, I'm in the locker room chatting it up with a bunch of the girls. Women, to be more accurate – the age range this morning is twenty to eighty. It strikes me I am dead middle in that range.

I'm right in the middle in other ways as well. Appraising myself in the floor-length mirror, I note that I'm neither thin nor fat, short nor tall, dark nor fair. My body is still trim, my skin unwrinkled, and I wear my pink and purple leggings and matching sports bra well. My light brown hair falls in soft curls around my unlined face – at least it does when I'm not perspiring this much. How long will I keep looking forever young, a female Dorian Gray? For quite some time, if my seventy-seven-year-old mum is any indication.

Whitney is there, along with a petite blonde named Jill, and an older woman whom they call "Paulette" or "Paulie." I don't know anyone's last name, not even Whitney's. When she typed her contact info into my cellphone earlier this week, she listed her name as "Whitney Gym." As for the other women in the locker area, since I don't have a clue about even their first names, I invent little descriptive phrases to remember them by. My favorite is Amazon Lady, an impossibly tall woman with strawberry blond hair and a luscious body – golden-skinned, flat-bellied, and perfectly proportioned. She often sits naked on one of the benches, all six feet of her sprawled in a relaxed pose for everyone to admire. She is so pleasant, I don't find her display of nudity to be boastful or exhibitionistic. It seems natural and lovely.

"Hey, how are you today?" she says with a welcoming smile. I can tell she doesn't know my name either, but she sounds as if she *cares* about how I am doing.

"I'm great. And you?"

"Wonderful. It's nice to see you."

A sense of warmth spreads through me, filling up the holes of deprivation. After months of isolation, this simple exchange of meaningless pleasantries is just the ticket.

"Has anyone eaten at that new Mexican restaurant over in the Village Shops?" asks Dame Donut. She has a peculiar ring of flab that surrounds her waist, giving her otherwise normal sixtyish body a misshapen appearance.

"The food is very upscale. It's being touted as the best new restaurant in the South Bay," says Tattoo Woman, who boasts serpentine etchings along her upper arms and shoulders.

"I didn't have dinner there, but they serve fabulous signature cocktails in the bar. Creative stuff," says Patch - given this secret name by me because of the patchy, thin layer of greasy dark hair interrupted by bald spots on her head. The poor woman must be suffering from a horrific scalp condition, but the name helps me to remember her. Will I ever be able to learn the real names of these women now that the nicknames have become indelibly burned into my brain?

I'm distracted from this conversation when I notice Whitney staring at the wall-mounted TV in the room's corner, a look of discomfiture on her face. The rest of us have our backs turned to the video screen, so I can't see what has caught her attention. Now Amazon Lady glances up at the TV, and I follow suit. The set is tuned to a local news program with the sound muted. Amazon Lady's usual beatific expression fades into a frown. "What's going on?" she says, then she stands and reaches up one long graceful arm to adjust the volume control on the set.

We learn that another shooting has occurred, this time at a shopping mall somewhere in the Midwest. The preliminary body count is three dead and six wounded - including the shooter, who has been apprehended and hauled off in a rescue truck to treat his shoulder wound.

"Oh God," says Amazon Lady.

"This is the third one in—what—a month?" Patch says.

Whitney's expression has gone from uncomfortable to horrified. She races off to the bathroom and slams the stall door shut. I follow her and stand outside the stall, waiting for her. "Are you okay?" I ask when she emerges.

"I—I feel a little queasy." Her lips form a smile, but when she glances at me, her eyes are wide with panic. She blinks hard and turns away as if blinded by headlights.

"Why don't we go out to the pool deck for some fresh air?" I say. She follows me outdoors to the club's harbor-view deck. I move two cushioned lounge chairs close together and gesture for her to sit down. She does so, tilting her head back, eyes closed.

"I'll be right back." I go inside and purchase a Coke for Whitney from a vending machine in the hallway. It seems incongruous for a gym to have a soda machine, though not as incongruous as the bowls of pretzels and chips they place in the lobby every afternoon. Maybe their strategy is to fatten up club members to stimulate increased use of the facilities, like a dentist passing out lollipops to young patients.

Whitney makes a face when I hand her the Coke can. "I know. I don't like soda either, but it will help settle your stomach," I say.

She clutches the can in two perfectly manicured hands and gives it a tentative taste, like a toddler drinking from a sippy cup.

"Whitney, what's wrong? You looked so shaken when we saw the news report on the shooting."

"It's awful. So horrible. How can people do these things?"

"I know."

"But you don't seem upset."

"To be honest . . . it happens so often now, I've grown kind of hardened to it." I shake my head and sigh. "At least this time, there are only a few fatalities. Nowadays, it takes twenty or thirty dead at minimum to have any major shock value."

"That's so unfeeling," she says.

"Oh gosh, I—I didn't mean to sound sarcastic. Of course, it's awful. Sad—really sad we've come to this."

Now she seems wary of me. "You were kind of sarcastic in power sculpt too."

Not only do I regret what I just said, I also wish I hadn't given her a hard time during the class I attended on her recommendation. I determine to make it up to her. "Sorry, I'm having a bad day myself. Listen, are you free tomorrow night? I thought we might have dinner at that new Mexican place. My treat."

Her face brightens a little. "That's nice of you. I—I guess we could do that. If my stomach trouble goes away."

Whitney takes another sip of Coke as I study her perfect fingernails. I picture Alice with those same high-gloss crimson nails, administering an expert neck massage to Henry as he sits in his executive office chair. Perhaps they were in mid-massage when I called months ago and she answered Henry's phone, cooing hello in that syrupy voice.

Whitney says, "So . . . Mar, I'm still not feeling great. I'm gonna go home." She stands up slowly and retreats into the building, then turns. "Thanks for the Coke."

In the locker room, the women are back to comparing notes on new local eateries. For them, like me, the shooting has already been relegated to the background. Antsy to return to my routine, I take my leave. The women all wave and wish me a nice day.

Late in the afternoon, before dusk sets in, I'll take my usual solitary walk along the esplanade by the beach - an hour-long break from my editorial duties. I take this daily walk not only to stretch my legs but also to clear my head, sorting through whatever personal issues are weighing on my mind at the time. I'll run into Dog Lady, a pretty, full-figured young woman I see almost every afternoon, and we'll exchange friendly greetings as I stoop to admire her Wheaten terrier. Then I'll swing by Whole Foods to pick up salad and a piece of grilled salmon from the food bar for my dinner. Aqua Girl, the young checker at the market - so named because her spectacles are rimmed with big, round, turquoise-colored frames - will comment on my daily take-out selections and note how she shares my disdain for cooking. Apart from that, I will have no more human contact until I return to the gym tomorrow.

And that's absolutely fine with me.

3.

The trendy new place in the Village Shops is inexplicably called The Kitchen – not La Cocina, the Spanish translation that would better suit a Mexican restaurant. The Kitchen does not accept reservations, and when I arrive, I discover that there is a long wait for tables. I hadn't expected this on a January weeknight. Surveying the dining room and adjacent bar, attractively furnished with big armchairs and banquettes upholstered in turquoise-and-beige Southwestern print fabrics, I conclude this is a much more upscale establishment than the touristy waterfront resto where Whitney and I met earlier in the week. This new place is aimed at the foodies and the hipsters who like to see and be seen.

Though I invited Whitney tonight, she takes over the role of host. Whatever was bothering her at the gym yesterday seems to be forgotten. She ushers me to a small table in the crowded bar, perusing the drinks menu and insisting we both order the signature cocktail of the week, cutely billed as a "Marvelita." It's a creative mix of high-end tequila, agave syrup, lime, blood orange liqueur, and three other foreign-sounding ingredients I've never heard of.

"I prefer to order wine," I say.

"Oh, but I don't want to drink alone."

"Wine is a drink."

Her lower lip juts out in pouty defiance.

The bar is filled with patrons imbibing either conventional salt-rimmed margaritas or the blood-orange-colored specialty version, all served up in oversized stemmed martini glasses. Not a wine drinker in sight. "Oh, what the hell," I say. "All right."

When the cocktails arrive, I take an exploratory sip. The Marvelita is sweet, but not in a cloying way. I taste the mingled flavors of fruit and tequila, something peppery, something flowery. As I continue to drink, now with greater enthusiasm, I realize I am not only thirsty but also ravenous. I glance around the tabletops for bowls of salsa and chips, but there is no sign anywhere of the Mexican restaurant staple. For once, lowbrow munchies would be a welcome addition to the table; I ate a small cup of yogurt this morning and have not had a bite since. I drink faster, figuring the fruit and sugar will provide at least a small measure of nutritional value to tide me over until dinnertime. I suck greedily on the slender blood orange wedge that garnishes my drink, although I doubt it supplies more than six calories.

Whitney orders a second round. "Been to any good movies lately?" she asks, and then she sings the praises of the new chick flick showing at the Regal. "It's about four twentysomething women who book themselves into a dude ranch on accident."

"How do you go to a dude ranch *by* accident?" The editor in me can't resist correcting Whitney's English. Why do millennials persist in mangling their prepositional phrases?

"So . . . they confuse the ranch with a famous spa that has a similar-sounding name. But they still think they're in a spa – like, when they practice riding on a mechanical horse, they mistake it for some kind of special massage – there's a lot of stuff like that. It's fricking *hilarious*," Whitney says, though I find the assertion improbable. "I thought I'd pee my pants."

I know this is a movie I will never watch, even if it is the only entertainment available on a fourteen-hour airline flight. Nor will I tune into any of the favorite TV shows she then reels off, mostly police procedurals and reality programs. Whitney displays a similar lack of interest in the news, documentary, and history programs that top my TV watch list.

Midway through round two of our cocktails, I'm feeling buzzed from the pleasurable yet dangerous sensation one gets from too much strong alcohol consumed too fast on a stomach too empty. I regret having opted for tequila over wine. As if by magic, two more Marvelitas appear. "Did we order these?" I ask Whitney.

"I signaled the waiter a couple of minutes ago. Guess you didn't notice. You're good with having one more, right?"

You might have consulted me before you ordered, I think, but I nod and flash her a dopey smile, wondering if it's a dead giveaway that I'm already hammered. I can't stop thinking about how hungry I am, so I keep slurping away at my cocktail to satisfy this insatiable craving to funnel any form of sustenance into my stomach.

Whitney resumes her edgy critique of television and film. "I'll never understand why that Quentin Tortorino is so popular. His movies are so creepy and gory."

"Tarantino. Not Tortorino." My voice sounds echoing and inhuman to my ears. I think my figurative buzz has devolved into a literal one, like I've contracted some sort of alcoholic tinnitus. I stand and say, "I need to find the women's room." I lurch in the direction of a long corridor that holds the promise of restrooms at the end, praying I will make it there without calling attention to myself. I slow my pace down to keep from ricocheting into a wall.

The restroom has cobalt blue and white tiles on the countertops and curved wall alcoves decorated with flickering LED candles. I zigzag into the nearest stall and unleash a torrent of pee. When I come out, I view myself in the mirror with a mix of curiosity and horror. The face peering back is dimly familiar, but my skin is a pasty grayish green, my forehead glistens with sweat, and my eyes are bloodshot and filmy. Frozen in place at the counter, I grip my face with both hands, resting my elbows on the cool hard tiles.

After a few seconds (minutes? hours?), a gentle voice beckons me. "Are you all, right? Can I help you?"

I revolve my head an inch at a time (*no fast movements, please*) to face the woman who addressed me. I calculate she's around my age—no, probably a few years older. "Earth mother" is the description that comes to mind. She is bulky and bosomy, her long graying hair thick but not fashionably cut or styled. She wears a multi-colored patchwork sweater coat, the kind they sell at street fairs, over a formless black dress. You would not say this woman has a single attractive facial feature, but I warm to her endearing smile, deep dimples etched in both cheeks. Her eyes smile, too, and they sparkle with compassion. She is so toasty-warm and cheerful, I can't help but like her. Maybe this kindly woman can replace Whitney as my new best friend.

She grabs a couple of paper towels from a stack on the counter and wets them with cold water. As she hands them to me, I notice her fingers look stubby, the nails bitten down to the quick. "Here. Use these to wipe your face and neck." Her voice is likable as well. It has a musical tone, sweet and reassuring. I nod and follow her instructions like an obedient child.

"Did that help?" she asks.

"A little. I think I'll go back to my friend now." As I turn to leave, I wobble on my feet.

She folds her arm around mine with a firm but gentle touch. "I'll help you back to your seat."

Grateful for the help, I let her guide me back into the bar, where I sink onto the upholstered chair. "Your friend could use something to eat, I think, if she can manage it," she says to Whitney. "Better still, maybe you should take her home." The woman gives me a comforting pat on the shoulder before strolling back to the dining room.

Her melodious voice reminds me of someone, but I can't think who. I can't think too coherently about anything right now. I observe her as she walks back to her table, where she is greeted by a man who rises with his back to me. He turns far enough for me to recognize the familiar profile – the beer belly straining against the golf shirt, the roundish cheeks and jutting mouth, the dark, deep-set eyes – and he greets her with an embrace followed by a warm kiss on the lips.

It's Henry Schuyler. *My* Henry. My once-upon-a-time-in-suburbia Henry. Which means this woman must be Alice. Alice Hanley, the other woman, my nemesis. No wonder she sounded familiar. I should have recognized that voice from when she answered my phone call to the office.

I cannot believe my eyes. This is the woman Henry has left me for? During all these lonely months, I have been convinced she is young, sexy, and gorgeous, the quintessential trophy girlfriend. The revelation that I've missed the mark by a thousand miles has an instant sobering effect as if I've been doused with a bucket of ice water. I gulp down the remainder of my third cocktail in an ill-advised attempt to escape this harsh new reality. How could I be so clueless about my husband of twenty-eight years?

What else have I gotten wrong?

I peek at them once more, then avert my gaze, staring into my empty cocktail glass. The only saving grace of this whole encounter is that Henry doesn't know I'm here. If he should spot me in the bar, his new partner will have total justification in saying, "Who can blame poor Henry for walking out on that falling-down drunk?"

I try to steady myself, but the shock to my system has been too great. My heart races, my cheeks burn with heat, and my stomach sloshes with all the liquid refreshment. I need to get out of this place, and fast. "I—I have to get some air," I say to Whitney in an urgent whisper. I run out of the main entrance and hang a sharp left towards the adjacent parking lot. There, I bend over and "blow my lunch," as the expression goes . . . except I have no lunch to blow. With nothing in my stomach but the contents of three generous Marvelitas, what emerges is mostly bile and spit.

When I straighten up and wipe one sleeve across my mouth to catch a final trail of saliva, Whitney is standing beside me. She stares at me with a stunned expression I've seen on her face once before, when she—well—when *was* it?

I remember. This is how she looked when we heard the report about the mall shooting on the locker room television. She freaks out. "Omigod, I knew you looked familiar. Omigod, omigod, omigod—"

"What is it?"

"The woman in the Vegas shooting."

"What are you talking about?"

Now tears stream down her cheeks, and her body trembles violently. "You know the shooting at that music festival in Las Vegas? The one where hundreds of people were killed and wounded?" she asks.

"Of course."

"I was at the festival and . . . and . . . these people next to me . . ." She is sobbing now, crying so hard I can tell she is struggling to speak.

I coax the story out of her. "What about the people next to you? Tell me what happened to them." I dread the answer, though I can't imagine what it has to do with me dry heaving in a restaurant parking lot.

"The man—the man next to me was shot in the arm, and he fell to the ground screaming. The woman with him crouched down and put her arms around him. Then she stood, and when she found his blood all over herself, she clutched her stomach just like you were doing and threw up. She looked exactly like you . . . the same hair, the same height and build. Why didn't I realize this before?" She raises her voice, almost screaming. "Was that you, Mar? Were you the woman in Vegas?"

I wonder if this is a serious question. "Oh, Whitney, of courshhh not." The two of us are quite the pair - Whitney hysterical, me slurring my words. I guess her liquor-laced quest for "fun, fun, fun" is rooted in unhappiness, the same as mine. So much for my labeling this young woman as baggage-free. We may be toting different brands of luggage, but both of us are burdened by a heavy load.

The rest of the evening is a blur. But as I remember it, Whitney stops crying and grows calm enough to say, "You said you'd treat tonight. Okay if I grab a few bills from your purse?" I nod and she does so, then she says, "Wait right here. I'm going inside to pay the tab and ask the bartender to call you a taxi."

I retreat into the shadows to avoid recognition if Henry and Alice should emerge from the restaurant. Whitney comes back out to wait by my side. The taxi pulls up - an old-school yellow cab - and as it inches along in the valet parking and pickup lane, Whitney breaks up with me.

"So . . ." she begins, "I'm so sorry, Mar, but I don't think I can hang out with you anymore. You know, Vegas was—it was, like, a huge trauma for me, and I'm still working through it. It's not your fault, but, like, you remind me so much of that woman at the shooting, I don't think I can get away from that. Every time I look at you from now on, I'll think of that horrible night."

"Wow. Okay, I get it."

Relief washes over her face. "So . . . you're not mad?"

"I'm not mad. I promishhh." The fact is, Whitney is doing me a huge favor. I need to find a new acquaintance who is closer to my age, or at least more like-minded.

As I pile into the back seat of the cab, shit-faced and shaky, the weirdness of the situation strikes me. Whitney is ditching me because I remind her of a traumatic event in her past, but I, in turn, associate her with a trauma of my own. Because in my mind's eye, whenever I pictured Henry with Alice, the woman I saw in my tortured imagination was . . . Whitney. Not literally her, of course, but a woman who looked and acted a lot like Whitney, a doppelgänger of sorts.

How ironic that Whitney and I are both doing such a piss-poor job of running away from the past. Only a short time after seeking each other out in friendship, we've come face to face with the very demons we're trying to escape - and the demons are each other. And it is Whitney, not me, who understands that we can never continue as friends because of that.

The girl has a lot more brains than I gave her credit for.

PART TWO: FEBRUARY
JUDITH

4.

I'm huddled in the small lounge area of the women's locker room with a few other members, all of us confined indoors because of the teeming rain outside. Sometimes in LA, entire winters can pass with little or no meaningful precipitation, but this is not one of those years. It's poured for six of the last eight days, setting new rainfall records.

Amazon Lady is there as usual, along with Patch, Dame Donut, Jill, and a middle-aged woman I've taken to calling Effy because she drops so many F-bombs. It's the last thing you'd expect, given her coy demeanor. Tidy and clean-cut, with tightly styled gray hair, a little upturned nose, and a sweet smile, she is the picture of all-American wholesomeness. But the expletives that gush from this innocent-looking woman like lava from a volcano are anything but genteel. Right now, Effy is regaling us with a story about how her husband overreacted when she went out of town for a girls' weekend, leaving him on his own.

"I don't know why he falls apart when I go away for a couple of days," she says.

"Maybe he misses having home-cooked meals," says Patch.

"Are you fucking kidding me? He does all the cooking around our house. And when I'm there, he hardly even notices me, he's so busy watching every sports program on TV. Football, basketball, golf . . . *bowling,* for Christ's sake. I didn't give him sex for two months, and he never noticed that either."

We nod solemnly at this.

"Not that it's a big deal whether we do or don't. I mean, when we *do* get it on, you could measure the whole thing from start to finish on an egg timer."

This elicits gales of laughter from the group, but Effy's is the loudest of all. For someone with such a tiny nose, she has an unexpectedly nasal voice, and when she laughs, it comes out as a gooselike honk.

"I take it he survived your absence?" I ask.

"Oh, hell yeah. But the house barely survived. When I got home, the place looked like a fricking crime scene." More laughter. "We're talking books and magazines all over the floor, open drawers with clothes hanging out, dirty dishes in the sink, toilets not flushed . . . the place stank like an elephant enclosure at the zoo."

"It must've made you crazy to come back to such a mess," says Dame Donut, absently scratching her ring of waistline flab. "I bet you had to summon all your professional skills to straighten things out."

"What do you mean?" I ask.

"Judith is an organizational specialist," Patch says.

Effy—Judith—turns to me and grins. "I help people sort out their shit."

"Sounds unpleasant," I say.

Judith snickers at this. "I consult with clients on how to declutter homes and offices, and I re-design closets and shelves, stuff like that."

I flash on a brief image of my chaotic apartment, where file folders and magazines are scattered across my office and unpacked boxes are piled in every available space.

"Are you withholding sex in punishment?" asks Amazon Lady with a wry smile.

"Ha-ha," Judith says. "Not that it's anyone's business, but we shared three minutes of intimacy last night during a commercial break from the national miniature golf championship. Afterward, he pissed and moaned about how lonely he's been while I was away."

"Men are such crybabies," Amazon Lady says.

"Amen to that," Dame Donut agrees.

Patch grunts in agreement, but I say nothing. I don't want to open the door to a conversation about my solitary domestic status and the rapturous relationship between Henry and Alice. I take a swig from my disposable water bottle.

"Is that alkaline water?" asks Effy, eying the label with suspicion.

I nod. "I used to get heartburn, but not since I started drinking this."

"It's a rip-off. Four bucks for that thing; are you kidding me? You can make any water alkaline by adding lemon juice."

"I've tried that. The lemon gives me sour stomach," I say, my tone defensive.

"Oh hon, forget it. Let's not argue over some crap bottle of water, right?" She winks at me and all is forgiven. This woman tickles my funny bone.

I head upstairs to the cardio equipment room. I don't have a lot of time to work out today - I'm scheduled for a rare lunch with my son Michael - but I squeeze in thirty minutes on the elliptical trainer, enough to work up a good sweat.

It's been unusually busy at the club this week. The rain has driven all the walkers, joggers, and tennis players indoors for their exercise. Striding on the machine next to me is Sexy Eyes. Most likely in his early fifties, he is tall and nice-looking, with strong, pleasing features - particularly his long-lashed, gray eyes, which are a standout. I've always been a pushover for a nice pair of eyes. Henry was never a handsome man, but one long, soulful gaze from his deep-set, nearly black eyes was enough to reel me in.

I usually think of gray as a cool color (is it even considered a color at all?), but the gray eyes of my new gym acquaintance are warm and intelligent – eyes I could dreamily gaze into given half a chance. I've seen him around the club a few times, though he's never spoken to me . . . until now, when he steps off the treadmill, wipes his head and neck with a towel, smiles, and says, "Try to keep dry," before walking away.

Is he commenting on the pelting rain outside? Or, heaven forbid, on my perspiring brow?

5.

For lunch, Michael suggests we meet at Jake's Place, a hole-in-the-wall deli tucked away in one of the endless strip malls along Coast Highway. I've never understood the appeal, but he loves their pastrami Reuben and orders it every time, accompanied by a platter heaped with well-done fries. As we greet each other with a stiff hug, I am struck by the way Michael's resemblance to his father increases with age. He has my coloring, but his dark eyes and full lips are the spitting image of Henry's as a young man.

When the food arrives, I wrinkle my nose at the sight of my sandwich: pre-sliced turkey, wilted lettuce, and a pale hunk of tomato on dry whole wheat toast. I am living in the wrong time and place. Had I been a magazine editor several decades ago in Manhattan, I'd be enjoying a martini lunch right now with a young executive from one of the big PR firms, dining on a three-course menu of things stuffed with other things: lobster-filled avocado, Dover sole with scallop mousseline. And for dessert, profiteroles filled with vanilla ice cream and drizzled—no, make that *lathered*—in hot, rich, dark chocolate sauce.

I nibble on the tasteless turkey, focusing as intently as if it were a Michelin-starred meal. Anything to delay conversation. I haven't seen Michael for longer than I care to admit, and I'm not sure where to resume with him. Relations have been strained for the past year, ever since Henry moved in with his little tart. Okay, I know now she isn't a tart, and she certainly isn't little, but still - I never expected my only child to embrace the new arrangement with such enthusiasm. So I find it easier to maintain a safe distance. I try to see Benny every week or two, usually when Michael is off on one of his frequent business trips. I relieve Heather for an hour while she goes to an appointment or runs a few errands.

"Mind if I have a fry?" I ask, helping myself before Michael can respond. Even cooked well-done, it is bland and mealy on the inside. At least I'm not tempted to eat more. Michael, however, is shoveling the fries into his mouth with mechanical efficiency. I note with despair that at twenty-seven, my son has his father's sagging belly and puffy jawline. Poor Michael. He's inherited Henry's looks and my irascible nature.

Between scarfing fries, he gets the conversational ball rolling. "How's the apartment coming along? Have you settled in?"

"Yes and no. I still have piles of boxes everywhere, and more stuff stowed away in a mini-storage locker. There's no way it will all fit into my cozy apartment, that's for sure."

"You didn't have to move into such a small place. For that matter, you didn't have to move at all."

"We've been over this," I say, trying to keep my tone upbeat. "I didn't want to live there alone, after—I needed a fresh start."

"Benny liked visiting the house."

My marital home was conspicuously large for a family of three, let alone a single woman. Michael knows a big house and fancy cars aren't important to me like they are to his father, but he would have me remain in his childhood home to indulge a toddler's whim.

"Benny's three. I'll bet he's forgotten about the house already. Besides, I've set up some toys and books for him in a corner of the living room. And my new health club has a pool where I can take him. He'll love that," I say, borrowing

Whitney's suggestion. "How's *your* place?" I ask, segueing (I think) into neutral territory. "When are you starting the kitchen remodel?"

"Sore subject." This is how Michael responds whenever he wants to block off a particular avenue of discussion. He has an ever-growing list of sore subjects, at least a couple of hundred by now.

"Never mind." I rack my brain for a topic that won't lead to bickering and hurt feelings. "Tell me what brilliant and adorable things Benny is doing these days."

"He's great," Michael says, grinning for the first time. He talks about how verbal Benny has become and how clever about many things. "Yesterday he said, 'Daddy, I want to make a picture of the park. Mix the yellow and blue paint together so I can paint the park green.' Can you believe that? He knows red and yellow make orange too."

"I'll bet even Picasso hadn't figured that out at three. Benny's a great little guy. You and Heather should be proud of him and proud of yourselves as parents." It's true. I smile thinking of my grandson and my daughter-in-law, a young woman who has my affection and respect.

Now Michael is beaming. "Thanks, Mom. I have to give most of the credit to Heather. She spends so much more time with him than I do."

When he rewards me with a smile like this, one that lights up his entire face, it makes my heart clench with joy and sadness at the same time. Joy at sharing such a warm moment; sadness because it's rare for him to radiate pure glee. Michael has always been subject to mood swings and bouts of sullenness, a tendency that's grown worse since the divorce. I have wondered a thousand times whether Henry and I caused Michael to turn out this way. How much blame must parents bear for their children's problems? Lately, his ill humor is often aimed at me without explanation, as if *I* had been the one to jump ship and paddle off with a new partner.

"How's work? Business still strong?" I ask.

"Oh yeah. Ridiculously busy. We acquired a company that makes safety surfacing for playgrounds. It's a good extension of our product line since we already sell to schools and municipalities."

"What are you going to name it?"

"Nothing. I mean, it will just become part of Schuyler Enterprises."

Schuyler Enterprises is Henry's family business, founded as a manufacturer of office furniture by Henry's father, who ran the company until his death. Henry and his older brother, Steve, now share the helm. As Mister Inside, Steve runs the business end of things and handles all the hiring and firing. Henry avoids any distasteful activity that might make him less lovable. A born salesman, he adores schmoozing customers, hosting hospitality events, and handing out promotions and bonuses to the sales force he heads up. What Henry lacks in looks, he more than makes up for in amiability and charm. Under the two brothers, Schuyler has branched out into additional markets: schools, libraries, community centers, theaters. The expansion strategy has paid off. Thanks to Schuyler, we all enjoy a comfortable lifestyle, even post-divorce.

"How about calling the new product line Schuyler Surfaces? Has a nice ring, don't you think?"

"Thanks for the unsolicited advice, Mom, but I think we've got it covered," Michael says with more than a hint of sarcasm. What he means to say is that I've relinquished the right to offer strategic marketing guidance to Schuyler Enterprises.

This has nothing to do with the divorce. Years ago, when Michael was still a young boy, Henry's family wanted me to "hop aboard" (Steve's actual words) as Schuyler's advertising and PR manager at more than double my editor's salary. I dismissed Steve's recruiting efforts, and the Schuyler men took my incomprehensible rejection as an affront to the family. A model wife would not deign to be so ungrateful and uninterested. Henry never could understand why I clung to my unglamorous, low-paying editorial job, or why I had to add insult to injury by devoting further time to free-lance work. "You know, Margaret, you don't have to lift a finger if you choose not to," he said countless times.

"I like to lift all my fingers and tap away on the keyboard."

But whenever I worked late, traveled on business, or spent hours at the computer on weekends, Henry would make unfunny cracks in front of Michael about my tireless dedication to the powder-handling community of America. Now, after Michael rejects my marketing idea for the company, my mouth sags in an unintentional frown.

"Mom. Don't give me that look."

"What look? There was no look."

"I think there was."

"I swear, I'm totally lookless." Now, he gives *me* a look. "Is Alice still working for the company?" I ask.

This takes him by surprise. "Yes."

"Tell me about her."

"I thought you didn't want to meet her or hear anything about her. That's what you've been saying all this time."

"I don't want to meet her." Of course, I don't mention the inebriated brush with Alice at The Kitchen restaurant. "But I'm ready to find out more about what she's like."

"Why?"

"I was married to your father for twenty-eight years. Now he's with someone else, and she's spending a lot of time with my family both at work and outside of work."

"We're not exactly your family." As soon as he says this, Michael knows he's gone too far. "I meant, Dad and Alice are, like, a separate unit now. I didn't mean the rest of us."

I'm not so sure. But I ignore his hurtful comment and say, "It's important for me to learn more about her. I shied away from it for a long time, but I accept that I have to face it."

"She's friendly. Down-to-earth."

I already know this. "Is she still doing inside sales? Or did your father promote her to the marketing department?" I'll admit, I'm trolling to see if she has glided right into the job I refused all those years ago. Why not? She's glided into every other aspect of my former life.

"He's given her a few marketing assignments. But her job title hasn't changed."

"Ah."

"Alice is very selfless. She volunteers at a soup kitchen on Sunday mornings."

"Oh, isn't that nice." I'm laying it on pretty thick, and Michael again grows suspicious.

"You're being sarcastic, aren't you?"

"What makes you say that?"

"You've made it clear how you feel about volunteerism, Mom."

I shrug with genuine chagrin. "I don't know what you mean."

"A few years ago, one time when Heather and I were at the house, I overheard a conversation between you and Dad. He wanted you to serve on some charity board, and you told him your work didn't leave you with time for 'fluffy stuff' like that."

I try to laugh it off. "Oh, you know how I am. Sometimes I say things without thinking them through. Don't take it literally."

"That's not all you said." He is determined to air some age-old grievance. "Dad told you not to be so selfish with your time, and you said all people are fundamentally selfish, even if they're doing good works."

I have to admit that sounds like something I would say. But he's taking it out of context. "What I meant was, we all try to do the things that make us feel good," I say. "Like, if a woman juggles three volunteer jobs, she's ultimately doing it for her own satisfaction - not just to help others, but because she derives pleasure from the work."

"Suppose a woman had to choose between herself and her child," Michael says.

"Choose how? Like, there's only one ticket to the Lady Gaga concert, and the choice is who's gonna get it?"

His eyes roll. "Let's set the stakes a little higher, okay?"

"How high?"

"Life or death."

Now I have to struggle to keep *my* eyes from rolling.

"Let's say they both have some deadly virus," says Michael, "and there's only enough of the anti-viral medicine to save one life. If the mother sacrifices herself so her child can live, you can't tell me *that's* a selfish act."

This whole line of discussion is bizarre, but I want to treat it seriously so I consider my response. "Maybe the mother knows she can't live with the knowledge that she's condemned her own child to die. Deciding to die in her child's place is unselfish in one way - but it's also self-serving because it's the only choice she can stand to make."

"But what if the child—"

"Michael, please. Can't we lighten up?"

He picks up a fry but then tosses it back onto the plate to signal his annoyance with me. "Oh, right. You want to get back to pumping me for information about Dad's relationship, don't you?"

"I'm not pumping you. I'm simply curious about your opinion of Alice."

"I already told you, she's friendly. But I'm not gonna get in the middle and act like some kind of informant. If you have questions, ask Dad yourself. Or ask them both. Alice is very kind and direct. She's not a game-player."

Unlike his mother.

Things go downhill from there. Michael lets his churlish side take over. At first, I try to keep the conversation alive with light chatter about the gym, but he starts scrolling through the messages on his phone. Slighted by his inattention, I grow silent too. I guess he'd rather be in the company of someone warmer and free of cynicism. Someone like Alice. I envision her on her birthday, receiving an avalanche of Hallmark cards festooned with adorable kittens or sprays of colorful spring blooms, and the sentimental messages inside that say *Birthday greetings to a wonderful, caring person.* The few cards I get invariably feature cartoon figures who are swearing, farting, or giving someone the finger. Sometimes all three. That's the difference between Alice and me. That, in a nutshell, is why Alice is the popular favorite with Henry, Michael, and his family - and I am on the outside looking in.

As often as Michael and I grate on each other's nerves, I love him fiercely and would, in fact, give my life for him if faced with such an ultimatum. I could never tell him this, however. He'd dismiss it as another instance of his mother being a sarcastic wiseass. He only sees the tough, pragmatic side of me - not the side that hurts from his cool insensitivity.

Later, on my beach walk, I'll replay our lunch conversation in my head, rewriting the dialogue to edit out all the remarks Michael found disagreeable. If only I could read from a script every time we had a conversation, the outcome would be much more satisfying. He would emerge less hostile - and I, less wounded.

Back in my office that afternoon, I go through emails and phone messages. I play back a message on my office voicemail.

"Hello, Margaret dear. This is Nancy Ostrowski. From next door."

I would know that raspy old voice anywhere. She and her husband, John, were my neighbors for over twenty years.

"Will you call me back, please? I need to talk to you about something."

A week after I moved to the apartment, she had phoned to inform me that the automatic sprinklers in my former yard were turning on several times a day at odd hours, and since the new owners hadn't yet moved in, she wasn't sure who to tell. "Sorry, can't help you with that," I'd said to her at the time.

The Ostrowskis were a thorn in my side for years. Or at least, *he* was. John's always been a cranky old man who complained with relentless displeasure about everything we did. I thought we were courteous neighbors overall, but it didn't matter. He was a cantankerous geezer who took pleasure in finding fault no matter what.

I don't miss him for a minute. As for Nancy, I can't say I either like or dislike her, though I pity her for having to put up with such a nasty man all these years. Meek and diffident, she has a peculiar way of walking with her narrow shoulders hunched, her elbows bent and fists clenched, as though she is fending off blows. I suspect she's calling to tell me about the sprinklers again, or some other irrelevant problem I can't be bothered with right now, so I save the message and resolve to get back to her another time.

Walking from the kitchen with a glass of water, I stub my toe on one of the many boxes I've stowed outside the door to my office. I need to do something about all my crap. Maybe I should talk to that woman, Effy—I mean, Judith—next time I run into her at the gym. I could use a professional organizer.

6.

One week later, Judith and I are heavily into it. She begins by giving me a lengthy questionnaire to complete, in which I'm called upon to detail my belongings and state my goals for our project. This proves to be a useful exercise as it forces me to think about my possessions in a more clinical light.

We spend an afternoon at my mini-storage unit. Here, we divide the contents into three groups, color-tagging each item: green for *must go*, red for *must keep*, yellow for *undecided*. Somehow, Judith convinces me to relegate half my stuff into the *must go* category. She accompanies this with her usual unfiltered commentary. "A sleeping bag? A pup tent? Are you planning to pitch it in the middle of the fucking apartment?"

"I thought Benny might enjoy it when he's a little older."

"Buy him a new one when that day comes. Nobody uses camping gear like this anymore. This crap smells like it's from the last millennium." She divides the green items into two subcategories, the throwaways and the charitable donations.

"Can't we give everything to charity?" I ask. "Like, why not this bed frame and headboard set? It's got a few scratches, but it's not in bad shape. We bought it from Ikea when Michael was in college." I flash back to the day when Henry and I helped him move into the off-campus apartment, and how the three of us hugged at the end of moving day, emotional over this latest passage into adulthood.

"This bed is *particle board*," Judith says, spitting out the term like someone spewing a mouthful of milk that's gone sour. "Salvation Army won't touch this with a ten-foot pole." I defer to her greater wisdom upon learning that she will arrange for pickup of all the green-tagged items. "I'll make a couple of calls to my people, and this stuff will be flushed out faster than shit through a sick goose," she says in a cheery voice.

The "undecided," or yellow-coded items, are trickier. These include a huge box of schoolboy memorabilia and cheesy plastic trophies that Michael earned on his various sports teams, from T-ball through middle school flag football. He was never a brilliant athlete, so most of these are awards for mere participation *(good job showing up for the games)*, or for most improved player *(you sucked to begin with, but you're no longer a total embarrassment)*.

"Don't make me throw these out. I can't," I say in weak protest.

"Honey, here's what we're gonna do. You tell your son if he wants the trophies and shit, it's his call. He's got six months to move them outta here, and if he hasn't taken them off your hands by the deadline, you're chucking the whole sorry lot."

I have to admit this is a good idea. Judith assures me this is the biggest obstacle that all her clients face. They can't bear to part with sentimental junk from the past, but who the hell wants this worthless crap? She makes me sign a form agreeing that in six months, any possessions that remain unwanted or unused must go. It's like a contract with myself. She also directs me to post the deadline on my cellphone calendar. It's bossy but effective. If I can stick to Judith's plan and rid myself of enough additional junk in the next half a year, I'll be able to downsize from my current premium storage room to a smaller and more economical locker.

Hiring Judith to create order out of my new life is a stroke of genius. She's competent and efficient, yet entertaining too – outspoken and irreverent. In some regards, she reminds me of *me*. But whereas I'm forever regretting my verbal indiscretions, Judith seems unfazed by hers. What must it be like to say anything you want without shame or remorse? It might take the sting out of my uncomfortable brushes with Michael.

Maybe I could learn to follow this woman's example.

Famished after hours of sorting and tagging, I dig a nutrition bar out of my purse. It's a popular brand, rich dark chocolate filled with chopped toasted almonds. I peel off the foil wrapper and hold it up to Judith. "Would you like half? Happy to share."

Her eyes narrow into disapproving slits. "Why don't you hook yourself up to a cyanide drip instead?"

"Meaning what?"

"These bars are full of pesticides. There should be a law against marketing this crap in the 'nutrition' category."

I flash back to the day when she expressed similar disapproval over my alkaline water.

Undeterred by Judith's dire health threat, I shrug and take a bite of the tainted snack.

The next day, working together at the apartment to organize the rest of my belongings, Judith rips into me big-time. She starts with my super-comfy Israeli walking sandals, which she deems too extravagant. "You could buy U.S.-made shoes that are as good for a third of the price."

"I know, believe me. They were a gift from my ex the year before we broke up."

She freaks out when we open a large bag containing about ten pairs of patterned workout leggings, all with matching tops. "I didn't realize you were opening a Lululemon outlet here. Guess I'll earn my money figuring out where to fit all this stuff."

"Not Lululemon. These are knock-offs." It's true I've been updating and expanding my wardrobe for a fresher look – but

I've always been frugal, and I pride myself on being low-maintenance. "Except for a few new outfits, I've been working on downsizing," I say. "Like I only own this one little TV. We had a movie-theater-sized set in my old house, but I left it for the buyers. And I bet I'm the only tenant in this building who isn't leasing an Audi or BMW."

"If you want to help the planet, get yourself an electric plug-in model like mine," she says, referring to a vehicle scarcely larger than a golf cart.

We proceed to the kitchen, where I continue to self-promote my modest lifestyle. "This is the only appliance I use regularly." I point to the wall-mounted microwave.

Sitting on the counter is a new refillable plastic water bottle, the price tag and label still affixed. She examines it and says, "This bottle isn't BPA-free," and emits a dejected sigh as though she's already written me off as a hopeless case. I'm not sure what BPA is, or why it's advisable to be free of it. I don't ask.

Judith glances inside the refrigerator and then opens the pantry door, looking up and down as she surveys the shelves. I await a compliment on my healthy food choices. She says, "This is what you eat? Jesus."

I can't imagine saying this to anyone, even if I were to unearth a stash of Doritos, sugary desserts, and institutional-sized tins of mashed potato buds. I believe my own selection of vegetables, dried beans, whole grains, and other "good" carbs should be commended, but she tells me all the foods I once thought to be healthy are apt to cause premature death or dementia.

"Then what should I be eating?"

"A strict anti-inflammatory diet like the kind I'm on," she says. "It's all about the lectins."

"What are those?"

"Lectins are proteins that occur naturally in a lot of plant foods."

"Well, plant protein is good for you, right?"

"Not in this case," she says with authority. "Lectins *block* the absorption of nutrients, which makes them bad actors." Then comes the grim news – the list of lectin-containing no-nos. All legumes and beans. Wheat. Gluten. The nightshade vegetables (my favorites): eggplant, tomatoes, peppers. Most dairy foods. *Any* food that's white.

"How about nuts? Those are healthy in moderation, right?"

"Not if they're almonds, cashews, or peanuts," she says, reeling off three of the staples in my pantry.

"If I can't eat any of those foods, what's left?"

"Oh, lots of yummy things. Fatty fish. Broccoli. Berries. Oranges. Avocados. And olive oil. You can slather everything in as much olive oil as you like."

Can I survive on a diet of nothing but these half-dozen items? I think not. Trying to put a cheerful face on it, I point to the big bag of fresh kale in my crisper bin and ask, "I can eat this stuff till it's coming out of my ears, right?"

"Wrong," says Judith with a contemptuous snort. "Kale is full of heavy metals like aluminum, lead, and nickel . . . not to mention thallium, which is used in rat poison, for Christ's sake. Let me dig into this pantry and throw out everything that's past its sell-by date. That'll free up some space."

"*No.*" I slam the pantry door. "I mean—that won't be necessary. I bought all new groceries when I moved in here." No way is she tossing my beloved ancient grains. Judith's unexpected push to reorganize not only my closet contents but also my stomach contents has left me unsettled. A little chardonnay might help to calm my nerves. I followed my humiliating performance at the Mexican restaurant with a record period of abstinence – not a drop of alcohol in days. But if I've been waiting for the right moment to resume drinking, surely this is it.

When I invite Judith to join me, she gives me a disapproving look and I brace myself for another lecture. "I never drink white wine. It sends my fasting glucose up into the stratosphere. Red wine is *so* much better for you. Would you mind if we open a bottle of red?"

"Be my guest." Relieved that she's onboard with the drinking, I'm hopeful a little wine will make Judith more mellow as well. I uncork a Malbec and pour a generous glass for her and a chardonnay for myself.

"I'm starving," I say, pulling out a wedge of cheddar from the fridge and slapping it on a small cheese board with a few whole wheat crackers. Then I remember Judith will not touch this. "Is there anything in my kitchen you can eat?" I ask. "Help yourself to whatever you like."

Judith retrieves a large avocado from a bowl on the counter, slices it in half, removes the pit, and fills both cavities with olive oil - it must be half a cup. Then she slurps it up with a spoon, the way one might enjoy a bread bowl of chowder, as she swigs the Malbec. Halfway into the first glass, Judith kicks off her shoes. The wine is doing its job.

"How did you get into this line of work?" I ask her.

"Hah. For years, I drove my husband nuts, keeping detailed inventories of our stuff, alphabetizing the magazine rack— "

"You have an alphabetized magazine rack?"

"Doesn't everyone?" she says with a wink. "Anyway, one day he said, 'Why don't you channel all this energy into something profitable?' When I decided to become an organizational consultant, he was all for it."

"You enjoy the work?"

"Oh yeah. It's gratifying to be helping people so much, even if the money isn't so great."

Right now, I'm not all that positive about her helpfulness. And when I think of the big fat checks I've been writing to Judith, I'm not sure I agree about the money either.

"I meet interesting people too. Last month I had a hell of an experience. Wanna hear about it?" Before I can respond, she barrels ahead with her story. "Okay, so this lady hires me and tells me she's a recent widow, which is surprising because she's pretty young. We need to get rid of all her late husband's stuff because she can't bear to see it around the house, you know? I arrange for charities to pick up his clothes and shit. There's also this big easy chair, like a brown leather BarcaLounger type of deal, and when they're about to haul it away, she fricking throws herself across the chair and starts sobbing, the perfect picture of a grieving widow." She chuckles at the recollection.

"How is this funny?"

"Just wait. The next day she asks me to come back to take care of a few final things, and in walks the husband. The dude is definitely not dead. Can you fucking believe that?"

"No, I can't."

"He notices right away that his favorite chair is missing, and he goes to the bedroom and discovers that his half of the closet is empty. He turns to me and says, 'What the hell is going on?' I tell him, 'Your wife said you'd passed away.' Then he gets all mad at *me*, like the whole thing is *my* fault. Can you fucking believe that?"

"No, I can't. Do you think he came home early from a business trip or something?"

"No, I think the wife set the whole thing up. She *wanted* him to walk in on us getting rid of his stuff. She knew exactly what she was doing."

"But why would she do that?"

"I'm coming to that. She screams, 'Serves you right, you goddamn cheating son of a bitch.' Right to his face, she accuses him of being unfaithful to her every time he travels out of town. Can you fucking believe that?"

This strikes a bit too close to home. I stiffen my back at this latest revelation and say to her, "*That* I can fucking believe." I'm so rattled, I'm not sure what to do but self-medicate with more food and alcohol. I pull a container of hummus from the fridge and offer her some.

"No way," she says with a fierce shake of the head. "Lectins."

"Oh, hummus has lectins too?"

"Honey, I told you beans are off-limits. Hummus is full of garbanzo beans."

"Forgive my ignorance," I say, though my tone is unapologetic. "I'm the editor of *Powder World* – not *Lectin World.*"

How did I ever find this woman agreeable? Her opinionated responses and endless guilty verdicts are rankling. I'm not sure why she's getting under my skin so deeply, but I come up with a new and even better nickname for her: Judge Judy.

• • •

Maddening as she is, Judge Judy creates order out of chaos over the following week. We finish sorting through all the boxes, discarding unwanted items; and she organizes my storage space with shelf dividers, hanging racks for shoes and accessories, and various-sized plastic stacking bins. She finds a file cabinet that's a perfect fit for the corner of my office and a bookcase for the adjacent hallway. Appreciating that I'm in a rental unit, she takes care to avoid any built-in carpentry work. "We'll only use storage components you can take with you when you move," she says.

She's good at what she does, I'll give her that. She has rid me of clutter and helped me in my quest to continue shedding my former skin. And I still enjoy her sense of humor. On her final visit to my place, she brings me a BPA-free water bottle and a cookbook titled *Lose the Lectins*, presenting the gift to me with a wink and one of her honking laughs. But I no longer want to emulate her mean-spirited behavior, nor do I want her in my daily life. I've figured out why she bothers me so much – the last thing I need is another person who makes me feel bad about myself. Michael is already doing a bang-up job of that. I will be polite to Judge Judy at Seaside Fitness, but I won't hang out with her.

To celebrate this decision, I order dinner delivery from a nearby Italian restaurant. Not only do I ignore as many of Judge Judy's food prohibitions as possible, but I also put aside my own healthy Mediterranean diet preferences for the night. While I'm entering the online order, my mother calls from New York. We haven't talked in a couple of weeks, but that isn't unusual. She has always taken a hands-off, almost indifferent parenting approach to me, her only child.

"Margy, dear." Margy is the pet name Mum has called me since childhood. She pronounces it with a hard *g,* as in *margarita.* Though she moved to New York from London as a teenager, Mum still retains more than a trace of an English accent and a lifelong adherence to that old-fashioned, never-wear-your-emotions-on-your-sleeve school of manners.

"Hi, Mum. I'm in the middle of something. I'm getting ready for a lasagna dinner."

"Lasagna—how fattening, dear. Are you layering it?"

"Have you met me? Of course I'm not layering it. I'm ordering it."

"I'll make it quick. I got a call from *Henry* today." She emphasizes his name in a breathless, almost worshipful tone, as if it were Brad Pitt who'd phoned. Mum has always been partial to Henry - even now, after all that's happened. She seems to blame the collapse of our marriage on some deficiency in my character rather than Henry's infidelity. It's that slippery charm of his. "He's concerned about you," she says.

"Henry? Concerned?" He didn't seem so concerned when he dumped me for Alice.

"Michael told him you're cramped in a tiny apartment, and you've had to put half your belongings in storage. He wishes you were in a better living situation."

I groan. "My apartment is cozy, yes, but it's great. Right on the water. I've got a gorgeous view of the harbor."

"You know, most men want their ex-wives to live in a *smaller* place after the divorce, not a bigger one. You're lucky Henry is so generous."

"Yeah, I'm lucky, all right."

"Glad you agree," she says, my sarcasm sailing right over her head. Mum places great importance on the comfort and financial security that Henry gave me and Daddy gave her. In her view, being a good provider is a husband's number one job.

"Listen, Mum. You know Henry always wants to look like a good guy. That's what this is all about."

"You really think so? Oh, he also mentioned he's getting ready to go to Mammoth Mountain, but he's missing a box of ski accessories. He thinks maybe they got mixed in with your things."

"Aha. Now we cut to the chase. Henry has sent you on a spying mission."

"Well, you won't communicate with him, and he doesn't like putting Michael in the middle."

Last week, that box - which contained ski gloves, goggles, and other top-of-the-line accessories - went out with the charitable donations. I can't hide my annoyance as I say, "You can tell Henry I don't have it." Which is true.

"All *righty* then. No need to shoot the messenger."

"Sorry, Mum. I'll call you tomorrow. Love you."

"Love you too."

While I'm unpacking the food delivery, I munch on a few metal-laden kale chips from the pantry. Then I settle down to dinner, a generous helping of lasagna. It's delicious and cheesy, with a rich pink sauce, and the house-made white noodles are tastier than the high-fiber whole wheat pasta I'm accustomed to eating. Henry wasn't crazy about lasagna, so I never served it when we were married. This makes my enjoyment even sweeter.

Also on the menu is a savory vegetable side dish laden with forbidden ingredients. I'm up to my eyeballs in nightshades. Eggplant! Tomatoes! Peppers! I tear off a crusty heel of Italian bread, also white. And though the meal might pair best with a nice Italian red, I've decided instead on a chilled pinot grigio with a crisp, clean flavor and straw-colored hue. Maybe I'll allow myself a full bottle tonight.

At the end of this enormous meal, I stretch out on the couch with my final glass of glucose-elevating white wine. Happy to eat and drink what I please, when I please, I pat my belly with contentment - sated, blissfully unencumbered, and oblivious to the hot mess of lectins churning in my gut.

PART THREE: MARCH
SUNNY

7.

The sun hasn't yet risen on the March morning when I wake feeling fuzzy and sleep-deprived. Five-thirty—*ugh.* Last night, I labored at the computer until well past midnight, so it's no wonder I'm exhausted. But I know I won't fall back to sleep.

I'm scheduled to meet my new pal Sunny at the club around nine. Though Sunny is her real name, it could just as well be one of my pet names, given her long, glossy blond hair. Her personality reminds me of sunshine as well, but not the blazing sun of a hot August day; it's more subtle and low-key, with a tinge of melancholy, like the muted sunlight of winter. Sunny is not given to false cheer or over-effusive greetings like Whitney, nor is she bossy or negative like Judge Judy. I scroll through emails and then double-check my business voicemail to make sure I haven't missed anything. There are now *two* messages from my old neighbor, Mrs. Ostrowski. I meant to get back to her last night, but by the time I remembered, the hour was too late. Maybe today . . .

Nine o'clock is hours away, so I might as well go to the club early. I examine the class schedule on my Seaside Fitness phone app and decide on 7:30 a.m. hatha yoga. I haven't tried yoga in years, and it's never been my favorite thing. But it will be good to challenge myself with something different, something I wouldn't have done in the time of Margaret.

As I enter the yoga studio, Sexy Eyes is walking in front of me, carrying his rolled-up purple yoga mat. Uh-oh. Are we expected to provide our own mats? Then I see an open supply closet. I grab a mat, bolster, strap, and two blocks, mimicking the others who have claimed their places and are sitting or reclining, already engaged in pre-class warmup poses, dedicated yogis all. Sexy Eyes rolls out his mat and settles into a spot in the front row, and I position myself behind him.

Marlene, the teacher, enters a few minutes later. She is easily the oldest instructor at the club – in her mid-sixties, I'd guess – slender and muscular, with a mane of beautiful silver hair tied back with a ribbon. "*Namaste*, everyone," she says as she sweeps across the room, all lightness and grace. I thought *namaste* was something people said at the conclusion of a class, but apparently you can use it to mean hello or goodbye, like *aloha* or *shalom*.

She instructs the class to start in a cross-legged seated pose and tells us to place our hands in a position that sounds something like Angelina Jolie. Then she repeats the phrase and I now understand it to be *anjali mudra,* which describes the simple gesture of pressing your palms together in front of the heart. What follows is a succession of poses that Marlene calls out in rapid-fire Sanskrit. We engage our *mula bandha,* drop down in *Chaturanga,* perform a swooping *vinyasa,* invert ourselves into a V-shaped *Adho Mukha Svanasana,* find our *drishti* as we balance one-legged in *Vrksasana* to resemble a tree, squat down into an imaginary chair in *Utkatasana,* salute the sun with *Surya Namaskar*, and so much more.

My comprehension of Sanskrit is about on par with my fluency in Mandarin, but I stumble along, trying to keep up. I find it helpful to watch Sexy Eyes and follow his lead. His long body is agile and lithe, flowing from one pose to another with effortless skill. He has a light winter suntan that suggests an affinity for outdoor activities. His hair is dark on top but graying around the edges, straight and thick, in a boyish cut that tumbles across his face whenever he lowers his head or turns sideways in the twisty poses. His biceps and triceps, thigh muscles, and calves all tauten as he moves from pose to pose. His limbs are well-sculpted, but his is not the bulging physique of a bodybuilder – which is fine by me, since I regard the muscleman look as a major turnoff.

The truth is, I'm not watching Sexy Eyes to guide me through the poses as much as I'm ogling him. And why not? I haven't been with a man in a long time, and without question, this man is highly ogleable. I reflect with catty pleasure that there's no way Alice can derive this kind of pleasure from observing Henry, whose pale limbs and long bloated torso have gone soft and fleshy from years of inactivity – though in the bedroom, I guess, he hasn't exactly been inactive. *Stop thinking about Henry,* I command myself. I steal another glance at Sexy Eyes for distraction.

Near the end of class, as we execute a recumbent spinal twist, Marlene sits in a serene lotus pose, organizing small towels into a neat pile. I'm all in favor of multi-tasking, but is it appropriate for this woman to be folding her laundry? It isn't until we assume our final corpse pose, or *savasana,* and she tiptoes around the room to distribute a warm towel to each of us, that I understand the lavender-scented cloths are to enhance our final relaxation with aromatherapy.

I nearly burst out laughing at my own cluelessness, but Sexy Eyes turns his head toward me as he adjusts his pose, and our brief eye contact stifles my impulse to laugh. As I take in the soothing scent of the lavender, my eyelids grow heavy. The next thing I know, Marlene is summoning the group back to consciousness with a gentle voice to lead us through the final *om.* I'm so drowsy it takes a massive effort to pry open my eyes.

On our way out of the studio, Sexy Eyes asks me, "Did you enjoy the class?"

I smile up at him. "I did. But all those yoga terms go way over my head. I need a cheat sheet with translations and drawings."

"You might try Marlene's Introduction to Yoga class. Only English is spoken there." He must see my smile fade because he adds, "Kidding. Keep coming back and you'll catch on in no time."

Is he being polite, or is that an invitation? I've no idea, but I float downstairs to the lobby, my body humming with an unexpected frisson of excitement. I can hardly wait to get back to hatha yoga to work on all those unpronounceable poses.

As I'm pouring myself a cup of java at the free coffee bar in the lobby, Sunny arrives and fixes herself an herbal tea sweetened with two packets of raw sugar. It's a beautiful morning, unseasonably warm because of the Santa Ana weather that can bring the hottest temperatures of the year to the coastal sections of Los Angeles. Today the mercury is predicted to top out in the mid-eighties. To take advantage of the delightful weather, we stroll out to the deck with our hot beverages, passing Sexy Eyes along the way.

"Hey, Sunny, how's it going?" he asks, smiling at her.

"I'm good. You?"

"Same." He and I lock glances for a moment as we cross paths. My cheeks feel hot, and I hope my blush isn't visible.

Sunny and I settle into adjacent lounge chairs facing the water. The deck is deserted right now, but that will change in another hour when the water aerobics contingent arrives to take over the pool. They are mostly an older group, not the fittest people in the club, but definitely an enthusiastic bunch.

"The man who just walked past us—who is he?" I ask.

Sunny peers back at me, her eyes a tranquil emerald sea. She's around forty, and though she's not beautiful, she has an earnest, trustworthy face, with regular features and white teeth that gleam when she smiles. "Charlie," she replies. "Charles Kittredge."

"You know his last name?"

"He's like the rock star of the club."

"That man is a rock star?"

"Not literally," she says, laughing. "He's a *novelist*, and a pretty famous one." She emphasizes the word with a tone of hushed respect that one might reserve for a Nobel Prize recipient. "But he doesn't act like he thinks he's a rock star. Charlie's a nice guy. A really nice guy."

"I haven't heard of him."

"You don't read fiction?"

"Not much. I mostly go for biographies, political books, that sort of thing." Though I don't say it, fiction seems a bit like a waste of time to me.

"He's published a lot of literary fiction. One of his novels even came out as a movie a while back. *Bicoastal*. Have you heard of it?"

I shake my head, again professing ignorance.

She leans toward me and lowers her voice. "He's a *widower*." Sunny imparts this latest bit of information in the same reverential tone as if to suggest that widowhood is a distinguished and even desirable state.

"That's so sad. Did his wife die recently?"

"A few years ago. I don't recall the exact timing; except I heard it was sudden. Why do you ask about him? Are you interested?"

"Oh no. Simply curious. Are *you*?"

"No, although . . ."

"Although what?" If there is anything between Charlie and Sunny, I will certainly want to back off. I mean that in the hypothetical sense. I would back off *if* I was interested—which I'm not. Ogling isn't synonymous with need or desire.

She blinks and looks away from me when she replies. "Nothing," she says. "We're friends. I've read a few of his books. You should check them out."

"I'll go to his Amazon page right now," I say, pulling out my cellphone. On my screen is a text message from Michael, sent about twenty minutes earlier.

Michael: Call me ASAP. Important.

"Shit," I say. I silenced my phone at the beginning of yoga class and forgot to check it until now.

"Anything wrong?"

"I'm not sure. I need to call my son." I stand and walk over to the railing at the front section of the deck, away from Sunny, to speak to Michael in privacy. I can never predict when he might have a bone to pick with me about something.

He answers my call immediately. "Oh good, you're there. Mom, we're kind of in a fix. Heather's come down with a nasty stomach bug and a fever. She's too sick to take care of Benny, and I've got to get to the office. I'm late as it is. Can you watch him?"

Since Heather is a stay-at-home mom, they don't have a regular daytime sitter. "Sorry she's sick," I say. "Won't Boss Daddy give you the day off?" I regret this question the moment I ask it.

"*Boss Daddy* needs me in the office. We've got an important new business pitch today, and I'm in charge. The presentation starts in an hour."

I sigh. I made it clear to the kids a long time ago that although I may work from home, I still have a real job and can't be at their beck and call during the week. But Michael's voice is fraught with tension, and it occurs to me this might be a good opportunity to mend fences.

"Sure, I'll watch him. At my place, not yours."

"But all his stuff is here—"

"Look, I don't want to catch whatever Heather's got. Anyway, I'm expecting a few calls later on the business line, and I need to work while he takes his nap. Throw some stuff in a bag, whatever you think he'll need, and I'll pick him up in about fifteen minutes." I walk back to Sunny's lounge chair and explain the change of plans.

"Is there anything I can do to help?" she asks.

"Thanks, but no. I have no idea what I'm gonna do with a three-year-old all day, but I don't want to babysit him at their house with my sick daughter-in-law."

"Why don't you bring him over to Seaside Kids?" she says, referring to the childcare center here at the club.

"Oh, I don't know . . ."

"They've got that great playground in the back, and the bounce house, and lots of toys. The kids here always look like they're having a blast."

I pause, then nod my head. "Maybe you're right. I'll take Benny there and we can both check it out. It could be a lot of fun for him."

For the next couple of hours, all goes well. I collect Benny, who is excited to see me, throwing his arms around me as he shouts "GrandMar" in a joyful little voice. Since he was two, Benny has called me this name, coined by his mother. It's original, pronounceable, and cute all at the same time – far more memorable than the generic Grandma, Grammy, or (God forbid) Granny. And it has inspired the current abbreviation of my full name to "Mar."

I bring Benny straight to the club. In the company of a staff member, I escort him hand-in-hand around the childcare center and study his reactions.

"Look, GrandMar." He points at a ride-on car. "That's like my car at home, but this one is bigger. And it's yellow."

"What color is yours?"

"Blue. I want to go on this one."

"Soon," I promise. When we lead him out the back door to view the playground and bounce house area, his eyes light up. "Do you want to play here for a little while? While GrandMar gets some exercise?" I ask.

He nods, and I am satisfied that he will be okay.

The aide ushers us back to the check-in desk, where I complete the required paperwork and hand over a sandwich and snacks that Michael has stowed in the child's little Spiderman backpack. Benny's face crumples when I turn to leave him, so I rush back and grab his hand.

"How about a ride on that yellow car you liked?"

Benny nods and I lead him to the car. I help him into the seat, and he pushes the vehicle around as I give him a goodbye wave and turn to leave. His expression turns solemn again, but the aide swoops in and distracts him by showing him how to work the horn, giving me a thumbs-up as she does this. I reconnect with Sunny, who is still lounging on the deck, and we go to a cycle class. I find it a tad boring to sit on a stationary bike pumping my legs for an hour, and my thoughts turn to Benny as I wonder how he's doing in childcare. The woman at the desk promised to pull me out of class if there were any problems, so I guess everything is all right. I'm pouring down sweat by the end of class, energized by the rigorous if repetitive cardio workout. "Do you want to meet for a drink somewhere later? After I drop Benny at home?" I ask Sunny.

She hesitates. "To be honest, I'm not a big fan of the happy hour crowd."

I remember she declined a similar invitation last week. "You're welcome to come to my place instead. I've got a balcony with a view, and it should be warm enough tonight to sit outside."

This time, she breaks into a grin. "That sounds terrific."

I agree to text her with the time and address as soon as I learn my schedule. Still dripping from the cycle class, I take a shower and go to pick up Benny. To my relief, I find him jumping up and down in the bounce house at the rear of the Seaside Kids area, wispy blond hair flying, a mile-wide grin on his little face. I let him bounce for another ten minutes, figuring he'll have a good nap this afternoon. He cries when I inform him it's time to leave.

We run into Charlie again on our way out. When he sees me hand-in-hand with the weepy child, he crouches down to Benny's level and smiles at the boy. "What's wrong? Did you lose a thumb?" He shows Benny that trick where you bend both thumbs at the joint and slide one thumb along the side of the opposite hand, creating the illusion that the thumb is in two pieces. Benny's eyes widen and the sobs turn to giggles.

"Thanks. Great diversion." I grin at Charlie as we continue on our way.

I turn on my cellphone as we're climbing into the car, and what comes up is not good. The screen is cluttered with multiple messages and missed calls, the earlier ones from Heather and the rest from Michael.

Where are you? We are very worried is the central theme, expressed in escalating degrees of urgency over a period of nearly two hours.

Crap.

I strap Benny into his car seat, unwrap a stick of string cheese to occupy him, and call Michael at once.

"Is everything all right? Where's Benny?" he asks, his tone panicky.

"He's fine. Couldn't be better." I shoot the child a pleading look that says *whatever you do, don't start crying.* Fortunately, his attention is riveted to the string cheese. "We're about to drive home from Seaside Fitness," I say to Michael.

"What are you doing there?" Before I can respond, he says, "Heather and I have been frantic. She tried texting and phoning you, and when you never answered, she called me out of my meeting. She thought something had happened."

"Nothing happened, I just—"

"I had to leave the new business presentation to drive to your apartment. When you weren't there, I was at my wit's end. We were sure you were in a car accident, or Benny got hurt and you took him to the ER—"

"He's absolutely fine. I brought him to play at the childcare place here at the club."

"Are you kidding me?" Now Michael is shouting into the phone.

"They have a bounce house. He had the greatest time. I'm sure he'll tell you all about it later."

"I cannot believe this. We entrust you with your only grandchild for the first time in weeks, and your response is to stick him in daycare with a bunch of strangers?"

"Michael—listen, please," I say, more apologetic now. "I'm sorry you and Heather were frightened, but let's all try to calm down. They have a terrific facility here, and the childcare workers are all licensed, or certified, or whatever you call it. It's not like I left Benny with a band of Hell's Angels."

Silence. At least Michael has stopped shouting. After an audible intake of breath, he says, "How soon will you be at the apartment? I think I should pick him up and take him home."

"Please don't. Listen—there's no reason for you to disrupt the rest of your workday. I've got this covered. We'll have a bite to eat, then nap, and then later I'll take him down to play by the tide pools. He'll enjoy that."

"All right," Michael says, but his tone is grudging.

"Why was Heather trying to reach me?"

"She wanted to tell you Benny doesn't always nap anymore. If he can't sleep, give him a few books to occupy him. I put some in his backpack."

"I keep books for him at my place too. We'll be fine."

"Don't forget, all right? Set a timer for twenty minutes, and if he's still awake, give him the books then."

"Twenty minutes. Got it."

"He'll be okay as long as he has books, and he understands this is quiet time. You'll still be able to do your fucking work."

I chafe at this last comment. My work has always been *fucking* work as far as Michael is concerned. He has inherited the Schuyler contempt for my career choice. But I let it go. "We'll be fine," I say once again.

At the apartment, Benny finishes his partially eaten sandwich from Seaside Kids, followed by a few apple slices and strawberries. I settle him down on my bed, cradling him in my arms as we examine a book about tide pools. "Tell me how many things you can name in the tide pools," I say, giving him a light kiss above the ear as I take in the innocent scent and soft feel of his silky hair. Michael had exactly the same hair at this age. With this recollection, a lump catches in my throat.

Benny points to the familiar objects one by one. "Snail. Crab. Seashells. Rocks. Seaweed."

"Very good. Later when we go down to the water, we'll count how many of these we can find," I say, feeling a sweet sense of tranquility from sharing such a gentle time together.

He gives me a sleepy smile. "Can I ride on the yellow car again soon?"

"Sure, little lamb."

Thinking of Michael's snarky reaction, though, I'm not at all sure – and my serenity dissolves. Why is he so compelled to micromanage every aspect of Benny's care, even though the boy turned three last fall? Honestly. You'd think I had never put a child down for a nap. Still, I set my cellphone timer for twenty minutes as I'd pledged to do.

• • •

That evening Sunny and I are sitting on my balcony, enjoying the spectacular Santa Ana sunset – the twilight sky a palette splashed with a dozen brilliant shades of orange and pink. We nibble on brie and crackers and enjoy an Italian red blend that Sunny presented on arrival. I'm familiar with the wine - it's one of those bottles you can purchase for five or six dollars at Trader Joe's. Despite the bargain-basement price, it's eminently drinkable, and Sunny's sharp eye for a good value wine increases my respect for her.

We discuss the book I'm reading, by an Ivy League-educated psychiatrist whose patients report past life experiences in their sessions. "He documents cases in which his patients reveal things they *couldn't* have known unless they had lived these past lives," I say. "It's pretty compelling. Unless he's made it all up." Part of me wants to believe in this phenomenon, while the other part remains a skeptic.

"I believe in reincarnation," says Sunny.

"In the religious sense—like Hindus or Buddhists?"

"I guess so, though I wouldn't call myself a follower of any specific faith. But I do think our actions in this life have an impact on future lives. Like good deeds can make for a better life next time, while bad behavior can lead to suffering in the next life."

"What about fine, upstanding people who suffer tragedy unfairly in *this* life? Are they paying for previous misdeeds?"

Sunny pauses before answering. "I've thought about that a lot. I don't know, but maybe. It *would* provide a rationale for why bad things happen to good people."

"I guess."

"What about you?" she asks.

"I'm inclined to believe in multiple lives too. But I don't think they're connected, or that one life influences the next. It's all random."

"Do you think there's a final destination, a place where you arrive after all these lives?"

"You mean like heaven or nirvana?"

Sunny nods.

"Well, I don't believe in heaven. I can't picture myself in some paradise, reconnecting with all the people I've ever loved in my life, partying and rejoicing, or whatever the hell you do in heaven. Nirvana is more spiritual, isn't it?"

"Yes. It's a release from human bondage from the cycle of life, death, and rebirth. What happens at the end – if you get there – is peace and happiness and liberation from suffering."

"Sounds better than heaven to me, but I can't see a path to nirvana in my random universe."

"But if events are random, then nothing you ever do as an individual makes a difference," says Sunny. "I can't believe our actions don't influence the future. I believe in cause and effect, and in, I don't know . . ."

"Consequences?"

"Yes." She nods fiercely. "I believe in consequences."

Later, when we've emptied the wine bottle and decimated the cheese plate, I offer to prepare something more substantial. "I don't cook, but I'm a genius with a microwave. I keep a stash of TJ Reduced Guilt meals in the freezer, and I always have fresh veggies on hand."

"Thanks, but I must've scarfed half a pound of cheese. I'm stuffed." She starts toward the front door. "Are you coming to the club tomorrow?"

"I plan to unless the kids need me to watch Benny again."

"If I can help, I'm happy to do that," Sunny says. "I love little kids. And I know you have work to do."

"I gather you're not working right now?"

She looks down at her hands. "No. Not for a while now."

Sensing her discomfort, I don't ask her to elaborate. After she leaves, since I'm not hungry either, I head straight to the computer to work on a freelance assignment. My brain is stimulated and I'm ready to sink my teeth into some productive writing. As I pound away at the keyboard, I reflect on how nice it is to have a new friend with whom I can discuss topics that run a little deeper than weather patterns and restaurant openings.

8.

As it turns out, the kids need me again the following morning. Michael calls first thing to inform me that Heather is no better today. He says he *really* has to get to the office early to crank out a proposal following yesterday's new business presentation, and he'll drop Benny off at 8:00 a.m. sharp. He makes me swear on the proverbial stack of Bibles that I will keep Benny in the apartment, that I'll text him first before going outdoors, and that under no circumstances will I take him to Seaside Fitness again.

This all happens so fast that I don't even have a moment to think about my rudely interrupted workday until Benny has arrived and I've fed him a bowl of instant oatmeal. When I review my daily calendar, I find an appointment that has slipped my mind. Bill Bayliss, an important advertiser from Phoenix, is visiting LA, and I'm scheduled to have lunch with him in Marina del Rey, about a half hour's drive from here.

Robert has arranged the lunch himself. Our advertisers enjoy it when the publisher trots me out to meetings, where I give my little rehearsed speech about how we couldn't attain our lofty editorial goals without their dedication and support. When Robert is present, he follows with a talk about all the awards my team has won and the independent studies rating us as the preferred publication among engineers for twenty years straight. It's a crock, but it impresses the clients . . . and it's kind of an ego trip for me. There is no way I can blow off this meeting.

What to do? Seaside Kids might have offered a solution, but Michael has declared it off-limits. And I don't dare call him to renege on helping with Benny. I'm already skating on the thinnest of ice, and it won't take much for me to plunge through the cracks into more frigid and turbulent waters.

I call Sunny to accept her offer of help. She arrives at the apartment less than fifteen minutes later.

"I didn't realize you lived so close," I say.

"Well, actually, I—" She hesitates. "Never mind. Hi Benny. My name is Sunny. Like the sun in the sky, you know?" She gives him a warm smile.

He nods shyly.

"The sun is shining this morning. Would you like to draw a picture of the sun?"

He considers the idea. "I want to make a tide pool picture. Maybe I can draw a sun smiling over the water."

"That's a really great idea," she says.

"We went to the tide pools yesterday after we read this," I say, handing Sunny the tide pool book. "Maybe you two can read it again today, and Benny will tell you about what we saw. Or you can use it to help him with his drawing."

Benny settles down to play with a plastic firetruck while Sunny and I empty his backpack. Then I show her around the kitchen, where we discuss options for his lunch and snacks. Thanks to her prompt arrival, we can spend more than an hour together before I have to go.

The three of us play with his dinosaur activity box for a while, and as Benny becomes gleefully absorbed in hatching dinosaur eggs with Sunny, I retreat to my office to do a little work. When the time arrives for me to leave for my lunch appointment, I bend down and encircle Benny in a hug. "Sunny is going to be your babysitter for a few hours."

"I thought you were my babysitter."

"You're so lucky to have *two* sitters to play with you," Sunny says. "Your GrandMar won't be gone too long."

"Okay," he says, appearing to be on board with the plan. Today there is no crumpling of the face, no need for distraction. He has warmed to my friend in no time at all.

As she walks me to the front door and out of Benny's earshot, Sunny asks, "Do you think he'll be okay with me?"

"I do. And I'll keep an eye on my phone so we can stay in close touch."

"Sounds good."

"Sunny, thanks again. You're a lifesaver."

On the drive to Marina del Rey, a fluttery sensation stirs in my belly, followed by a rush of heat. This is the physical response that occurs when I'm overcome with guilt. It's like an internal blush of shame that follows self-centered behavior. I first noticed this reaction when my former housekeeper had to cancel because of emergency gall bladder surgery. My immediate thought was not one of concern for her, but rather: *Why did this have to happen now? We've invited twenty people for a cocktail party, and I'll have to clean the house myself.* Bring on the guilty flutter and the slow burn in my tummy.

Trying to ignore this feeling, I ponder what I'll say to Michael when he arrives later to pick up the child. Before Benny spills the beans, I will have to confess to leaving him with Sunny. I think Heather will be okay with the idea, but Michael is another story. He's such a nervous hoverer that the term *helicopter parent* doesn't begin to describe him. How can I frame my actions in the most acceptable light?

I'll jump off that bridge when I come to it.

• • •

There's a saying, "Be careful what you wish for," and right now I'm regretting that I wished for a return to the era of the three-martini luncheon. If there was ever a day I did not want to resemble a character in a 1950s Madison Avenue drama, today is it.

It's 2:30 p.m., and we've occupied our window table at Marina del Rey's most popular seafood restaurant for over two hours now, admiring the sailboats that glide past as Bill Bayliss sips vodka gimlets contentedly. That mid-century alcoholic classic, which features four parts gin to one part Rose's lime juice, served on the rocks with a wedge of lime, is my client Bill's beverage of choice. He's demolished three thus far.

I select a low-alcohol French rosé and limit myself to a solitary glass, which is like total abstinence given my usual habits. My nerves are so raw from worrying about Benny that I don't experience even the tiniest buzz. It's not Benny I'm worried about as much as Michael. He texts me once an hour to confirm that everything is fine. I, in turn, text Sunny for updates.

She responds lickety-split:

Sunny: He ate a big turkey sandwich, everything but the crusts. And a banana. I cut it into pieces and made it into a happy face.

I excuse myself and walk outside for five minutes to call Sunny and Benny. I speak in turn to both of them, relieved to hear Benny's little voice chattering about all the fun things they're doing.

Half an hour later, another text update:

Sunny: He isn't asleep yet, but he's quiet. I've given him three books, and he's lying on the bed looking at them.

I forward this information to Michael as if I were supervising Benny myself. With every text, the lie elongates like Pinocchio's nose. My conscience is troubled by this deception, though I know Benny is safe and content. Still, I'm impatient to get back home, and I devise every trick in the book to conclude this tedious meeting. When Bill and I study the dessert menu, I cluck and say, "Strictly *entre nous*, the desserts are not good here. I've tried a few, and . . ." I tip both hands into a thumbs-down posture.

"Oh, thanks for the warning. In that case, I'll have a little *fromage*. They can't screw up cheese, can they?" Bill says with a chuckle. He summons the server and orders a small cheese plate, along with a glass of port to "go with" as I try to mask my disappointment.

Half an hour later, I glance at my phone—no more messages from Michael, thank God—and I say, "Oh my gosh, this has been so pleasant, I lost all track of time. Can you believe it's three o'clock?"

Responding with only a dopey smile, Bill has reached an even mellower state than the overripe wedge of camembert that drips across his cheese plate.

"I hate to spoil the party, but if you and your driver don't hit the road soon, you'll be stuck in nasty rush hour traffic going back to your hotel," I say with a wag of my index finger.

"At three o'clock?"

"You'd better believe it. Los Angeles evening rush starts about now and doesn't end until after seven. Come to think of it, I don't understand why they call it rush *hour*."

At last, I've caught his attention. "Let's be on our way, then," says Bill.

I raise my hand to scribble a faux signature in the air, signaling the waiter to bring our check. I thrust a credit card into his hand with only the briefest glance at the itemized bill - though I look long enough to note the daunting total damages. Robert has been grumbling that ad revenues are off, and he's nitpicking our expense accounts, which is uncharacteristic. Still, I'm under his strict instructions never to let an advertiser pay. As I hurry out to retrieve my car from valet parking, I shoot a text to Sunny:

Mar: Heading home from client meeting. Thanks for covering with Benny. And no argument, I am totally paying you.

It's about a quarter to four when I turn my key in the lock and open the front door. Michael is perched on the couch, rigid with attention, lying in wait for me, and there is no sign of Sunny or Benny.

My eyes widen. "Michael? What are you—"

"*Shhhh.*" He interrupts me in a fierce whisper. "Benny's taking a nap."

I lower my voice. "What's going on? Why are you here?"

He picks up his cellphone from the coffee table and thrusts it in my face. "I'm here because of *this*."

Displayed on his screen is my last text message to Sunny, thanking her for covering. I realize with a sinking heart that I didn't send that text to Sunny. I sent it to Michael. *On accident*, as Whitney might've said.

"When I read this message, I drove right over here to find out what the hell was going on." Though Michael continues to speak in a whisper, his voice drips with venom.

"So you sent Sunny home?"

"That is correct. Wait—no. I couldn't send Sunny home because she *has* no home."

Now he might as well be speaking in tongues, so incomprehensible is this latest remark. "What are you talking about?"

"I thought it was negligent yesterday when you stuck Benny in the childcare place," Michael says, "but today you left a *homeless* woman in charge of him?"

"She's not homeless."

"She *is*. I asked her where she lived, and she told me she was between places right now."

"That doesn't mean—"

"Let me finish." His tone is growing darker by the minute. "You never listen. I pressed her on it, and she admitted she's living in her car. Maybe you could've bothered to find this out yourself before entrusting your only grandchild to her."

Dear God.

I puzzle out how best to keep the situation from escalating. Benny is fine, I reason to myself, so it's likely that Michael is reacting more to my deceit than my negligence. It's not like I left the kid unattended at the water's edge. "Even if Sunny doesn't have a home right now, that doesn't mean she's mentally deficient or incompetent. She's intelligent, calm, and totally responsible," I say to him, struggling to sound calm and responsible myself.

"So you're confident this woman's credentials are impeccable, even though you've only known her a few months." A few *weeks* is more like it, but I won't correct Michael on the math.

"She kept offering to help with Benny for a couple of hours, and I had an important work meeting, so I took her up on it. I didn't want to bother you—"

"It's always an important work meeting with you, Mother."

I'm in deep *caca* whenever he calls me *Mother.*

He continues. "Nothing has changed. You were pulling the same crap when I was a kid, leaving me alone all the time."

"I never left you alone until you were much older than Benny," I say, protesting the unfair comparison. It's true when Michael was ten or eleven, I'd sometimes go out for an hour to meet with a client or freelance writer in the late afternoon. But latchkey kids were common in our area back then. Some of the neighbors' children were unsupervised for hours after school every day until their parents returned from work. "You were fine with being alone."

"How can you be so sure? You weren't there. There were lots of times I *wasn't* fine with it."

"You never gave any sign of that."

"You never asked. Even if you had, it wouldn't have changed anything. Like I said, you don't listen. Your work life has always come first."

The conversation is going nowhere, so I change course. "Can I get you a cold drink or something to eat while Benny finishes his nap?"

He shakes his head. "No. If he naps any longer, he'll never get to sleep tonight. I'm going to wake him up and head home."

"Do you want to bring him again tomorrow?"

"No, I do *not*. I can't believe you would even suggest it after everything that's happened these last two days."

"I know you're upset, but keep in mind that Benny has been fine through all of this, and he hasn't been unsafe for a moment. Everybody is trying to juggle a difficult situation - you with a sick wife at home, both of us with a lot of work stress right now."

"Riiight," he says, but the way he draws out the word, I know what he really means is "wrong."

"Michael, it's not easy being under this kind of pressure when you're in your mid-twenties. I went through it myself. I hoped you and Heather would wait longer to start a family and not repeat the same mistake your father and I made—"

"Mistake?" He no longer bothers to lower his voice. "Is that what I am to you, a *mistake*?"

"Oh God, of course not. All I meant was that it's harder to handle that kind of responsibility when you're young. We struggled with it big-time ourselves."

"Oh, now Heather and I are the irresponsible ones? That's a fine one coming from you after all the terrific 'help' you gave us this week." He makes air quotes with his fingers when he says the word *help*. As he storms toward the bedroom where Benny is napping, he says, "Don't worry, we won't need any more of your 'help.' If you want to talk about mistakes, leaving you in charge was *my* biggest one."

Ouch.

On their way out, as Michael carries the sleepy child against his shoulder, Benny says, "Bye-bye, GrandMar," and gives me a sad little wave. Even the kid can tell I'm up shit's creek. For twenty-seven years Michael has been my son, my sole offspring, but whenever we have a dispute, I still don't know how to make things right with him. My well-meaning words tumble out twisted into knots that only tighten when I try to unravel them. Every time we part on bad terms, the ache of regret in my chest is palpable. After he leaves with Benny, I find a text from Sunny.

Sunny: So sorry about what happened. We need to talk. TMO morning?

Mar: Sunny, none of this is your fault. Yes—tomorrow.

9.

As we sip coffee on the club's pool deck and munch on the fresh croissants I picked up at the Village Shops bakery, Sunny reveals the whole sad story. "It's true I'm living in my car. I didn't mean to tell Michael, but I'm not a good liar, and when he pressed me for specifics, the truth spilled out."

I sigh. "You don't need to apologize for the truth, Sunny. But why didn't you ever tell me?"

"I almost did yesterday morning, but the time wasn't right. It's not something I'm proud of."

"How—how does that work, exactly? Living in your car, I mean." My privileged life has given me little first-hand experience with homelessness. In my naïve imagination, a homeless woman is the grimy figure who mumbles incoherently, her uncombed hair hanging down in oily strands as she pushes a shopping cart along back alleyways, her few grungy belongings stuffed into the basket of the cart. A homeless woman is not supposed to look well-groomed, hygienic, and *normal* like Sunny.

"The way it works is that Seaside Fitness has become my primary residence. The club is open from six a.m. till eleven at night, so it's a place where I can shelter indoors, exercise, watch TV, read on the sundeck, and drink the free coffee."

"But doesn't it arouse suspicion for you to be hanging out here all day long?"

"It would, so I don't. There are other safe places where I like to spend time . . . the library, the mall, the beach on nice days."

"So the club is more of a home base."

"Right. I can shower as often as I like and use all those nice-smelling amenities in the locker room . . . shampoo, lotion, all that. Rosie in the housekeeping department has taken me under her wing, and she sneaks a load or two of my clothes into the club laundry every week."

"Where do you sleep?"

"The parking lot around the back of the club is for employees, and a section of that lot is off the beaten path. I can park my car there overnight and nobody will hassle me."

I lick buttery croissant crumbs off my fingers. My brain is exploding with questions I'm reluctant to ask. As if reading my mind, Sunny says, "You must be wondering how I came to this sad state of affairs."

"Yes, I am. But you don't have to talk about it unless you want to."

"I *do* want to. It'll be a relief to clear the air. And even though we haven't known each other long, I think of you as a friend I can trust."

"Thanks. Same here." I reach over and take her hand. "I never would have left you in charge of Benny otherwise. Learning about your circumstances doesn't change that for me."

She smiles for the first time today. "I figured you'd drop me like hot coals when you found out. I wouldn't blame you if you did. Anyway, it's been about four months since I had to give up my apartment."

"What happened?"

"My mom had Alzheimer's for the last few years of her life. While she could still make decisions, she asked to stay in her own home. It was a costly choice, but I went along with her wishes."

"You were a good daughter. So you were close to your mother?" I shudder, thinking of how Mum and I would fare in that situation. At least money wouldn't be an issue.

An unreadable look crosses Sunny's face. "Mother was—both my parents were in their forties when they had me. It caused problems for them. We had a complicated relationship."

"My mum was in her twenties when I was born, but my dad was forty-two and never had the energy to keep up with me." I smile at the memory of him. "He was a dear though."

Now Sunny is the one to shudder. "*Dear* isn't a term I'd apply to my father." Her green eyes darken as though a storm cloud has settled over her. Despite her name, I suspect my kind-hearted friend has not had such a sunny life after all.

"Do you want to talk about him?"

"My father? Not really." She sighs. "Anyway, for the first year or so after the Alzheimer's diagnosis, Mother managed okay on her own—well, with me helping out with shopping, appointments, that sort of thing. But as time went on, I had to hire a caregiver. Eventually, her money went. Then *my* money went. Then my boyfriend didn't like the way I was handling the situation, and *he* went." She utters a mirthless laugh.

"Lovely of him."

"Oh, there were extenuating circumstances; he had a job opportunity out of town. Anyway, I can't put it all on Todd. I made some bad decisions. When I saw the money running out, I panicked and cut back with the caregiver. Then I had to keep missing work to stay with Mother myself. Eventually, I got fired."

"Sounds like a no-win situation," I say. "I take it she's gone now?"

"Yes, she died about six months ago."

"Weren't you able to make money from the sale of her house or live in it yourself?" I think of my own windfall when I opted to leave our marital home and put it on the market.

She shakes her head. "Mother lived in a rental property. I never imagined something like this happening to me, not having a roof over my head. But it's not as awful as you might think. Sometimes I make it into a kind of game, like a survival challenge on reality television." Then she smiles. "Sounds too dramatic, doesn't it?" Sunny gestures at the sparkling Olympic pool near our lounge seats, the boats bobbing in the harbor, the water lapping against the jetty with a lulling rhythm. "This place isn't what you'd call a hellhole. The club has been a godsend, no question about it. Except . . ." She frowns.

"What?"

"My annual membership runs out at the end of the month. I can renew on a month-to-month basis, but even that will be unaffordable for me at this point."

"What will you do?"

"I'll figure something out."

I pause, mulling over how to tell her what I'm about to say. "Listen, Sunny. I stopped at the ATM this morning. I've got cash in my glove compartment. How much are the monthly dues?"

"One hundred and ten dollars. But Mar, I can't accept money from you."

"Why not? For one thing, I owe you for babysitting."

"Maybe so, but not a hundred bucks. Anyway, I don't—"

I thrust out one arm, my hand flexed back with fingers splayed in a gesture that says *stop*. "I'm giving you two hundred dollars. That will take care of next month's membership and maybe help a little with your other expenses. Do you need more?"

"No. I'm getting unemployment benefits, but it's not enough to live on. This would be a huge help, but I'm concerned it might be a financial strain for you. You've never told me your story either, but you're a single woman living in a small apartment. A small but *nice* apartment."

"I assure you it will not be a strain. I'm fortunate I don't have to worry about money." I've said this before, but until now they were empty words. It took Sunny to help me appreciate how blessed I am by comparison. Though I don't get into the details with her, the truth is Henry has been generous in the divorce settlement, I am gainfully employed doing work that I love, and it's never a struggle to put food - or expensive wine, for that matter - on the table.

"You *are* fortunate, and I'm glad for you. But I'll only take the money if we agree it's a loan to be repaid, not a gift."

"Yes, a loan. There's no timetable for paying me back, and if things haven't improved by this time in April, we'll revisit the situation."

Sunny nods. "Perfect. I'm pursuing a couple of things, and depending on what happens, I might have to leave the area. For now, I'm taking it month to month."

"Okay, fine. One other thing. I have a futon where you could crash—"

"Absolutely not. Your place is small, you work from home - it would be a huge imposition. In a few days, you'd resent my being there, and I'd resent your resenting it. Besides, with me around, Michael will never let you have Benny over."

My mouth curls into a tight-lipped smile. "I don't think he'll let me have Benny over for a long time, anyway. And that's on *me.* All the lying to Michael, making dumb choices to cover up my actions . . . now I'm paying the price. You were right about life not being a series of random acts. What was the word we used?"

"Consequences."

"Ah, yes. Consequences. Let me run to the car and get you that money."

"You're a generous friend." She reaches out for a hug. As we hold each other in a warm embrace, I think about the consequences of Sunny's bad decisions - decisions rooted in filial duty and respect for her mother's wishes. Unlike mine, her character is selfless, honest, and pure. But she is the one who ended up broke and living out of a car.

• • •

Sunny leaves ten days later. Her cousin Eleanor has opened a day spa in Northern California and reports the place is "printing money," according to Sunny. It's proving difficult to find reliable employees, and Eleanor thinks Sunny will make a perfect hostess. Before departing, she asks me to meet her at the club for a farewell coffee. "My job is to man the front desk and greet customers, answer phone calls, book appointments, that sort of thing," Sunny says. "I've done similar work, so I have no anxiety about whether I can handle it. The real question is whether I can handle that insipid canned harp music they play all day long in spas."

"Are you worried you'll get too relaxed?"

"I'm worried I'll get sick to my stomach." We laugh in unison.

"That's great news. Well, except for the nauseating music. But isn't it expensive to live up north? Rents are supposed to be even worse than here."

"Eleanor has a little guesthouse above her garage where I can live. I don't even have to pay rent as long as I take care of the cats whenever she and her husband travel. They became empty nesters this year and it's pretty lonely, so she says she'll be excited to have me around."

"It sounds ideal. You can keep each other company, but you'll have your own private space."

Sunny pulls a hundred-dollar bill from her purse and hands it to me. "Here. I held off on paying next month's club membership fee because I wanted to wait and see if the job offer would materialize. I can't repay you the full amount I owe you, but I should be able to send you the rest in a couple of months."

"I appreciate that, but why don't we forget it? I owed you for babysitting, and the difference isn't worth worrying about. You can buy me a glass of wine next time you're back in town."

"Fair enough." She stands and says, "I'd better hit the road. I want to make it up north before I get stuck in the evening rush at the other end." I nod in agreement. In California, our comings and goings are governed by an often fruitless quest for traffic avoidance.

When Sunny and I hug each other, her soft cheek against mine, hot tears prick my eyes. I marvel at how quickly I've become involved in Sunny's life. In one sense it's a good thing she's going. If I'm to hold on to my newfound independence, it's wiser not to grow too close. Still, her departure leaves a void that will be difficult to fill. Sorrow wells up in my chest as I think once again about the hardships in Sunny's past. I try to be hopeful about my friend's future. And my own.

PART FOUR: APRIL
NIC

10.

The day begins with bad news.

I'm going through my first emails of the morning when I come across one from my boss containing a big red exclamation mark. Robert almost never resorts to this overused flagging device, the same way he abhors the use of exclamation points or all caps in the subject line to lend a message greater urgency. My pulse quickens as I click on the email to open it. Robert informs me that ad revenues are "*down, down, down.*" For trade magazine publishing to be profitable, we have to maintain a prescribed ratio of ads to editorial pages. When the paid advertising commitments fall short, articles end up on the cutting room floor. Robert writes that the special sixteen-page pollution control insert we'd planned for the next issue must now be slashed to eight pages due to lack of advertiser interest, making it more of an excision than an insertion.

"Damn," I say aloud. I haven't had my morning coffee, and my voice sounds like gravel. As editor, it's my job to decide what goes, and it's never fun to tell a contributor that the article we accepted weeks earlier will now be pushed back to an indeterminate month on the editorial calendar. I open up a spreadsheet containing the special insert plan to review my options.

The landline rings, and caller ID displays an unfamiliar New York number. I should let it go to voicemail as usual. But I somehow worry, absurdly, that Robert might be phoning from another location in New York, and I don't want to miss his call.

"Hello?" I answer in my still-croaky voice.

A brief pause, an intake of breath. "Oh no. I think I woke you up."

I clear my throat and sound a bit more human when I ask, "Who's calling, please?" Definitely not Robert.

"I am so sorry, Ms. Meyer. I'm Nicolas Rodriguez. That's Nicolas with no 'h'."

"Yes?" The name is unfamiliar.

"I'm the new account supervisor working on L&M Processes, and I'm a total idiot. They told me you worked from California, and here I am calling you in the middle of the night."

I laugh. "It's actually six-thirty, and I was already at my desk."

"Are you sure? Or are you being tactful?"

"Oh, I'm rarely tactful. I turn off the phone at night, so I assure you there's no danger of you waking me up."

"Oh, thank *goodness*," he says. He has a theatrical way of speaking.

"You're with Bentley Communications?" I ask, naming the small New York agency that handles publicity and advertising for L&M, one of *Powder World's* biggest advertisers.

"Yes, I joined the agency two weeks ago. Nice to meet you by phone—though I still think an apology is in order. It can't be fun having to start your workday this early to keep up with New York."

"On the contrary, I *love* the Pacific Time Zone. It has so many advantages."

"Such as?"

"Like, you can host people for the Super Bowl or even the Oscars and stay awake through the entire event. All the guests are gone by a civilized hour." To hear me talk, you'd think my lonely little rental unit was Party Central.

"I never thought of that," he says.

"Good thing you called. You folks owe us a feature article for the July issue, and it's almost the deadline. With the account changes going on at Bentley, I wasn't sure who to contact."

"I'm your man," he says in a self-assured tone that inspires immediate confidence.

"Do you need me to send you a copy of our article submission guidelines?"

"No, I'm good. Already got 'em. Remind me, what's the drop-dead date?"

I glance at the calendar. "Three days from now. Can you submit it by then?"

"You can count on it. We immigrants know how to get things done," he says, paraphrasing a line from Lin-Manuel Miranda's smash Broadway show, *Hamilton.*

"Ah—a *Hamilton* fan, huh?"

He lets out a whoop. "Sounds like you're a fan yourself. Have you seen the show?"

"Yes, I saw it here in Los Angeles. Ticket prices for the touring company weren't too crazy. I don't think I could afford the Broadway production." This is not true, since Henry's settlement has left me with wiggle room for splurges, but I would prefer to project the image of an earnest and hardworking publishing professional rather than a pampered divorcee.

"Well, we can solve *that,*" Nic says. "Management has given me a generous budget for entertaining important editors. And spouses, of course . . . if you're married."

Though he hasn't known me for five minutes, this man has already scoped out how to get on my good side - quoting one of my favorite shows, flattering me professionally. A junket to the New York production of *Hamilton* with such a fun individual might be just what I need this spring. I'm already imagining us after the performance, enjoying post-theater supper and champagne at Joe Allen or one of the other old-school Times Square haunts. "I take it you're an immigrant, then?" I ask, circling back to his reference to the *Hamilton* song.

"I will admit to taking liberties with that reference, Ms. Meyer. I'm a born and bred New Yorker. My parents immigrated to the Bronx a few years before I was born."

"Please call me Mar. Where did your parents emigrate from?"

"Puerto Rico."

"Just like Lin-Manuel's folks."

"Marvelous. A-plus-plus for you on Broadway trivia," he says. "In fact, I think I'll call you Marvelous Mar. And you can call me Nic with no 'k'. My intuition tells me we're gonna get along fine. Let me see if I can guess your tastes. Rodgers and Hammerstein – good. Rodgers and Hart – even better."

"Nailed it."

"Let's try another. You can't bear Disney musicals, but you adore Sondheim."

"Nailed it again, but that was too easy," I say with a laugh.

"How many times have you seen *Sweeney Todd*?"

"Four."

"I've got you beat – six times. Not including the film version, which I think we can agree is best forgotten." This time we laugh together.

"Okay, my turn. What's your favorite Sondheim that nobody's ever heard of?"

"Oh, good one," he says, then pauses before responding with, "*Road Show*," one of Sondheim's later works that was not a commercial success. "What's yours?"

"*Evening Primrose*."

"Come again?"

"It's a musical set in a department store, starring Tony Perkins. Sondheim wrote it for television in the mid-sixties," I say.

"Wow, you're good. But I hope you know, we're in serious geek territory here."

I *love* this guy.

• • •

Four days later, there's no sign of the promised feature article. I've been so focused on cutting eight pages from the special insert that I've forgotten about the article until now. Nic picks up the call on the second ring when I phone him to ask about the status.

"Good afternoon, Marvelous Mar."

"It's still morning out here, but no matter. I'm following up on the article, checking to make sure it didn't get lost in cyberspace."

"Oh, my dear, I haven't sent it yet . . . but I have not forgotten you, trust me. I've finished the copy – and if I'm allowed boasting rights, it looks *terrific* – but I'm still waiting for a couple of people at L&M to sign off on it and send me the photos they promised. I am *so* sorry if I've thrown off your whole schedule."

"You haven't thrown it off – yet. I always build a little air into these deadlines. I can give you an extension until the end of work Monday. But I need to get it by then at the latest."

"You're the best, Mar. I promise you shall have it." Nic changes the subject, telling me about a Broadway preview he attended the previous night.

"I'm not familiar with that show. Is it a musical?"

"No, a straight play."

"When I was younger, I thought a 'straight' play was one that had only heterosexual characters. I didn't know it meant a play without music."

He finds this hilarious. We discuss a few more theatrical developments – major productions scheduled to open this season, other shows that are trying to hang on by the skin of their teeth until the Tony Awards. I don't have a lot of theater pals, especially in my current self-imposed friendless period, so I enjoy the banter. I've let Nic off easy about missing the editorial deadline, but no big deal. I'm sure everything will be fine. Monday comes and goes, however, and still no sign of the article. Late in the day, I shoot off a one-line email: *Hi, Nic. Checking back with you on the article status. I need it asap, thanks.*

I don't expect a response until the next morning, since it is already dinnertime in New York. I slip on a warm hoodie and go out for my afternoon walk along the esplanade, and as usual, I'm able to put work matters aside for the hour. It's a coolish day in the fifties. Living near the beach, I've developed a mere fifteen-degree comfort zone, from about sixty to seventy-five Fahrenheit. Anything lower or higher and I complain. Like now, when the marine layer has settled in and the ominous dark gray cloud bank envelops me in its chilling mist.

Occupying my mind today is the vexing situation with my son. In the weeks since I bungled my babysitting duties, Michael has rebuffed my attempts to set things right. To complicate matters, he's been traveling a lot, and I don't want to contact Heather and put her in the awkward position of either rebuffing me or going against her husband's wishes. I reach out to Michael with short chatty emails every few days and hope he'll get over what happened before too much time passes.

Meanwhile, I keep replaying our last argument in my head. It's now clear to me that Michael resents being left alone when he was a boy, and that he regards my putting Benny in daycare and leaving him with Sunny as a similar form of abandonment. What did he say to me on that dreadful day last month? "There were lots of times I wasn't fine with being alone." But there is only one time I recall him being upset - the day his bicycle was stolen.

I rack my memory to recall the sequence of events that led to the incident sixteen long years ago. We'd given Michael a new red bike for Christmas. He was thrilled for the first couple of weeks, watching over it like a new baby and even wheeling it into his bedroom at night. But he quickly grew careless about using the shiny metal padlock and chain we'd given him with strict orders to secure his prized possession whenever he left the bicycle outdoors. More often than not, he'd leave the bike laying on its side, unlocked, on the front lawn or the edge of the driveway where anyone could come along and take it. Though we lived in a safe neighborhood, I tried to impress on Michael that it was never wise to tempt fate.

I remember coming home one afternoon from an editorial meeting to find Michael in tears. I hadn't been gone much over an hour. "What's wrong?" I asked.

He let out a pitiful sob, his reddened face streaked with tears. "My bicycle is gone."

"*Gone*? Oh, Michael. I warned you about this. I told you not to leave the bike lying around the yard."

"It didn't get taken from our yard."

"Where, then?"

"I—I don't want to say."

"Tell me what happened. Did you go to the park?" He often rode to the neighborhood park at the end of our block to use the playground equipment.

Michael paused before answering. "Yeah. I—I rode to the park."

"And where was the bike when this happened?"

"I—I'm not sure."

"You're not *sure*?"

"I guess I leaned it against a tree." Now he was crying harder. "I climbed up the jungle gym, but I was only gone a few minutes. When I went back to the tree, the bike was gone."

It relieved me that the theft had occurred in a public park and not on our property. But that knowledge did nothing to mitigate my annoyance with Michael. "You knew not to leave the bike unlocked. And now see what's happened?"

"I'm really sorry, Mom." His face contorted with pain and loss.

I couldn't bear to look at him when I said, "You'll be a lot sorrier when you have to walk everyplace because there's no more bike to ride."

He was shocked at this as if the idea hadn't occurred to him. Did he assume Henry and I would go right out and replace the stolen bicycle?

"Will I have to walk to Luke's? Or can you drive me?" he asked, referring to his best friend who lived a few blocks away.

"Neither. You're grounded."

Maybe I was being a little harsh on the kid. Losing his treasured bike was probably punishment enough in itself. But my disciplinary actions soon became irrelevant when Henry - always the good cop on our law enforcement team - overruled the grounding after he came home later and heard the story. He even treated Michael to a ski weekend up at Big Bear. So much for discipline. Though there were still consequences to pay. Michael remained bike-less for the rest of the school year at my insistence. What rankled the most - Henry made sure Michael knew he would've had a new bike a lot sooner had it not been for his hard-ass mother.

Still, thinking back on the whole episode, it doesn't add up. The theft of Michael's bike may have left a traumatic scar, but what did that have to do with my leaving him alone? If I'd been working in my home office that afternoon when he rode to the park, the result would have been the same. I couldn't understand how it was *my* fault for going out. Perhaps the events had become muddled in his young head after this disturbing episode. Or perhaps he needed someone to blame other than himself.

"You don't listen. Work has always come first with you," he'd said to me the day he was so angry about Sunny. It's all connected, I think, but I can't fathom *how*. I can't get the pieces of the puzzle to fit, no matter how much I shuffle and rearrange them.

My troubled musings are interrupted when I run into Dog Lady and her Wheaten terrier. The dog jumps up and plants his furry paws on my shoulders, then licks my chin as if I'm his favorite friend in the entire world. "Off, Petey," Dog Lady commands, tugging sharply on the terrier's leash. "Gosh, I'm sorry. We call that the 'Wheaten greetin', but he knows better than to jump up on strangers." She says *gawsh* instead of *gosh,* and *bettah* instead of *better*. I hadn't noticed until now that she has such a pronounced New York accent. Make that New *Yawk.* It fits well with her expression of wry amusement, the look of a city girl who's wise to everything.

"Oh, we're not strangers. We've been running into each other for a long time. Haven't we, Petey?" I extend both hands to scratch the terrier behind the ears. Wheatens have curious but delightful ears that lift out from their heads at jaunty angles, and then fold down in bluish-gray triangles in vivid contrast to their sand-colored coats. Petey presses his shaggy square head into my hands and closes his eyes, luxuriating in the massage.

Don't stop. Don't ever stop, I imagine him saying.

"He loves that," says Dog Lady. "I'm Audrey, by the way."

She extends a pudgy hand and I reach over to shake it. Petey looks up as if to inquire why I interrupted the ear-scratching. In my mind, he's speaking to me again. *I told you not to stop.*

"Nice to meet you. I'm Mar. Petey is beautiful. Is he a show dog?"

"No, but he's a busy boy. I put him through a therapy dog training program last year and he's been making rounds with me every week at a retirement home. The folks there are crazy about him—aren't they, Petey?" She strokes the dog's back like a proud parent. "He's gentle with the residents. He never jumps on anyone when he's on duty."

"I guess I should be flattered that he doesn't mix me up with the old folks."

Audrey laughs at this. "I don't think anyone would confuse you with old folks." She sweeps one hand across her forehead to brush away the dark bangs that are falling into her eyes. I note that wry expression again.

"Thanks. I'll see you next time. I need to get home and finish up some work."

"You work from home? Doing what?"

I give her the abbreviated answer about my editorial job, the one where I don't mention the name of the publication. When I say *Powder World,* people think it's a magazine about skiing, or maybe women's cosmetics. I'm not in the mood to have that conversation right now.

"I work from home too. But I'm out on the road a lot."

I learn she is a regional sales representative for a pharmaceutical company. "What about Petey?"

"If I'm going out for a long stretch, my boyfriend, Nathan, pitches in, or my parents. In the winter, when the weather's cool, sometimes I take him with me on my customer rounds and he sleeps in the car. But he's okay by himself at home most of the time. He's a good boy."

I stoop to give the good boy a final scritch and continue on my way. My thoughts return to Michael and this mysterious anger he's holding onto - but I'm no closer to figuring it out.

11.

When I fire up my computer the next morning, I'm relieved to see an email from Nic Rodriguez. But relief turns to frustration when I read the message.

Marvelous Mar (or should I call you MM for short). Please don't be TOO peeved with me. I will send you the article tomorrow, I promise. Anyway, isn't this deadline kind of crazy-early for a July issue? It's only the middle of April.

Nic's charm is wearing off, and fast. I reply at once: *Our official deadline for the July issue was last week. We have a review process involving a team of editors and advisors; and we must allow time for this review, and time to repeat the process with a revised draft if needed. If I don't receive the manuscript from you by tomorrow, I will plug another article into that slot.* I'm not sure whether this sounds snippy or merely formal, but I hit the send button. I receive Nic's response ten minutes later.

No worries, MM. I assure you, I'm not throwing away my slot. He is parodying another lyric from *Hamilton.* He adds: *Anyway, there won't be a need for a revised draft.*

We'll have to wait and see, I think. I type a reply. *I hope so. I have every confidence you'll deliver a great article, Nic.* No. He's being a wiseass and does not deserve an obsequious response. I delete it and write: *We'll have to wait and see.*

Well past the close of business in New York the following day, Nic emails the long-awaited article. I normally begin my beach walk at this hour, but curiosity gets the better of me. The beach can wait.

Two pages into the manuscript, I already regret the decision to forgo my afternoon exercise. Disappointment is too mild a word for my reaction as I slog through the murky prose. From a standpoint of grammar and syntax, Nic is an even weaker writer than Doctor Dave, our celebrated dust diagnostician. But each month Doctor Dave serves up a sizzling platter of meaty advice that our engineering readers can sink their teeth into. Nic has delivered nothing more than a lightweight plateful of sickly sweet confections, sugar-coated and devoid of flavor or substance. The article is a shameless commercial plug for L&M. I debate whether to call my boss. But this article is such a flagrant violation of our editorial guidelines, I'm confident Robert will back me up as he always does. No reason to disturb him with this.

I also consider calling Nic to discuss the submission, but there needs to be a paper trail. I pour a glass of white wine to soothe my frazzled nerves and settle down to the task. It takes a full hour to draft a reasonable and measured response. I inform Nic, with apologies, that this article is not something we can publish in its present form. I attach a copy of our "Guidelines for Authors," the document he clearly didn't bother to review earlier. So Nic won't accuse me of being negative or unfair, I then offer suggestions on how he might approach the next draft. I highlight several areas of concern for our readers and provide a series of questions to be answered. To placate him, I write: *These revisions will be time-consuming, and it's now impossible to include the piece in July. The good news is, we've reserved a slot in the following issue, which is one of* Powder World*'s best-read every year. Please reply to confirm your agreement with this plan.*

Hitting the send button, I'm confident I've addressed the problem with an abundance of fairness and diplomacy. Yet I don't hold out high hopes for anyone who could submit such a piece of unmitigated rubbish in the first place.

• • •

I wake up early again, on edge about the unresolved situation with Nic. Business hours have begun in New York. Perhaps his answer awaits me already. But when I get to my desk, I see I have no voicemail, no email. Maybe he's at a meeting, maybe he's read my email but is still mulling it over. I turn my attention to editing another article, but I can't resist checking the inbox every few minutes in my impatient search for resolution. I ditch plans to go to a strength training class at the gym because I'm reluctant to leave my desk until I know something.

Another two hours go by before the phone rings. "Ms. Meyer? Nicolas Rodriguez here." No more Marvelous Mar. He's all business now.

"Good morning, Nic."

"I reviewed the email you sent me last night."

"Good. Do you have any questions?"

"No questions. I think you need to call your boss. Robert Carlson, the publisher."

"Yes, Robert is the only boss I have. Why do I need to call him? Perhaps I should have emphasized this before, but I make the editorial decisions at *Powder World.*"

"Just call him," says Nic. There's an abrupt click on the line as he disconnects the call.

My hands are shaking as I speed-dial the office. "Robert, have you spoken to Nic Rodriguez, the new L&M account guy?"

"Margaret." Robert's voice is dull, expressionless. He's once again forgotten he is not supposed to call me by my old name, but this is no time to split hairs.

"He told me to speak to you, and then he hung up on me. What the hell is going on?"

A heavy sigh. "We have to run the article."

"*What*? Have you read it?"

"Yes, he emailed it to me this morning."

"Then you know it's a steaming pile of horseshit."

"I recognize that. Listen—he threatened to cancel the advertising if we don't run the article. Not only the ad in the July issue. He's threatening to pull the entire schedule for the rest of the year."

"Then talk to Ed Matthews," I said, naming the vice president of marketing at L&M. "Ed's a reasonable guy. I can't believe he'd support his agency doing something this outrageous."

"Of course, I tried to do that. I stalled Nic, told him I'd get back to him, and phoned L&M immediately. But it turns out Ed is on a three-week South American cruise for his twentieth anniversary, and he left strict orders not to be disturbed. He instructed his assistant that 'the agency can handle any decisions in my absence' - and the problem is, 'the agency' now means Nic Rodriguez. I'm up against a wall here."

I take a deep breath, trying to collect myself. "But this kind of thing has happened before, and you've never given into it. You're the one who taught me, we mustn't ever let advertisers hold us hostage."

"That was then - this is now. Our first quarter bottom line was lousy. In fact, it stank like last week's garbage. We can't afford to lose one of our biggest advertisers right now." His voice cracks a little with the strain. "It'll break us, I'm telling you. It'll break us."

"What if it's all a big bluff?"

"I don't think it is. Anyway, I can't take the chance. I called Nic back and told him we'll run the article in July, but he has to make a few concessions."

"Like what?"

"He agreed to eliminate the section where the article criticizes competitors. And he's letting us cut out two of the brand name mentions."

"Only two? But not eliminate all of them? There were way more than two product plugs in the manuscript."

"Correct."

"I still can't believe you're telling me this. Have you considered the blowback from our other advertisers and contributors? They're all going to come to *me*, as the editor, and ask, 'Why did you let L&M run a puff piece like this when you've always held us to a stricter standard? What happened to editorial integrity?' I'd like to know how I'm supposed to answer them, Robert. What *has* happened to editorial integrity?"

"Defending our integrity doesn't do a lot of good if there's no magazine left to defend. Believe me, I don't like this any better than you do, but we're running the article. My decision is final on that."

My heart is crashing in my chest. "And I'm resigning as editor, effective today. *My* decision is final on that." I slam down the receiver, unplug the business phone from its cord, and hurl it across the room. I won't be needing it anymore.

12.

It's too early for wine, so an hour of relaxation yoga appears to be the best alternative for warding off a full-blown anxiety attack. I consult the schedule and find a suitable class at three o'clock. I compose a brief, formal email to Robert confirming my resignation - again, always wise to have a paper trail in matters of importance - before I shut down my work email program. Now that I'm offline and my work phone is out of commission, I won't have to worry about Robert trying to talk me out of resigning. But I turn off my cellphone as well, to be on the safe side.

At yoga class, Sexy Eyes—I mean, Charlie—is in his usual spot. Since the row behind him is fully subscribed today, I must plant my mat to the right of his. This sidewise proximity will limit my ogling opportunities, but at least I'll get to gaze at him every time we twist or turn to the left. And I won't embarrass myself in his presence by bungling difficult balancing poses or pretzel-like moves since this class is limited to seated or reclining stretches and relaxation postures. By the end of the hour, I am indeed calmer and more optimistic about my professional future.

Outside the yoga studio is a second-floor outdoor walkway, where I pause to gaze over the railing to the sparkling pool area below and the dark blue harbor beyond, which is speckled with small sailboats at this hour. Charlie walks up and grips the railing with both hands, stretching out his long arms as he takes in the view. "It's hard to think about going back to work with a tempting vista like that in front of you, isn't it?" he asks. His voice is like a smile.

"Do you always work late in the day?" I ask, turning to face him.

"Only when I have to meet a publishing deadline."

"Oh. I actually prefer working late afternoons and evenings. I work from a home office."

"Doing what?" he asks.

"Editor of an engineering journal." For years, my identity has been so defined by this job, it isn't until after the words spill out that I realize they are no longer true.

"An editor," he says. "Well, well. I should confess that editors are the joy of my career and also the bane of my existence. The editor is my inspiration and my nemesis. My protector and my attacker. My liberator and my enslaver. And all at the same time."

Wow. If he can speak off the cuff with such eloquence, what must his writing be like? I should take the time to find out. Evidently, he knows *I* know he's a novelist. Perhaps Sunny has discussed me with him.

"My current editor is the relentless pest who calls my agent every day and screeches, 'Where are those pages Kittredge promised?'" he says. "But without her and the others before her, I'd be nowhere."

"You make the editorial profession sound so glamorous . . . and powerful."

"It is," he says.

I must have a stricken expression on my face because he gives me a curious half-squint and tilts his head to one side, causing his long boyish bangs to flop from one side of his forehead to the other. "Maybe in the engineering world, being an editor is different?"

"Oh yes," I say as I heave a sigh. "I can assure you it is." As much as I've been enjoying the quiet conversation and the tranquil view, this stark reminder of my present situation has planted me back into reality, and all at once, I'm itchy to be alone. With a sad smile, I wish him a nice day and I head out to the esplanade.

Pausing in the lobby to refill my water bottle, I listen in on a conversation between Dame Donut and a red-faced man I haven't seen before. Although it's an unwritten rule among members to avoid controversial topics, this man is expressing his uninformed opinion that climate change is a big fat hoax. Dame Donut says to him, her tone silky-smooth, "An accomplished man like yourself is much too intelligent to believe that, so I'm going to assume you were joking just now." She gives him a gracious smile and glides away.

Well done, Dame Donut. In the same situation, I would've muttered "asshole," stomped off, and then berated myself for the inelegant response. As a professional writer and editor, how is it I so often allow my words to betray me, as they did when I quit my beloved job on impulse? Part of me already regrets my blurted resignation.

Right or wrong, what's done is done. During my walk today, I compose a mental list of all the clients for whom I've free-lanced. I'll call or email my contacts at these companies and drum up a little business for myself. As long as I'm proactive, I believe my efforts will yield results. I *have* to believe this. Perhaps my search will lead me to a full-time job offer, though I'm not sure I want to go that route. It will be difficult, if not impossible, to find another employer willing to give me as much flexibility and freedom as Robert did, and I don't want to be chained to a nine-to-five (or worse) office gig.

When I cross paths with Audrey and Petey, the dog acts subdued, as if he's picking up on my sober vibe. Since he doesn't jump on me today, I squat down to scratch him under the chin, and he thanks me with a smelly kiss. Audrey and I smile and exchange greetings, but I resume my walk at a brisk pace. I have no stomach for small talk this afternoon. Back home, I pour a glass of a nice Chianti and fix myself an early dinner – TJ's frozen turkey Bolognese. All I have to do is nuke the package in the microwave for a few minutes. I boil a pot of salted water, throw in a handful of whole wheat penne, drain the cooked pasta in a colander, and toss the hot penne and sauce together with a tablespoon of grated parmesan. For a side dish, I make broccoli florets, also nuked. This is about as fancy as I get in the kitchen.

I top up my wine glass and settle at the computer for the evening, grateful to have a free-lance assignment to occupy my troubled mind. The task at hand is a five-page article for a building products company, a case study describing how an architect used my client's solar panels to save energy. After a couple of hours, I have a respectable first draft. It's not due for two weeks, but I need to stay productive.

The next day, I give the case study a fresh read and do a little fine-tuning. Then I proceed with my new business initiative. I make a spreadsheet of all my prospects and shoot out a brief email to the full list: *I'm pleased to announce that I am expanding my free-lance business and am ready to offer excellent availability and fast turnaround on all your writing and editing projects. Call or email me for a project quote. I look forward to working with you.*

I also make half a dozen calls to the people with whom I have the closest professional relationships. Nobody answers their office phones anymore, so I leave friendly voicemail messages to deliver my pitch. I summarize all these outreach activities on my spreadsheet to make sure I have a detailed record. By the time I finish this busywork, half of the morning still lies ahead. I'll walk over to the gym for a couple of hours, but then what? I can only spend so much time exercising and socializing in the locker room. After my workout is done, how will I engage myself for the rest of the day? And tomorrow, and the day after that, and all the days that follow? Panic stirs within me. This isn't about money – I have more than enough between the settlement and the house sale. It's about *time*.

Throughout my married life, between the magazine job, free-lance work, and family obligations, the pace was relentless. I used to imagine being bathed in time, never feeling rushed or overwhelmed. I envisioned myself luxuriating for hours in a Jacuzzi tub with fragrant bubbles, a good book, and a glass of champagne. I pictured long ferry rides to Catalina Island, hiking explorations of the Santa Monica mountains, daytime excursions to museums and lectures. But now that time has been handed to me like a gift, and all these pleasures are mine for the taking, the things that used to attract me are now repellent – like a Prince Charming transformed into a slimy frog.

Leisure is my enemy, not my friend. All I want is to work.

• • •

The following days are fraught with anxiety and boredom, which I try to relieve through a series of small tasks. Check email and voicemail again. Make another round of phone solicitations. Set up a new filing system that would make Judge Judy proud. But after two more weeks of this, not a single soul has responded to my new business overtures. Knowing the few free-lance assignments on my to-do list will be completed soon, I grow more despondent by the hour. If I weren't on the outs with Michael, this would be a perfect opportunity to spend more time with Benny. Remembering our day at the tide pools, I feel that ache of guilty regret again. If only I hadn't bungled things last month when Heather was sick. What was I thinking, leaving him with Sunny without their permission? I keep trying to call Mum, but every time I reach her, she says, "Now's a bad time, Margy," or "Frightfully busy this week."

At the club each day, I prolong my routine as much as possible. I work out in the equipment room, I attend a couple of classes, I chitchat indoors in the lobby and outdoors on the pool deck. Since I have nothing else to do, I no longer wait until late afternoon for my daily esplanade walk. I go out earlier, directly from the club, plugging in earphones and listening to music or podcasts to avoid reflecting on my personal circumstances. It's pleasant enough, I guess. But I no longer see Petey and Audrey because of the deviation in my schedule, and their absence has left yet another hole.

Back at the club one afternoon, desperate to fill time, I decide to use the women's steam room. Though sitting naked in a chamber filled with burning vapor can make me claustrophobic, today I spread a big towel on the highest bench, stretch out, and let the scalding steam penetrate every pore, hoping it will sweat the toxins from my mind and body. Fifteen minutes later, in the shower, I can't say the experiment has done any good, but at least it's allowed me to forestall my dreaded return home by another quarter of an hour. I dress, grab my gym bag from the locker, and am getting ready to leave when I overhear a conversation. Amazon Lady is talking to a woman I haven't seen before - another redhead, although her long thick hair reminds me of a chestnut mare, in contrast to Amazon Lady's finer strawberry-blond tresses.

"I don't know what I'm going to do," Horsehair says to Amazon Lady.

"What's wrong, Cheryl?"

"My sitter fell down the stairs and broke her leg. She won't be able to take care of Connor."

"For how long?"

"That depends on how it heals—but a long time. Like, *weeks*."

"Remind me, how old is he?"

"Four and a half."

"Why can't she sit for him anyway? He's not an infant who needs to be carried."

"Are you kidding? The way that kid runs around in the playground, you almost have to be a marathon runner to keep him out of trouble. A middle-aged woman on crutches is not gonna cut it."

"Oh yeah, I see what you mean. But can't you bring him to the daycare place here?"

"My time at the gym isn't the problem. I can work out in the mornings when Connor is in pre-school. But I volunteer twice a week, and I have my three-hour art class on two other days, so I need a private afternoon caregiver at home. Do you know anyone who babysits?"

I silently curse Nic Rodriguez for dragging me down to my current depths of despair. Then I stride over to the two redheads, straightening my back and shoulders as I walk. I want to project an air of authority while also exuding warmth and tenderness, like a woman who can control any situation but in a nurturing way. I reward Horse Hair/Cheryl with my brightest and most confident smile as I say, "I babysit."

PART FIVE: MAY CONNOR

13.

Connor looks like the child actor who would be summoned if you called up central casting and said, "Send me an impish little boy." With curly red hair, a tiny upturned freckled nose, and a mischievous grin made more endearing by a gap between his two front teeth, Connor is beyond adorable.

Still, mealtime with him presents formidable challenges.

The first day at his house, when it's time to feed him his lunch, I realize Connor's mom hasn't given me any instructions. In this same situation, Heather and Michael could always be relied upon to leave behind copious typed notes, so I'm unprepared for Cheryl's more lackadaisical approach. "How about a peanut butter sandwich?" I ask the boy, immediately regretting the offer. Supposing he has a peanut allergy? But wouldn't his mother have told me that? She couldn't be *that* lax.

"I hate peanut butter."

"Okay, then . . . turkey sandwich?" I say, surveying the fridge and pantry.

"Don't like it."

"Ham?"

"Don't like it."

"Macaroni and cheese?"

"I hate that more than anything."

I try a different tack. "Why don't you tell me what you *would* like?"

He responds without hesitation, "Chicken teriyaki."

Great. This kid has no idea who he's dealing with. "Connor, I don't think I can cook that for you. We don't have the right ingredients—"

"In the freezer," he says, pointing upwards.

I open the top freezer compartment and scan the contents. "Where?" I ask.

He holds up his arms to indicate I should lift him towards the open freezer, where he points to the right edge of the lower shelf. "There."

Sure enough, I see half a dozen small baggies, each containing two skewers of precooked chicken teriyaki. All I need to do is zap them in the microwave - my specialty. Connor eats the warmed chicken with relish, licking the soy sauce off his fingers. He also finishes a cupful of Goldfish crackers and a big bowl of blueberries, both specific requests.

After lunch, he introduces me to his toys and books. His favorite book is about the sounds that different animals make, and when he presses down on the electronic buttons on the animals' noses, the various bleats, moos, and neighs are replicated with stunning accuracy. The boy recites the entire book aloud without missing a cue. Is he a fluent reader, or has he memorized it all? I should be able to tell the difference. After a couple more books, he says, "Mar-Mar, time for my nap now."

He has already given me a nickname. Another name! I have so many, I don't know who I am anymore. I can't imagine Benny taking charge of his own schedule this way, but then I remind myself that Connor is half a lifetime older. That any child this age would nap at all is a miracle in itself. Benny is already on the verge of outgrowing his own afternoon quiet time. During the hour or so that Connor sleeps, I consider applying myself to one of my free-lance assignments; but given my current sparse workload, I prefer to save the writing for later, over a glass of wine at my computer.

The next day, in the kitchen with Connor, I say, "Chicken teriyaki time." The words come out in a sing-song voice.

"No, Mar-Mar. No teriyaki today." He looks stunned that I would make such an outlandish suggestion.

"Okay, what'll it be?" I'll let him decide. As I will soon find out, the menu changes daily at Connor's whim.

He holds up his arms again and we go to the freezer. This time he points to an individual serving of turkey tetrazzini, naming the dish correctly. As long as Connor knows his way around the freezer and I know my way around the microwave, we'll get along fine. The whole schedule, in fact, is close to perfect. After my morning gym routine, I pick Connor up at preschool around noon, drive him home for lunch, and play with him for an hour until he looks at the clock and announces his naptime. Is it typical for a four-year-old to tell time? I doubt it, but there's a lot about Connor that isn't typical.

When he wakes up, I give him a snack and offer him a choice of the playground at the end of the block or his own back patio, which resembles a showroom for Fisher-Price ride-on toys and playhouses. As usual, he directs the activities. "I'll drive the dump truck. Mar-Mar, drive the car. No, not the blue car, the *pink* car." He informs me there is a fire in the house and he's going to put it out. "Mar-Mar, go inside the house," he commands, pointing to the classic cottage playhouse with its red plastic door.

"But you said there's a fire inside."

"Just *go*." He promises to save me from the flames.

My cellphone buzzes during the fire rescue. It's Mrs. Ostrowski again. I acknowledge with a pang of guilt that I've never returned my old neighbor's calls, even though she's left me three or four messages in as many weeks. Come to think of it, it may have been longer than that. But I can't talk to her now.

I resolve to phone her back in a day or two. By four o'clock, Cheryl returns from her art class, or maybe it's the volunteer gig—I lose track of her day-to-day schedule.

On my fourth afternoon at the job, as I grab my purse and prepare to leave, Connor throws both arms around my legs in a fierce hug and says, "I love you, Mar-Mar."

Life is good. I have a charming new pint-sized pal who adores me without judgment. Though I spend long afternoons saying nothing more profound than, "Time to watch Daniel Tiger," or "Mar-Mar wants coffee," it's worth it to fill the gaping holes in my schedule. And I still have the freedom to do what I like for the rest of the day. After my babysitting gig, I go straight to my beach walk - where I unwind by the shore and enjoy my meetup with Audrey and Petey, who now resemble old friends.

• • •

At the gym, Judge Judy is in the women's lounge with Amazon Lady, Dame Donut, and the usual suspects. As I face a mirror in the adjacent dressing room, applying my lipstick, Judith delivers a familiar rant in her unmistakable nasal twang.

"So, it turns out the dude is not dead. His wife tells him he's a goddamn cheating son of a bitch, and it serves him right that she gave all his stuff away. Can you fucking believe that?" There is laughter all around as Judith re-tells the story of the embittered client who is settling a score with her unfaithful husband after he's strayed while traveling on business. Judge Judy can spin an amusing yarn, there's no doubt about it. Although this yarn is not funny. At least, not to me.

The thing is, Alice wasn't Henry's only partner in infidelity. There were other women - most or all of them one-night stands, as far as I know, which occurred during his business trips over the course of at least a decade. The first time I learned Henry was cheating, Michael was a teenager. It happened on a Saturday afternoon in autumn when the boy was off visiting his friend Luke. I remember how gray and chilly it was. We were contemplating whether to fire up the furnace for the first time that season. When I walked into the bedroom carrying a basketful of clean laundry to fold, I found Henry sitting on the edge of the bed, his back turned to me, his shoulders shaking.

I dropped the laundry basket and ran to him. "Henry—what's happened?" A multitude of frightening possibilities cascaded through my head in a split second. Was Henry ill? Or perhaps one of his parents? Was the company in trouble? Had he been hiding some financial problem from me?

He leveled his dark gaze on me, eyes brimming with tears, and grabbed my hand, squeezing it with urgency in both of his. "Margaret, I—I'm not sure how to explain this, but—"

"You're scaring me. Just tell me."

"I—I met a woman while I was on the road, and . . ."

"You're having an affair?"

"It isn't an *affair*. I—we had a few drinks at the hotel bar, and then we went to her room." He paused, reluctant to continue.

"And?"

"And we—*you* know . . ."

"No, I don't know. I need you to spell it out."

He sighed. "I slept with her. Once."

"When?"

"Wednesday night."

"Jesus, Henry. I'm trying to get my mind around this. You just went and picked her up at the hotel bar?"

"It wasn't like that," Henry said. "She was sitting a couple of barstools away from me, and she looked sad—distraught, even. She started a conversation and told me both her parents died in a car crash the month before. Then she broke down crying."

"So this was—what? A pity fuck?"

"The woman was coming on strong to me. I'll admit she was attractive, but I felt so sorry for her. The whole thing was kind of raw, emotional."

"Did you see her again Thursday night?"

"She checked out early that day to fly home."

"But if she'd stayed, you *might* have slept with her again?" Now I was a prosecuting attorney trying to corner the witness.

"I'm not sure if—*no*, it wouldn't have happened a second time. This was the proverbial one-night stand."

"One and done, huh?"

"This may sound like a cliché, but I swear to you it didn't mean anything outside of the moment."

"If it meant nothing, why make a confession?"

Henry blinked at me. "Oh, Margaret, I couldn't keep a secret like that from you. I would have felt terrible."

"So you chose to unburden yourself and make *me* feel terrible instead?"

"That's not how I meant it. I'm sorry. I never intended to hurt you."

Then something else occurred to me. "Since you slept with a stranger, do we now need to worry about—you know, catching some disease?"

"No, no," he said without hesitation. "I would never put myself at risk that way. Or you, of course."

I believed this. Henry was always good at taking care of Henry. But did this mean he carried condoms on his business trips, or did his bereaved partner considerately supply the protective device? I didn't want to know.

He kept grabbing my hand, repeating his apology, begging for forgiveness. That's the way Henry has always been. He hates it when anyone thinks ill of him, so he'll go to great lengths to absolve himself of whatever wrong he's committed. But with all the apologizing, there's one thing Henry *didn't* say that day. He never promised me it wouldn't happen again.

Over the coming days, I felt numb about my husband's revelation, as if the news of his betrayal and breach of trust had sent me into shock. I figured I'd come out of it in time - and when I did, I'd experience a delayed reaction of pain and anguish. I waited for that to happen. Then I waited some more. But it never played out that way. To my relief, strange as it sounds, I had to admit Henry's infidelity didn't bother me all that much. After all, lots of people had one-night stands, didn't they? Probably *most* people during the long course of a marriage, I rationalized - though most people exercised greater discretion, not confessing to one's spouse after a single false move.

Our marriage continued as before. We still enjoyed good health, a comfortable household, and a life free of financial worries. I pushed the incident out of my mind, locking it inside a safe compartment in the back of my consciousness.

I'm certain Henry continued to cheat on me two or three times a year, over a period of many years. I learned to recognize the signs. After returning home from a business trip, instead of vegging and dozing in front of the TV as usual, he would initiate enthusiastic sex. It had been ages since I'd felt any deep attraction to Henry. So when this happened, I was neither thrilled nor repelled. It was like dining at a fancy restaurant where an over-attentive waiter served a meal that failed to delight the senses yet wasn't bad enough to send back to the kitchen.

Sometimes I'd steal a glance at Henry's cellphone, where I often found text exchanges with unnamed recipients, confirming assignations. Though the messages weren't blatantly salacious, they were suggestive enough to leave little doubt in my mind that he was up to something. But I never confronted him with the evidence, and he never confessed to these other indiscretions. Don't ask, don't tell.

Did Henry become passionate with me on those occasions to assuage his guilt over cheating? Or did it happen because he was aroused by his trysts with new (and therefore more exciting) sexual partners? I didn't know, but I could always sense when he had been with someone. I told myself, *At least Henry's being discreet, life will go on as before, no need to be threatened by this behavior.*

Until he fell for Alice.

Michael knew nothing about the other women. In his eyes, Henry could never do wrong. He was always the fun parent, the easy parent, the let's-go-to-Vegas-for-the-weekend parent. Even the relationship with Alice could be excused, given that I'd never been the warm and devoted wife this wonderful man deserved. I should have been hosting dinner parties and organizing charity events and dedicating myself to Schuyler Enterprises.

I remember once, when Michael was in grade school, for Mother's Day the kids received an assignment to create a picture of Mom engaged in her favorite activity. Though I liked to believe I was a more attentive and nurturing parent than Mum, I knew Michael wouldn't be drawing us baking cookies together. He brought home a sketch of me seated at my desk, a curly-haired stick figure staring into a childishly drawn computer screen. That is how Michael has always seen me – as a woman who loves work above play, above family, above everything.

He's not entirely wrong. I've always turned to my work for comfort and shelter the way an overeater turns to food. I've taken the high road all these years, never saying a word to Michael about his father's philandering. Even when the affair with Alice came out into the open, I didn't denigrate Henry to him, not once. And where has it gotten me? In Michael's eyes, I'm still the bad guy, still the one to blame for the failure of his parents' marriage.

Maybe it's time for me to set the record straight about his father.

14.

About two weeks into my babysitting gig, I'm sorry to say the honeymoon between little Connor and me is over. The trouble begins in the kitchen, where he now rejects all his previous lunchtime favorites. The usual tour of the freezer, fridge, and pantry yields no requests, just repeated head shakes as he says, "No, no, no" to every item on offer.

He finally agrees to buttered pasta. I boil the macaroni and toss it in butter, but then I make the amateur mistake of sprinkling in a handful of parsley flakes for color. "I hate spinach," he says, pushing the bowl away in protest.

"It isn't spinach. It's a green called parsley, to make it look nice."

"Not nice. I hate green."

"Connor, please try it. You won't even taste the parsley."

"No. I don't want to eat that. I want charcuterie," he says, pronouncing it perfectly.

"Well, we don't have any." This elicits a loud whine from him, to which I respond, "Don't blame me, buddy. I'm the sitter in this house, not the shopper."

I talk him into cinnamon toast, but I screw that up as well. He wrinkles his nose after the first bite and says, "Too spicy." I have failed to dilute the cinnamon with an adequate measure of sugar. I shrug and push a box of Goldfish crackers across the counter. At least I can always count on Connor to gobble up the fish-shaped cheddar treats and a generous helping of fresh berries.

At playtime, he now finds fault with everything I do. When he asks me to help him build a house using his new Lego set, he criticizes my design skills. "Mommy makes nicer houses." He won't let me read to him, nor will he read aloud to me, looking at his books alone in silent protest and shaking his head "no" if I try to join him in the activity. And outside, the single game he will agree to is Jail, where I'm placed in solitary confinement and not permitted to speak or move as he rolls around the patio in his various ride-on vehicles.

Though Connor may be a precocious little imp, he's a poor substitute for Benny. Spending so much time with another young child now feels disloyal, which in turn makes me miss Benny even more. When Cheryl returns a few minutes past four, she asks if everything has gone all right.

I sigh. "Well enough," I say, not wanting to divulge the part about my failed culinary attempts. "Connor seems a little bored with the lunch selections. Maybe you could talk to him about it or restock the freezer."

Cheryl finds this adorable. "Oh, that's Connor for you. He always wants something new and different. He's so discriminating for a young child, isn't he?"

I hope my smile doesn't come across as phony.

She snaps her fingers. "I almost forgot. I have something for you," she says.

"You do? For me?"

"Well, for your grandson. What's his name again?"

"Benny."

"Right. Hold on a sec." She runs out of the room, then returns a few minutes later carrying a large cardboard carton. "These are some toys and books Connor has outgrown. They're all in excellent condition. I thought Benny might enjoy them."

"Cheryl, that is so nice of you." I peer into the box to examine the choice collection of goodies. "Wow, this stuff is great . . . he'll love it. Thank you very much."

As I walk out to the car to stash the carton in the back of my Prius, an idea occurs to me. This boxful of hand-me-downs provides the perfect excuse to stop by Michael's house and attempt to patch things up. If he's home, I'll do it today.

Walking on the beach, I call Michael from my cellphone. Fingers crossed he's not away on a business trip.

After several rings, when I expect the call to go to voicemail, he picks up. "Hi, Mom." He does not exude warmth or enthusiasm, but at least he's taken my call.

"Michael, I'm glad you answered. Are you traveling or in town?"

"No, I'm at the office."

"Could I stop by your house in a couple of hours? I have a few fun things to deliver to Benny."

"Heather's home all afternoon, so you could swing by anytime. Just call or text her before you come."

"Actually, I was hoping to come by when you're at home. I—I need to talk to you about something."

He pauses, then says, "Will it take long?"

"No, not long." We agree on a time. Before stuffing the cellphone back into my pocket, I glance through my emails to see if there's anything important in the inbox. A new message from my neighbor Nancy Ostrowski is there, with the subject line "*My News*."

Margaret, dear, I hate leaving this kind of message in an email, but I tried reaching you by phone and never could get through. I'm sure you're busy with that magazine job of yours. Anyway, I wanted to tell you that John (Mr. Ostrowski) passed away in February. He was only ill a short time. I thought you'd want to know. Sincerely, Nancy Ostrowski.

John Ostrowski died back in February? *Shit.* Here I am thinking my neighbor has been trying to reach me for three weeks, while it's been more like three months. And all that time, I've ignored and trivialized her messages. That hot, fluttery sensation of guilt stirs once again in my gut.

Is there a gene for empathy - and if so, is it absent from my DNA owing to some rare chromosomal disorder? Maybe my son is right to be critical. I find Mrs. Ostrowski in my contacts and am about to hit the call button when I think better of it. Nancy is the sort of woman who talks a blue streak, and I predict the call will take an hour if it takes a minute.

There I go again, putting my own selfish impulses above poor Mrs. Ostrowski's grief. My guilty conscience kicks in, igniting a fresh burst of fluttery flames in my stomach. But if I call her now, I'll be late getting to Michael's house, and he's certain to be cross with me. So instead of calling, I hit "reply" and send off a quick response to her email message:

Dear Mrs. Ostrowski,

I am so sorry about Mr. Ostrowski and also sorry I wasn't available to respond to your messages before now. Please accept my sympathy. I hope you're doing OK. I'll call you soon.

Best regards,

Mar (Margaret) Meyer

I spend the rest of the walk practicing what I will say to Michael when I see him. The news about his father's behavior will be upsetting, and I need to break it to him gently. If I do this right and take care in choosing my words, perhaps he'll regard me with a little more kindness.

Perhaps it will bring us closer together, after all these months.

When I arrive with the box for Benny, he jumps into my arms, thrilled to be reunited with his GrandMar. I'd like to say, "*See?*" - affirming that I've done nothing to traumatize the boy. But I swoop him up in a big hug, return him to the floor, and give Michael a kiss on the cheek.

He nods and murmurs, "Hi."

Meanwhile, Benny tears through the box like a tiger devouring its prey. "Wow." He pulls out a shiny police car. "Cool." Now he's examining a plastic shed filled with barnyard animals, wagons, and farmers in coveralls.

My eyes search the room. "Where's Heather?"

"She had to run an errand. What did you need to talk to me about?"

All business, my son. No "How are you, Mom?" or "Can I pour you a nice glass of wine?" Though the latter is wishful thinking.

"I think it's important for you to know something that happened—" I start. But then I'm caught short by his expression - a mix of impatience, intolerance, and can-we-please-get-this-over-with?

"What?" he asks.

I pause, uncertain how to proceed. "Something that—that happened when I was working with an organizational consultant a couple of months ago."

"What is it?"

"Oh, well, we found a box of your old stuff in the mini-storage unit. It's all your sports trophies, and souvenirs from trips, mementos from your school days—things like that."

"Okay, so what's the problem?"

"Well . . . I need you to decide whether you want to keep all that stuff or throw it away. Because I can't keep storing it. I mean, I don't need to know right away—"

"When, then? What's the deadline?"

I take out my phone and scroll through the calendar. "August."

"*August*? That's three months from now."

"Right. I wanted to make sure you had time to think about it. I can lend you the key to the storage unit, or we could go over together . . ."

"Can't you bring the box here?"

"It's kind of heavy."

He sighs. "Look, I'll go with you sometime, but I'm really busy this month. Summer will be better, all right?"

"Sure." I force a cheerful smile.

"*This* is the important thing you needed to talk to me about?"

"I—like I said, I wanted to give you time to decide." Although I haven't scored any points with this little charade, at least I've saved myself from confessing his father's sins - a confession which, I now acknowledge, would have been disastrous. Because if I were to tell Michael the truth, he'd shoot the messenger. It would drive an even deeper wedge between us. Thank goodness I lost my nerve.

As I turn to leave, he says, "You didn't tell me where the toys came from. Is there somebody we should thank?"

"They're from a friend at Seaside Fitness. Her son is a little older than Benny. I'll tell her you said thanks."

"Yeah, please do that."

I choose not to disclose that the "friend" from the gym is my new employer. Michael still doesn't know I've resigned from *Powder World*. I assume he considers me the least qualified babysitter in Los Angeles County, so the news that I've quit my editorial job to pursue employment in childcare is likely to provoke harsh disapproval. I haven't told Mum either. I can imagine her shrill laughter over the phone.

As I'm getting ready for bed that night, it occurs to me I forgot to tell Michael about John Ostrowski. It's too late to call him now, so I consider phoning him in the morning with the news. Better not. He's apt to say, "You interrupted me at work to tell me this?" I forward Mrs. Ostrowski's email to him instead, but all Michael writes in response is:

I hadn't heard.

15.

I'm sitting out on the deck with Sexy Eyes/Charlie. After morning yoga, we grabbed a cup of coffee, ambled outdoors, and settled into lounge seats side by side. Nobody invited anyone. It kind of happened on its own.

We're filling out questionnaires that the staff distributed upon check-in this morning. It's a survey asking what types of social activities might interest members. Wine tasting is one of the choices - and in reviewing the form together, Charlie and I discover this is an area of common interest. We compare notes. I like to attend wine tastings at the local food markets, where I can combine the activity with grocery shopping, but Charlie prefers the tastings offered by boutique wine merchants and some of the small restaurants. He tells me about weekly tastings at a new retailer in Hermosa Beach who specializes in domestic wines. "Not only California - they also stock lots of wines from Washington State, Oregon, and even East Coast wineries, including some small, hard-to-find labels. They've got an unusual inventory."

"How much do they charge for a tasting?"

"It's free," he says, then smiles. "Though I wind up spending a small fortune every time I go there."

"Why is it, if we pay ten or fifteen dollars to taste a flight of wines, we walk away at the end - but if there's no charge to taste, we feel obliged to spend sixty dollars on an overpriced bottle of cab?"

"That is so true. Sad that we can be manipulated so easily."

As he says this, my cellphone buzzes, and I glance at the screen. It's Robert, my boss. I mean, former boss. I don't pick up. But a couple of minutes later, a text pops up on the phone.

Robert: Nic Rodriguez is gone. The whole agency has been fired. Ed at L&M feels terrible about what happened. He wants you back and so do I. We need to talk, Mar. Please.

As unexpected as this message is, the part that jumps out at me is neither the news of Nic's departure nor Robert's pleading tone. It is the fact that my boss has addressed me as "Mar" for the first time ever. Is this a sign he'll play by my rules going forward? I stand and say to Charlie, "Sorry, but there's an important call I have to make. I'm going down to the lower deck for a few minutes where it's quieter."

"No problem."

"Can I leave my stuff here?" I ask, pointing to my gym bag.

"Sure. I'm not going anywhere for a while."

"Thanks. I'll be back soon."

Robert answers my call right away. He explains that when Ed Matthews returned from his long anniversary trip, he was horrified to learn of my resignation and how it resulted from Nic's threat to pull the advertising. "Turns out this is not the only funny business Rodriguez was engaged in," says Robert. "He also tried to pressure L&M's printer into giving him a kickback on a job - said he knew a better, cheaper printing house that could handle the work if they weren't prepared to cooperate."

"That's illegal, isn't it?"

"You betcha. Ed isn't going to prosecute though. He wants to put this whole sorry episode behind him."

"But why did Ed fire the agency? He could've just asked them to take Nic off the account."

"Long story, but he hasn't been happy with their work for several months, and this was the final straw. Oh, by the way, did Rodriguez tell you his parents are Puerto Rican immigrants?"

"Yes, why?"

"It's a load of crap. Rodriguez isn't even his real name. Turns out he changed it from Nicholas Rodgers."

"Good grief. Why would he do that?"

"Ed found out he changed it when he started exploring the job market after college. I guess he figured an ethnic identity would give him an advantage."

Though I'm vindicated by these developments, I'm still not sure I can go back to my old job as if nothing had changed. "But Robert," I say, "I've gotta be honest about something. I'm still concerned over the rocky financial picture. You and I clashed over this article because business was bad, and you didn't want to lose a big advertiser. Who's to say this won't happen again with another client?"

"Fair question. I was an asshole to give in to Rodriguez the way I did. I should've listened to you, I should've trusted that Ed would take our side—I should've done a lot of things differently. I panicked, and I made a bad decision."

"Well, I guess I did too."

"How so?" he asks.

"I—I shouldn't have been so quick to bail on you the way I did. It wasn't fair of me." It's true. Robert is a man I've known and trusted for years.

"It's not too late to undo our mistakes. At least, I hope not," he says. Then he dangles a carrot. "I can't give you a huge raise in pay, but I'm thinking a ten percent salary increase, effective the beginning of June."

"But how can you afford it if business is lousy?"

"Good news on that front as well. Turns out L&M is having a much better year than we are, and Ed has committed to buying sixteen more pages of advertising in our environmental inserts.

And we've signed up two new smaller advertisers who are coming on board for the second half of the year."

"Wow, that's great."

"Another thing. Pam is gone."

"Pam? What happened?" Pam was the weakest link in the advertising sales department, and I speculate on whether Robert has let her go - worrying, with a fiery pang of guilt, if he's done so to free up additional funds for enticing me back. But it turns out Pam's grown weary of the stress of advertising and resigned to work at a veterinary office. Instead of replacing her, Robert has split up her territory to give the three remaining regional managers more responsibility. They're happy to receive the additional commissions. And by eliminating one salary, Robert now has more dollars in the kitty to take good care of his other employees.

"One last thing," I say. "What happened with the article that I quit over?"

"Ed and I agreed it needs a total rewrite. It's on the back burner until they have a new agency in place. Oh, I almost forgot to tell you—Ed asked for our guidance in selecting the next agency, so I've referred him to the people we trust the most. Whoever he chooses will be an ally."

By the end of the call, we've agreed on the terms of my return, and Robert has promised to put everything in writing before end of day. I'm all smiles when I return to the upper sundeck, pumping one fist in the air to signify victory as I approach Charlie lounging in his chair.

"I guess your call went well?" he asks.

"Extremely well." I give him a heavily edited version. "That was my boss. I had a little problem at work, but it's been resolved in my favor. He's even giving me a raise."

"Well, that *is* good news. Sounds like a celebration is in order." Charlie raises his coffee cup in a mock toast, and I think that's the extent of the celebration. But then he says, "There's a wine tasting tomorrow night at the new store I told you about in Hermosa. They're featuring a little contest - Oregon versus California pinot noirs. Why don't you join me?"

His invitation sounds suspiciously like a date to me. Is this a good idea, at this difficult juncture in my life? But one glance into those beautiful gray eyes, and I know what my answer will be.

• • •

The next hurdle is to resolve what to do about my babysitting job. Of course, *Powder World* comes first, but I'm not the sort of woman to renege on a commitment. I decide a week's notice is adequate. When Cheryl returns home on schedule at four o'clock the next day to relieve me, I announce my resignation.

"Oh, Mar," she says with a strained smile, "this is quite a coincidence. I have news for you too."

It turns out her regular sitter's sister has driven down from Oakland to help out during her recovery, and she plans to stay for several weeks. The sisters have proposed to come over every afternoon to help with Connor - two for one at no extra charge. "I was going to suggest one week as well," says Cheryl. "I didn't think it was fair to turn you loose without notice. But now that you've got another job, maybe it's best for everyone if we make the change effective right away?"

"Yes, that will be fine." Relief floods over me at the news of this seven-day reprieve. "I'm sure Connor will be thrilled to have his regular sitter back," I say, though he's never spoken a word about her.

On my beach walk following this conversation, I greet Petey and Audrey with enthusiasm. The dog picks up on my elation, barking with excitement and jumping up to land a sloppy kiss on my nose. I lean down to stroke the terrier's silky coat, reflecting on how much I'm looking forward to the inbox full of articles to edit, the staff video conferences I'll be scheduling, and all the grownup assignments with which I will happily occupy my time once more.

"You seem happy today." Audrey grins at me.

"You've got that right. I have a lot to celebrate. From now on, no more endless games of Jail with Connor, no more worrying about whether I've hit on the correct ratio of cinnamon to sugar."

"I have no idea what you're talking about—but congrats anyway," says Audrey.

Petey barks again, and it sounds a lot like *congratulations* to me.

And to top off this sudden reversal of fortune, there's my newest acquaintance from the gym - the sexy yogi in whose company I'll spend the upcoming evening, trading observations on the relative virtues of Oregon and California pinots.

PART SIX: JUNE
CHARLIE

16.

Charlie is perched across from me at a high-top table on the lower deck of Seaside Fitness. He has pulled a fresh sock from his gym bag, drawn a face on it with a ballpoint pen, and is now wielding it as a hand puppet. "Hey there, Mar," says the puppeteer, in that falsetto voice people like to use when manipulating hand puppets, "wanna see a movie with me tomorrow night?" The puppet bops me lightly on the tip of the nose as if to add an exclamation point to the invitation.

"What movie, Socko?" I ask.

"Socko? That's your name for me? As in Sacco and Vanzetti?"

"Not exactly," I say with a snicker.

He tells me the name of the film. A comedy about a quirky friendship between two middle-aged couples, it's a Hollywood remake of a popular British movie. Charlie tells me he's seen the original version, though I have not.

"I'll go if you promise not to spill the ending."

"Oh, but I'm not good with secrets," the puppet says. "At the end, Alexa tells Mickey that—"

"No, you don't, buddy," says Charlie in his own voice. Now he's pushing the puppet down onto the table with his free hand in a mock-serious arm-wrestling match.

"You are a madman," I say to him, laughing.

"Are you speaking to me or the puppet?" Charlie grins.

"Both."

Every day Charlie finds creative new ways to amuse me. He is often cheerful and lighthearted. He revels in watching sitcoms, stand-up comics, even chick flicks. "I have a lot of women readers," he explains.

"So you follow these shows to connect better with your audience?"

"That's my official position. But the truth is, it's what I like to watch."

I didn't expect to find such a temperament in an award-winning author of serious works, and a widowed one at that.

We'd gotten off to an uncertain start the last week of May at that wine tasting, which proved to be more or less a non-event. Charlie and I met at the Hermosa store, where he showed up in shorts and a t-shirt, causing me to feel overdressed in slacks and a tailored blouse I might've worn to a business lunch. Charlie introduced me to the store owner and his wife, and we sampled pinots from Oregon's Willamette Valley and a few of California's Sonoma wineries. As Charlie ushered me around the aisles, we compared wine preferences. Though I didn't buy any of the sampled wines, I purchased a couple of rosés, feeling sorry for the owners because the event was so sparsely attended.

"Now is the perfect time to stock up on rosé. We're heading into the summer solstice . . . long, sunny days, and we've had no sign of May Gray all month," the store owner said to me while ringing up my order. She was referring to the coastal weather phenomenon that could bring depressing overcast conditions to the region for days or weeks on end. Depending on the timing, it was poetically referred to as *May Gray* or *June Gloom.*

Charlie walked me to my Prius, kissed me on the cheek in farewell, and held the car door for me. And that was our so-called date – about forty minutes in a wine store together. Maybe I read too much into his invitation.

• • •

But here we are a week later, going to a movie on a real date, and our second evening together takes on a more intimate quality.

For starters, he insists on picking me up at the apartment. I dress down this time, in white capris and a turquoise hoodie. Charlie shows up in black jeans and a soft gray sweater that matches his eyes. His hair also looks different – he's used a light gel to keep it off his face, highlighting those eyes with even greater prominence. So dazzling is that gray gaze, I almost have to blink and look away, as if I've been blinded from staring into the sun. I should've brought a handkerchief to mop up the drool. I'm sorry to report that the snappy greeting I come up with is, "You clean up nicely."

"So do you," he says, with a light peck on the cheek as he delivers the obligatory returned compliment.

After thirty years with Henry, I find it strange to sit in a darkened theater next to this tall, attractive man. Feeling like I've been hurtled back in time, I wonder whether my date will slip his arm around me halfway through the movie, and I speculate on where the evening might take us.

Charlie does not make any moves during the film, but the evening does take us next door to a little bistro where we share a bottle of wine and three small plates. "The film was funny, hilarious at times. But I couldn't buy the relationship between Alexa and Mickey," Charlie says. "I don't remember having that reaction when I saw the British version. It's a weakness in the script."

I shake my head. "I think it's more of a casting problem. The actor who played Alexa wasn't right for the role. I pictured somebody younger and a little less stodgy."

He considers my comment. "You know, you're right. If a film is flawed, I always blame the writing. If it's brilliant, I credit the writing. I need to consider other elements like casting, or music, or visual effects. That's why I would never make it as a screenwriter."

"But one of your books was made into a movie, right?"

"Two of my books. And two others were optioned, but the movies never got made. *Bicoastal* was the only film that enjoyed any real success."

"Were you involved in writing the screenplay?"

"Oh no. The producers didn't want me anywhere near it, though my contract gave me a modicum of control over the script. I wasn't allowed to mess around with dialogue or make any granular changes, but I had veto power if they tried to introduce drastic revisions, like turning the protagonist into an axe murderer."

"Were they allowed to change the ending? I'm ashamed to admit, I haven't read the book or seen the movie."

"No shame in that." Charlie seems to like the fact that I'm not a card-carrying member of the Charles Kittredge fan club. But I'm still embarrassed I haven't read a single word of Charlie's novels, though I've done my due diligence by reading book reviews and author profile pieces on him. I've learned that his works are, unlike their author, serious in tone - especially his two most recent books, which are described as *dark* and *brooding* by the critics.

"There was never any discussion of changing the ending," he says in reply to my question. "Not to sound immodest, but the conclusion of *Bicoastal* is the strongest part of the book. I think the producers recognized that."

"I must read it and see for myself."

"No pressure."

This leads to a discussion of writing, and next thing I know, we both have so much to say, we keep talking over each other. Charlie likes to make up little stories about people he observes in the course of his day-to-day life. "I jot down my ideas at the first opportunity. Every so often, one of these stories will expand and deepen, finding its way into a novel or short story. But most of the time, the stories remain untold. I must have hundreds of them by now."

"How about an example?"

"Here's a funny one. I pulled up to a traffic light and looked over to the car stopped next to mine in the left-hand lane," Charlie says. "A red-headed woman had her head turned away from me to face the driver. Her head kept bobbing up and down, and I was pretty certain the woman was speaking to the man in an agitated way. In my imagination, she was chastising him. I concocted a story in my head that she was upset because the boyfriend had taken her for granted, he wasn't responsive to her needs, and she was breaking up with him, right there at the stoplight."

"How did you come up with that scenario?"

"Well, the driver really *wasn't* responding to her. He sat there, not saying a word, while she continued to bob her head. But then, right before the light changed, he opened the passenger side window halfway and his companion turned her head toward the open window . . . and stuck out her snout."

"Her *snout*?"

"Yes. She wasn't a redheaded woman at all – she was an Irish setter."

I'm drinking from my water glass when Charlie delivers the punchline, and I respond with an embarrassing spit-take, during which I choke a little as water dribbles out of my mouth. Smooth move, Mar. I daub my mouth and chin with a napkin. To my relief, Charlie glosses over this. "How about you? Where do you get your ideas for the magazine content?"

Regaining my composure, I say, "To tell you the truth, I don't have to come up with all that many ideas. Most of the article topics are determined by our editorial calendar, which doesn't change much from year to year."

He wants to hear everything about my work. Do I edit other pieces, or do I write bylined articles as well? Do I enjoy working from home, or does the isolation bother me? Do I work on a strict schedule? What training did I have for the job? "I assume you have an engineering background?" he says.

"No, not at all."

"So you picked up the technical expertise along the way."

"Not exactly. I don't even understand many of the pieces I edit. I mean, I can address the grammar and sentence structure, and the general organization of the piece, and whether the article is successful in communicating what the reader needs to know—but I often do that without really 'getting it' myself."

Charlie finds this fascinating. "I can't imagine editing copy I don't understand. It must take a special talent to do what you do."

"Thanks, but you're giving me way too much credit." My modesty is sincere. I'm unaccustomed to having anyone put my work on a pedestal - except maybe Robert, who has been uncommonly solicitous since my return to the job. But I bask in Charlie's compliment. In all our years together, Henry never exhibited much desire to discuss my professional duties and skills. When he couldn't lure me over to Schuyler Enterprises, his interest ended there.

When we finish the last of the wine and Charlie asks the server for the check, I experience a moment of uncertainty. Unsure of modern dating protocol, should I offer to pay half the bill? Then again, I can't be certain this even qualifies as a date. And friends usually split the check. "Can I participate in this?" I ask to be on the safe side.

"Thanks, but I've got it. You can treat another time."

Charlie drives me home and pulls into a parking spot near the main entrance of my apartment building. He shuts off the engine, turns to me, and takes my face in both hands.

The first kiss is gentle, soft, even tentative – as if he's making a preliminary exploration of my lips to see what will happen. I kiss him back, and next thing I know, we are kissing more deeply, mouths gradually opening to one another, our arms around each other.

We make out like a couple of high school kids for five minutes or so, and while we're kissing, I indeed feel like a teenager again. The sensation is foreign and yet familiar at the same time. Once again, I'm uncertain about the protocol. Should I invite him up to my place? And if so, how do I phrase the invitation? "Would you like to come up for a nightcap?" Are nightcaps even a thing anymore? And if he says yes and we are engaged in pleasant nightcapping, will I then be expected to ask, "Shall I go slip into something more comfortable?"

I can't imagine doing any of this . . . and I'm not ready for it. I thank Charlie and bid him goodnight, bestowing a light kiss on his lips one last time.

• • •

We continue to go out every few nights. I'm discovering that Charlie's humor is at times sophisticated and droll, and at other times, he devolves into corny jokes and puns a ten-year-old would find hilarious. He tickles me, literally as well as figuratively. He contorts his handsome features into goofy expressions, sending me into fits of laughter when I'm trying to concentrate on some sober task. He speaks in a variety of accents and can do dead-on imitations of Bill Clinton, James Corden, and Michael Caine. And like Shakespeare's Falstaff, he is not only witty himself, he inspires wit in others. My own words sound sharp and clever in his presence. The curbside end-of-evening make-out sessions are growing more intense, and every time they conclude with a hoarse exchange of whispered goodnights, I'm disappointed . . . and relieved.

This evening, following a fresh and simple dinner at a cozy seafood restaurant, we are back to the kissing marathon. There's a different atmosphere inside the car tonight as if the air itself is thrumming with anticipation, and I am responding to it.

This time, I invite him up to my place.

We don't waste time getting down to business. I pour us each a generous glass of chardonnay that we barely touch, Charlie acknowledges the stunning post-sunset view in the fading light of the June evening, and the kissing resumes - but this time, we take it to the bedroom. We both shed our clothes at the same time and crawl into the cool bed sheets, where he stretches out to his full six-foot length and presses his body against mine.

As for what follows, I wish I could report colorful bursts of exploding fireworks or similar orgasmic imagery. But as much as I enjoy the *idea* of Charlie making thrilling love to me, the reality is more unsettling. As hard as I try to relax and enjoy the marvelous sensations of his lips tracing a path down my neck to my breasts, as much as I try to lose myself while his fingertips stroke my skin with great tenderness, I can't help but notice how darned *peculiar* it is to be in bed with this new man and his unfamiliar body. Make no mistake - Charlie's toned and slender physique and his silky dark chest hair are infinitely more appealing than the fleshy body Henry had on offer. But Henry's was the body I knew for all those years. And though I try to respond to Charlie's touch and to please him in return, I'm unable to let myself go.

Afterward, he slips his jeans back on and I wrap myself in a kimono. We grab our wine glasses and sit on the loveseat on my balcony, gazing out wordlessly as the last sliver of pink light fades over the horizon. He puts his arm around me and pulls me to him, kissing my head softly right above the ear.

"Your hair smells nice," he says.

"Thanks." I stroke his face with one hand. "Charlie, I—I'm afraid I was a little nervous tonight."

He smiles. "I could sense that. Don't worry about it. You and I are going to be fine, I can tell. We'll find our stride."

I give him a grateful hug. "This was . . . the first time I've been with anyone since my husband. It'll take some getting used to."

"I understand. What happened with your marriage?"

"I—I'd rather not get into that right now. It's kind of a sore subject." I realize at once that's the phrase Michael utters whenever he wants to shut down a conversation. I don't like it when Michael uses that gambit with me, and by the way Charlie furrows his brow, I suspect he doesn't care for it either.

But he says, "Okay. You know, the first time I slept with another woman after Bet—my wife—I remember it was kind of surreal."

"Yes, that's a good word for it." Then I'm not the first woman he's had since being widowed. I wondered about that, after the physical encounters between us that never progressed beyond the kissing stage. "How long has she been gone?"

"Almost three and a half years."

"Any children?"

"No. When we got married, Bet and I were both in our late thirties. Neither of us was keen to start a family at that point in our lives."

So, they were married a relatively short time - ten, maybe twelve years, I calculate. I pictured them being together for much longer, though I had no basis for assuming their marriage resembled mine and Henry's. "Was it—sudden? When she died, I mean." I remember Sunny saying something to that effect months ago when we discussed Charlie for the first time.

"Yes . . . no . . . *yes*. There were events that led up to it over a period of months. It started with a bad case of recurring vertigo."

This triggers dim memories of the Alfred Hitchcock film of the same name. I have a vague recollection of Kim Novak up in a bell tower, everything spinning before she plummets to her death. "Did your wife die from a fall?"

"Oh no, nothing like that. It was—complicated."

"I'm sorry. I'll stop with the cross-examination. I didn't mean to make you relive painful memories."

"It's okay, Mar. I want you to understand what happened if you don't mind my telling you the story. Otherwise, you'll always be speculating."

He's right. "Of course I don't mind."

Charlie sips his wine as he talks, but he keeps his other arm around me, absently massaging my shoulder as he tells the story. "Bet went to the doctor because of these terrible vertigo episodes, and he diagnosed her with Meniere's disease."

"I've heard of Meniere's, but I don't know much about it."

"It's a disorder of the inner ear that causes excess fluid to build up. That's what triggers the vertigo. It's not a curable condition, but it's treatable. Bet started taking heavy doses of diuretics to drain the fluid and stop the spinning sensation."

"Did that work?"

"Yes, but it caused other problems. People on diuretics can be prone to potassium deficiency. Again, that's treatable, but Bet didn't follow the doctor's advice on diet and supplements."

"Why not?"

"She disliked taking *anything* unless she saw an instant payoff. Pop an Ambien and fall asleep. Take a diuretic and the vertigo will stop. Vitamins, supplements, other treatments that didn't make you feel any different - those, she couldn't be bothered with."

"What happens when your potassium gets too low?"

"It's called hypokalemia. I could write a book on the symptoms," he says with a humorless laugh. "The ones Bet complained about most often were fatigue, bloating, and muscle cramps. She attributed these to perimenopause. But over time, she started experiencing a more serious side effect - arrhythmia. Irregular heartbeat."

"That one, I know something about," I say. "My father had a-fib and had to take blood thinners and heart medications for it."

"Right. The doctor prescribed similar meds for Bet, but she didn't like the side effects. The arrhythmia drug made her clumsy, the blood thinner made her bruise . . . that kind of thing. So even though she took her diuretic faithfully to rein in the vertigo, she let the other problems go more or less unchecked."

"Couldn't you convince her how important it was for her to treat the other problems?"

"Perhaps, if I'd realized she was doing this. But it was a well-hidden secret." Though his voice is steady, I detect a flash of pain in his eyes. I nod in sympathy.

"Anyway, I had to go out of town for a couple of weeks on a book tour. I worried about leaving her, but she insisted she was fine. I got one of those pill organizers and filled it up with everything she was supposed to take. When I got home at the end of the tour, I walked into the house and found her lying on the kitchen floor."

"Oh God, how awful. Was she alive?"

"Alive, but unconscious. When they got her to the hospital, they determined she'd had a massive stroke. They think it happened just hours before I returned home. Her best friend had seen her the previous day and said she was all right then – though apparently Bet complained of dizziness. But it wasn't bad enough to seek treatment, or so she thought."

"Was she ever able to speak to you?"

"No. Bet lived three more days, but she never regained consciousness. I spent most of that time in the hospital with her, but when I came home to shower and catch a couple of hours' sleep, I found the pill organizer largely untouched. She'd taken the diuretics, but the other pills were still in their little compartments." He sighs and bites his lower lip. "I think she'd been doing that for a long time and concealing the behavior from me."

"This is a lot to take in," I say. "Then the stroke was the cause of death?"

"The direct cause. But the whole thing happened like a domino effect. All those other medical problems eventually triggered the stroke."

"Charlie, what a terrible story. Do you think you'll ever write about it?"

"I don't think so. There are little pieces of me in everything I write, but telling Bet's story would take too big a chunk out of me. It's too personal. Too raw."

"Of course it is. And you—you must have been so angry with her." As soon as the words slip out, I want to take them back. I'm reminded of all my verbal missteps with Michael. Here I go, delivering my usual insensitive commentary and then wishing I could revise the script. I rush to make amends. "I am so sorry, I should never have said that."

But Charlie pops up from the seat with a strange expression in his eyes that takes me a little time to decipher. It's a look of validation. "In over three years, you are the first one who's been candid enough to say that to me."

"I am?"

"Yes—*yes.* I always felt it would be in poor taste to suggest that Bet was even a tiny bit responsible for her own death. When your forty-nine-year-old wife dies in tragic circumstances, you don't go around telling people you're mad at her. That isn't done in the polite society we navigate these days. For the same reason, I guess, our close friends never dared to suggest it either."

"I, on the other hand, am the least tactful woman on the planet, as my son will testify. But Charlie—your wife clearly held some responsibility for what happened. If she'd taken everything the doctor prescribed, maybe she wouldn't have had the stroke."

"And if I hadn't gone on the book tour, maybe she would've taken the medications."

"But you said you believed this had been going on for a long time, and she was hiding it from you."

"That's true."

"She was an adult. You weren't her keeper. No matter how much you loved your wife, you're allowed to feel angry about what she did or didn't do."

He stares intently into my eyes, then pulls me to him in a fierce hug. When he releases me, I see that look of validation in his eyes again as he says, "Thank you."

For once, loose lips have not sunk my boat. It seems my candor has brought me closer to this man's heart. We stand on the moonlit balcony, facing each other, and the moment is so warm, so tender, that I don't stop to recognize our relationship has taken a turn into more serious territory.

17.

Two nights later, at my apartment again, Charlie and I are stretched out on my couch, the TV tuned to a rerun of a popular nineties sitcom. His arm is around me, his posture is contented and relaxed - perhaps a bit *too* relaxed, apart from his soft chuckling at a humorous scene. Charlie hasn't kissed me or made any overtures, and I pretend to concentrate on the program, but all I can think about is whether we are going to have sex tonight.

When we had sex that first time, I was hesitant, and perhaps that's why he hasn't made a move tonight. Though his hand rests on my shoulder and our bodies are touching, Charlie is reserved, holding himself back from me. Now *he* is the hesitant one, and his unexpected passivity ignites a flame of desire inside me. I start by snuggling up to him, running one hand along his chest as I burrow my face into his warm neck. His hand squeezes my shoulder, but he's still watching TV as though unwilling to be interrupted in his viewing.

We'll see about that.

Now I'm kissing him - light feathery kisses on the neck at first, but then I seek out his lips, prying his mouth open with my tongue. He's responding, but I don't want him to mistake this for one of our adolescent make-out sessions in the car. To make sure he understands my intent, I reach down with one hand and massage his crotch over his pants as I continue kissing him.

Now I have Charlie's full attention. He moans and returns my kisses now, encircling me in a tight embrace before flipping me over gently on my back. Though he has assumed a dominant position, I'm determined to remain the aggressor this time. I'm the one who undresses us both from the waist down, I'm the one who decides how long the kissing and stroking should continue before I open myself up to him. To express it in Charlie's lingo, I think we have found our stride. He was right when he promised we'd be fine.

• • •

On Sunday afternoon, we set out on a hike at Charlie's suggestion. High on the peninsula, there is a labyrinthine network of trails popular with the local Sierra Club chapter and other hiking enthusiasts. "Won't it be crowded on a Sunday?" I ask.

"Most of the groups go out early," he says. "We should be fine in the afternoon. And with this cool weather we're having, no worries about heatstroke." June gloom has set in at last, with daytime temperatures topping out in the mid-sixties. The sun teases us every day with a brief appearance around three or four o'clock, only to retreat behind threatening clouds a mere twenty minutes later.

The hiking area has two intersecting main trails and a countless number of smaller arteries that branch out from these wide primary trails, forming a crisscross pattern across the rolling hills. Views of the sparkling blue Pacific from this elevated terrain are distant but breathtaking, extending all the way to Catalina Island and beyond when the skies are clear. Charlie knows his way around and leads us off the main trail, and we thread our way down the smaller paths, which are much narrower and overgrown with brush in places. The vegetation has shot up to six or seven feet in height, thanks to the rainy winter. Right now, there are still random patches of greenery, but the plants, the tall weeds, and the remaining wildflowers are losing their colors and fading to brown.

"How do you ever find your way through here?" I ask him. "These side trails aren't even marked."

"I've hiked here so many times, I think there's a trail map etched in my brain at this point. I've memorized certain landmarks to guide my path. For instance, see the fork in the trail up ahead? And that small grove of cypress trees on the hill to the left? When we reach that fork, we need to bear right."

We continue on our path, stopping now and then to hydrate and enjoy the views. At one stop, he says, "There's something caught in your hair," and he reaches over and extracts the offending twig with gentle fingers. After doing this, he pulls my head toward his and kisses me warmly. I get lost in that kiss, oblivious to the world around me. When I open my eyes and look around, I notice there isn't another hiker in sight.

"I spoke too soon, predicting it would be crowded," I say.

"There are so many miles of trail, the hikers fan out. It can be kind of isolated - especially later in the afternoons."

"It's nice having the whole hill to ourselves."

Charlie smiles at me.

By the time we get back to the car, we've been out for over two hours. The trails are steep in places, and my legs ache from the strain of exertion. But I'm in good physical condition from all the working out, and it has served me well this afternoon. I'm tired and a little sore, but I had no difficulty keeping pace with Charlie's longer, more expert stride.

He has suggested I bring casual clothes to change into, and I've stashed a few things in my gym bag. We've agreed I'll go to his house after the hike, which I add to the list of the "firsts" in our month-long acquaintance: the first date, the first kiss, the first time together at my place, the first time making love. I like to think of these "firsts" more as adventures than milestones. A milestone sounds like such a heavy thing. But aside from our recent conversation about Bet, there's been nothing heavy about my relationship with Charlie.

He lives in a coastal section dotted with ranch houses built during the 1950s and 1960s. Most of the lots are spacious by California standards, so the area has become popular for new construction and remodels. As we drive through the area on the way back from our hike, he points out some of the more controversial remodel jobs - McMansions with overblown footprints that fill every available square inch allowed by local building codes, encroaching on neighbors' property lines and spoiling the symmetry of what was once a pleasing neighborhood of cottages. Charlie's house, too, has undergone a complete remodel. He had the plans drawn up right after securing the film deal for *Bicoastal,* he tells me.

The house has morphed from a single-story mid-century classic ranch to a two-story Mediterranean-style villa. But in transforming and enlarging the home, Charlie has taken care to maintain balance on the site, leaving space for a front garden, an ample back yard with a swimming pool, a detached garage, and a tiny side yard. The main residence features the Spanish-influence architecture that countless California developers have favored for decades, but Charlie's home has an air of authenticity that is lacking in many of the tacky, lower-cost imitations I've seen.

"You've done an amazing job," I say as we walk through the main floor with its Saltillo tile floors, arched doorways, and ornate woodwork.

"Thanks. It's been a work in progress for a long time. See the big garden out front with the old fountain? I commissioned that after optioning *The Chandler* to a Hollywood studio," he says, naming another of his novels. Other major projects include a large deck with a built-in barbeque and fire pit, and a guesthouse that's been built onto the garage. Every improvement to the property, he explains, can be linked to a large book advance or some ancillary revenue stream. "Do you mind if we have a bite to eat before cleaning up? I'm ravenous," says Charlie as he pours two tall glasses of water from a ceramic pitcher in the fridge.

"Oh, I'm glad you offered. I'm famished too."

"I've got chicken sausage lasagna I can reheat, if that sounds good."

"Perfect."

A few minutes later, he serves us each a generous helping of the savory dish, piled into deep porcelain plates with a dark blue glaze that echoes the home's Spanish motif. Though he's offered to open a bottle of rosé, I prefer to stick with water after our rigorous workout.

"This is delicious," I say, smacking my lips after the first bite. "Where did you get it?"

"I made it."

"You *made* it? Like, you layered it yourself?" Realizing this sounds like Mum, I blush. Just because I'm a slouch in the kitchen, why should I assume Charlie is incapable of cooking a classic Italian favorite? I worry that my remark will strike him as sexist or plain dumb.

But his eyes sparkle with amusement. "Yep. I layered it, I sauced it, I performed all the required steps."

"Whatever those might be. Damned if I know."

"You're not into cooking, then?"

"Oh no. I can't see investing all that time in something I will never be good at. Same with golf. Anyway, I figure I'm doing a service to the community."

"How's that?"

"Think of all the restaurants and take-out places that are staying in business because of my patronage."

"Good point. The kitchen can be a dangerous place, too, if you meet up with the wrong sort of people." Now he's chasing me around the kitchen island with a spatula, thrusting and parrying like a fencer with an epée as I dissolve into helpless laughter. I forget my momentary embarrassment.

He leads me upstairs through the master bedroom suite to a large bathroom with an oversized shower stall. The floor and inner wall are constructed of floral patterned dark green, pink, and white tiles with a distinct Mexican flair. The shower enclosure is partially glassed in, but the structure is open at the far end from the showerhead. This open design - combined with the natural light flooding in through a skylight overhead - gives it that *plein air* feeling often associated with tropical showers.

"Lovely," I say. The house Henry and I shared had an enormous master bath, all marble, with a Jacuzzi tub and large separate corner shower with multiple spray nozzles, like the kind you see in luxury spas. It's the one room in my grand former house that I miss.

Charlie smiles and draws me close to him, kissing me on the nose. "Would you like to shower together?"

I nod. This is a couple's activity we won't be able to enjoy at my apartment, where the shower stall resembles a telephone booth. He points out a white wicker basket filled with plush bath sheets, and two fluffy white terrycloth robes hanging side by side from wooden pegs mounted next to the shower door. "For afterward," he says.

I start unbuttoning my hiking shorts, but Charlie stops me and says, "Darling, please—you must allow *me*," with mock formality, in an accent that sounds part American, part British. I stand at obedient attention as he removes my shorts, my tank top, then my sports bra and panties. He folds each item slowly and deliberately, like a manservant in a PBS mini-series, but there's a wry twinkle in his eye. Then I realize who he's mimicking.

"Sir, you are very sexy when you channel Cary Grant," I say, going for a Katherine Hepburn vibe myself. "My turn, darling."

"Excellent."

I remove his clothing, careful to exercise the same calm deliberation with which he undressed me moments before. When we're both naked, he turns on the faucet, and, after double-checking the temperature, he leads me into the shower. We stand under the cascading water for a couple of minutes, allowing it to drench our hair and soften our skin with its moist heat. Then he grabs an oversized sea sponge and soaps me up, starting with my neck and working his way down. "We'll save the hair for last," he says.

After my body is slick with soap suds, I take the sponge from him and return the favor. When I reach his privates, I note a responsive twitch, but he doesn't become erect. Am I doing something wrong, or is Charlie saving his ammunition, so to speak? After years of married life, I've become inept at this kind of foreplay. Was I ever *ept* to begin with? It's been so long, I have no clear recollection.

He plants a warm, slick, wet kiss on my lips. Maybe he is responding after all? But I'm forced to break away unceremoniously from the embrace, my mouth curling into an expression of distaste that I'm helpless to prevent.

"Is my kissing that bad?" asks Charlie, half-amused, half-concerned.

"Soap," I say, choking on the word. I open my lips and indelicately spit out a mouthful of grayish-white foam. "I swallowed soap. It tastes *awful.*"

"You look like you swallowed moose dung."

We both laugh. Before long, I am collapsing against him in a fit of giggles, though my face is still contorted from the horrid aftertaste of soap scum. "It's not funny," I say, laughing even harder.

Charlie slips back into the Cary Grant voice. "Poor thing. Don't move a muscle, I'll be right back." He steps out of the shower, hustles to the sink, and comes back with a toothbrush to which he has applied a stripe of red and white paste. He pries open my mouth and pokes the toothbrush in, running it across my teeth and tongue before putting the brush in his own mouth for a quick cleaning. This makes me squeamish for a moment – but then I think, as long as we're sharing saliva and other bodily fluids, what's the difference? His mouth finds mine again, and now the kiss is sweet and minty. We are like a couple in a romantic film, two people discovering each other in a gauzily filmed love montage. The shower ended, we wrap ourselves in the plush robes and walk into the bedroom. I expect this to be our next destination, but Charlie takes my hand and says, "Come with me. I'd like to show you something."

He leads me down a corridor to a carpeted alcove at the end of the hall. There is a yoga mat spread across the center of the alcove, and open shelves filled with additional mats, blocks, straps, bolsters, and blankets, all in a matching warm sand color. "There used to be a desk here, but last year I turned the area into a little yoga retreat."

I speculate the desk must have been Bet's. Charlie already showed me a large office on the ground floor where he does his writing and correspondence. "But you go to classes almost every day at the club. I can't believe you do more yoga here at home."

"I use this more for stretching and meditation. I try to meditate for twenty or thirty minutes a day. Twice a day if time allows."

"Nice." I respect people who meditate, the same way I respect people who never touch alcohol. Both are admirable practices I have no intention of pursuing myself. The alcove faces out onto a small balcony lined with dozens of potted plants, many of them flowering in brilliant bursts of color. "Oh, how beautiful," I say.

"The view is even better from the mat." He gestures for me to lie down.

I lower myself onto the yoga mat and gaze out towards the balcony separated from the alcove by a pair of French doors. The blooming greenery is tall and lush from this vantage point, and I'm in the middle of a garden of repose, a place of rare tranquility.

Charlie rolls out a second mat and lies down parallel to me. "Do you like it here?" he asks.

"Very much."

"It's too light out to show you, but I installed colored spotlights that shine down on the plants. It creates a whole different effect at nighttime."

I adjust my position and wince a little.

"What's wrong?"

"It's nothing. My neck gets stiff sometimes."

"Roll your head from side to side gently to lubricate the joints," he says.

I do as he suggests, but as I turn my head, a strand of wet hair gets caught in my mouth, and I'm once again wrinkling my nose. "I think I swallowed more soap."

"We must've been careless with the rinse cycle." He leans over to sniff my hair. "I detect a scent of cucumber and a little mint. It's pleasant. Kinda sexy."

"Not to me. Soapy." I pull a face, which gets us both giggling again.

He stops the laughter with another deep kiss, then slips the damp robe off to nuzzle my bare shoulder. "Are you cold?" he asks, pointing to the goosebumps on my arm.

"A little."

"Here, I'll get something." He grabs a yoga blanket and a couple of other items from the shelf, sheds his own robe, and lies down beside me, pulling the soft cover over us.

We're back to the love montage, I think. Nice.

What happens next takes us outside the realm of romantic films and into an altogether different genre. Charlie grasps a yoga strap, pulls my arms up over my head, and winds the strap around my wrists, tying them firmly together. I must look startled, because he leans in and says, "Just say the word and I'll untie you. We won't do this unless you're comfortable with it." He whispers this in my ear as though sharing a secret he doesn't want anyone else in on.

My heart is racing—but from excitement, not fear. In all our years, Henry and I never experimented with bondage. Not even the generic kind, let alone yoga bondage. "Keep going."

He looks me in the eye for visual affirmation. He has the same playful expression he wore when entertaining me with a sock puppet, dispelling any fleeting concerns I might've had about a sinister motive. I nod to confirm my approval.

Next, he slides a cotton bolster pillow under my hips, elevating me into a bridge pose. He parts my thighs with a gentle motion and pushes my ankles in close to my hips so that my knees are at a raised angle with my soles planted on the mat. The blanket covers us both, except for my bound hands poking out at the top. We're like a couple of kids playing under a tent, except it is a decidedly grownup game in which we're engaged. Charlie holds the power in this game - the power to do with me whatever he chooses.

And as it turns out, his choices are very much okay with me.

• • •

A little later, we're watching a stand-up comedy routine on HBO. The comic, a young Korean woman, delivers a hilarious rant about the terrible driving habits of Caucasian men, taking the old stereotype about female Asian drivers and turning it upside down. We're side by side on the couch, our bodies touching. But between the frothy entertainment and the chilled rosé we're now sipping, the temperature between us has cooled off a few degrees since our antics on the yoga mat.

The comedy special ends and a sitcom airs next, the one about the crabby comedian who elevates small annoyances into explosive but funny confrontations. "Okay if we watch this?" Charlie asks. Considerate to a fault, he always seeks my agreement, whether the choice at hand involves sexual predilections or taste in TV programming.

"I love this show."

"Me too. Some people find it mean and sardonic," he says.

"That's what I love about it."

Charlie grins. About ten minutes into the episode, he slaps his thigh and says, "Damn. The writing is so good and so tight."

"Have you thought about writing comedy yourself?"

"My publisher would be thrilled to see a little more humor. My books still do well, but they haven't been blockbusters like the earlier novels. My agent would like me to be 'less contemplative and more commercial.' But to answer your question . . . I don't think I have it in me to write comedy."

"Why not?"

"I'm sure you've heard the old saying, 'Dying is easy, comedy is hard.'"

"I wonder who came up with that."

"Lots of people have said it, but nobody can take ownership of the quote." He stands and stretches those long, chiseled arms in the air. "Hungry?"

"Now that you mention it, yes. I thought the lasagna would hold me for the rest of the day, but I could use a little something right now. A snack will be fine."

"Let me go to the kitchen and rustle up bread and cheese, olives, stuff like that."

"I'll help you."

I hoist myself up from the couch, but he shakes his head and says, "You relax and enjoy the show. I'll be back before you know it."

Ten minutes later, however, Charlie hasn't returned with the food, and my wine glass is empty. I walk into the kitchen to investigate. He is standing at the kitchen island with his back to me, but I can see him arranging an assortment of munchies on a platter. I'm in bare feet, so he doesn't hear me enter the room. His shoulders are shaking, which causes me to stop in my tracks. The sight fills me with alarm - an alarm that intensifies when an unwelcome memory floods back.

Henry. Henry sitting on the bed with his back to me, all those years ago, shoulders shaking in that same heartbreaking pose. Henry crying over his guilt about cheating on me, as it turned out. Charlie's cheating on me too? Already? It's only been a month. Recognizing my suspicion is absurd, I run over to him. "Charlie?"

He blinks at me through tears. "Sorry. I didn't mean for you to see this."

"What's wrong?"

"Today—today has been a big step for me. This is the first time I've brought a woman into this house since Bet died."

"But you said there've been other women."

"There have been a few. But I never invited them here. I couldn't handle it. Until you."

I digest this. "And now you—you feel it was a mistake to bring me to the house you shared with your wife? You're sad because you miss her?" Though these are both questions, my tone is flat, as if I'm delivering statements of fact instead.

"No. I'm sad because I *don't* miss her."

"Sorry?"

"For the first time since Bet's been gone, I'm finally ready to move on and leave my life with her behind, to pursue . . . whatever this is that's happening between us." He gives me an inquisitive look as though searching for an answer in my face. "I can't say for sure what *is* happening, but all my senses tell me it's something important. Something worth nurturing."

I don't say anything, and he continues. "This realization that I've moved on . . . there's something *final* about that, more final even than her death. Does that sound crazy? Anyway, that's why I lost it for a moment."

Whoa. I wasn't prepared for this. I still don't know what to say, but he wraps his arms around me, which saves me from having to reply. I slip my arms around his shoulders, hoping to offer comfort after such an important revelation. I'm flattered by what he's told me but not yet certain how to respond.

We nibble cheese, olives, and cherry tomatoes, finish off the rosé, and chuckle through two more episodes of the sitcom. As the marine layer continues to hang its heavy shroud over the neighborhood, the sky deepens in gradual shades from light gray to charcoal to black without benefit of a sunset.

Charlie reaches to clear away the cheese plate, then changes his mind and sits back down beside me. He takes my right hand in both of his and raises it to his lips, kissing my knuckles. As he does this, he gives me a searching look - the same expression I witnessed in the kitchen, right after he'd told me he was ready to pursue a more serious relationship. "Spend the night with me?"

I pause, deciding how to word my reply. "Sorry—I can't. I have an early conference call tomorrow morning with the New York office, and I need to be back at my own place. In fact, I should spend a little time tonight preparing." The part about the call is true. But with a pang of conscience, I acknowledge to myself that I'm using it as an escape strategy. After such an amazing day and evening, why am I now in such a hurry to leave?

Charlie nods. If he is perturbed or disappointed, he's not letting on. "Maybe some of your self-discipline will rub off on me," he says with a crooked smile. "Now that you mention it, I could benefit from an early start too. I promised my editor three chapters, and I've fallen behind. I'll drive you home."

"Before we leave, can I check out the lighted balcony upstairs? Now that it's dark outside."

"Sure," he says, looking pleased by the request.

We go upstairs, where I admire his floral light show with great enthusiasm, my guilty conscience assuaged. I try to convince myself that fawning over the balcony project will make up for my hasty retreat from Charlie's sleepover invitation and my nervous departure.

18.

Everything is spinning, spinning, spinning out of control. I'm strapped into one of those Tilt-A-Whirl rides you see at traveling carnivals. But it's turning much too fast, and I can't get it to stop. Charlie is seated directly across from me, but his face is a blur. Then, moments later, he's standing nearby, hands in his pockets. How did he get out? I'm too dizzy to undo my strap. For a moment, the woman on the ride is not me but Charlie's late wife Bet, and I'm witnessing an episode of her vertigo. But then the rider is me again, and it's not only Charlie on the sidelines. Henry has joined him at the perimeter of the ride and watches me, laughing. I try shouting to them for help, but my voice comes out in an incoherent squeak no one can hear. When I awaken from this nightmare, my gut is clenched with anxiety.

I try to shake off the dream and attribute my unease to the Monday morning blues that sometimes descend when I face a challenging work week ahead. But the feeling persists even after my early phone conference. The call is routine, even upbeat. The editorial plans for the next issue are ahead of schedule, advertising revenue is up, and the workload is slackening as we head into summer, when we only publish two issues instead of three.

Clearly, the anxiety has nothing to do with my job.

I decide to take my beach walk right away instead of waiting until late afternoon. The daily walk remains my favorite vehicle for clearing my head and thinking through personal issues, and that needs to take priority right now. Besides, I don't want to run into Charlie at the club yet. First, I need to figure out why I'm anxious. It'll be better when I sort myself out. But as I maintain a brisk walking pace along the shore, I concede I'm growing worse, not better. The more I try to identify what's nagging at me, the more I despair over the indisputable source of my anxiety.

It's Charlie. Dear, funny, smart, sexy Charlie. Why did he have to go and spoil everything by falling in love with me?

Granted, he didn't use the "l" word last night, but he might as well have said it. I harken back to those trembling shoulders and the whispered words about *what's happening between us.* Maybe I shouldn't be so rattled by his display of emotion. I guess a guy like Charlie is way more into feelings than the average American male. I once read a study concluding that devotees of literary fiction are more empathetic and attuned to emotions. I reason that a *writer* of literary fiction should be exponentially more sensitive.

But though Charlie may want to take things to the next level, I can't go down that path. Not this soon. Not when I'm still settling into my own space after Henry's departure. Even when Charlie revealed his innermost feelings about his wife's death, I refused to discuss my own marriage, keeping him at bay with my flippant "sore subject" excuse. Surely that must be a sign that I'm not ready. A serious liaison with Charlie—with *anyone*—would undercut my well-constructed game plan. I think last night's dream was a warning that I'm getting in too deep. It's different for him. He's had three and a half years to rebuild his life. I haven't had half that long.

Then I think, the poor man. After what he's been through with his wife, here I am adding to his pain. Though I'm sorry for

Charlie, I'm sorry for myself too. These last weeks with him have been filled with laughter and warmth and the joy of sexual reawakening. It will be wrenching to give all that up, but I don't see any other way forward. As long as it was fun and games, I could have continued. But this business of *something important . . . something worth nurturing* goes perilously beyond fun.

I now recognize my big error in judgment. I mistook levity of spirit for levity of feeling.

• • •

With the confusion cleared from my head, it's time to act before I lose my nerve, or my willpower, or both. I glance at the time on my cellphone. With any luck, Charlie will finish up a yoga class soon. I'll intercept him at the club and figure out a place where we can talk in private.

About thirty minutes later, I find him on the upper deck, staring out at the cloudy morning sky. The shoreline is shrouded in gray once again, with no end to the June gloom in sight. He wears a pensive expression as if he senses trouble. "Morning," I say.

"Good morning. Finished with your conference call?"

"Yes, it ended about an hour ago. Did you get any writing done?"

"No. As you can see, I came here instead. Procrastination is my middle name."

"Charlie. Can you take a little walk around the harbor with me? We need to talk."

He frowns at me. "Uh-oh. I've always regarded 'we need to talk' as one of the top entries in the lexicon of unwelcome phrases. I rank it right up there with 'it's not you, it's me,' and 'I'm referring you to an oncologist.'"

I laugh. Maybe we can keep it light after all. Maybe there's no need to make a complete break. Charlie and I can become friends with benefits or something along those lines.

But no. I have to go through with this.

He takes my hand in his as we walk, and I don't draw back from his cool grasp. We glance at the docked sailboats, the seagulls, the gray horizon as I deliver my unhappy speech. We don't look each other in the eye. I regret to say the theme of my breakup message is "it's not you, it's me." I assure Charlie he's a terrific guy who has done nothing wrong - in fact, most women would jump at an opportunity to win the affection of a man like him. But bad luck for Charlie, I am not most women. I'm a sorry wreck of an old girl who is still in emotional retreat after a long and unsuccessful marriage. I hope like hell he believes what I say because I mean every word. And I hope it makes my news a little easier for him to swallow.

Finally, he gives me a direct look as he says, "I have to ask. Does your decision have anything to do with—with what took place on the yoga mat? Did I cross a line?"

I say, "Oh no, Charlie, I swear that wasn't a factor in the least. Honestly, what happened there—it took my breath away." In my mind, though, he crossed a different line last night - an unmarked boundary between casualness and caring, between detachment and commitment.

"Ah, well. I'm glad I didn't frighten you off with any excessively kinky moves." He smiles at me, but his eyes are sad. "As with every cloud, I guess there's a silver lining."

"What's that?"

"I'll be more focused on my writing again. Being in your company has been delightful but also distracting."

"What's the new book about?"

"It's a love story. The beauty of writing about love is that you can mold it into any size and shape and color. It can be rough or smooth, it can be tragic or comic; you get to choose the outcome.

But when you experience love in real time, all that control goes out the window."

So now he *is* using the "l" word. Charlie starts to turn away, but then he spins around to face me again. "Mar, I have to ask one more thing."

"Go ahead."

"What you said before, about it taking your breath away . . ."

"Yes?"

"If it took your breath away, why run from it?"

"Because—because I can't afford to be breathless right now." Though I don't share this with Charlie, what I crave above all is breathing room, not breathlessness. I want controlled yoga breaths that warm and soothe me with a calming rhythm. I want a heart that beats with the cautious tempo of a metronome set at *lento*, my pulse immune to any sensual shocks that might send it racing. Slow and steady - that's the pace I'll maintain, going forward.

Give me liberty and give me breath.

PART SEVEN: JULY
JAX

19.

When I first toured Seaside Fitness before signing up, the assistant club manager encouraged me to try as many exercise classes as possible. "Even if you think you won't like a particular class format, you might surprise yourself," she said at the time. "I guarantee you'll get more out of your membership if you keep an open mind and you're willing to experiment."

I decide this is a good time to follow her advice. I'd like to avoid Charlie for the next few weeks at least, for both our sakes - and a change in routine might help lift me out of the doldrums in which I've been drifting since I stopped seeing him. I review the schedule with my eye on late afternoon and early evening non-yoga classes, geared toward the younger after-work crowd. I won't run into Charlie then.

For starters, I will give Zumba a whirl. The five o'clock class is packed to capacity, but I squeeze into a space near the back and pull a sweatband on to contain my hair, which has changed in the warm summer weather from its usual moderate waviness to frizzy curls. The dance moves are energetic but easy to follow, broken down into simple Salsa-like patterns that quickly become obvious to me. The music is up-tempo, loud, and Latin-sounding, which I don't care for. The participants all gyrate, shimmy, jump, and spin with unflagging zeal, shouting, whooping, and laughing as they move. In the short breaks between musical numbers, they continue to bounce on their toes and applaud with wild excitement. It's like everyone is at a big nightclub party but with no alcohol. I try to maintain a positive outlook. Maybe after half an hour the endorphins will kick in and I'll start enjoying it. Or maybe I'm too much of a tight-ass and I need to let go of my inhibitions, the way I did with Charlie the time that—

No. I mustn't go there.

By the end of class, I've gotten a good cardio workout, but the exaggerated moves and the overenthusiastic whooping and hollering strike me as false and even embarrassing. I half want to chastise the class for engaging in this stupidity, and I half want to apologize for being the only woman in the room incapable of sharing in the fun.

It's not you, it's me.

Okay, Zumba isn't my thing. No big deal. Unintimidated, I zero in on a hip-hop class two nights later. On the printed schedule is a little red asterisk flagging it as a new class taught by a new instructor billed as Jax. Great name.

Jax lives up to it. He is a cool-looking dude of medium height, with a compact golden-skinned body, curly black hair, and a sweet, toothy smile that I find irresistible. I guess him to be of mixed ethnicity - maybe part Asian and part African American, like Tiger Woods. His age could be anywhere between thirty and thirty-five, though who knows? These days, I'm lucky to guess within twenty years. I slip into the back of the studio to observe the class from a small gallery area in the rear. Jax is fascinating to watch. His feet move swiftly in an intricate pattern as he lifts one shoulder and alternately lowers the other. His head whips to the left, then right, then left again. He balls one hand into a fist and extends the other outwards in a "stop" gesture with the fingers spread wide. He angles his upper body forward, then moves into a sinewy backward curve with his hips thrust out.

He orchestrates all these motions with consummate style and precision.

I'm lost in concentration as I observe him, so at first, I don't know Jax is addressing me when he says, "Hey, Curls. Come dance with us." I'm oblivious that he's referring to me until he walks to the rear of the room and pulls me out onto the dance floor. Fortunately, he leads me to the back row where I won't be seen. Jax dances in the row in front of me for a while, giving me a close-up view of the dance moves before resuming his place at the front.

During the time I observed the class, I was memorizing the steps. Now that I'm physically working my way through the routine, I flush with pleasure to discover I am actually *getting* it. I'm dancing in unison with the group, I'm not making mistakes, and I'm even throwing a little personality into the moves. This is fun. I glance at myself in the side mirror and note that I look pretty damn good. *You go, girl*. I've found my perfect dance class.

At the end of the hour, Jax threads his way through the crowd, high fiving some of the dancers at random as he makes his way to the back. He rewards me with a dazzling smile and a double-high-five as he says, "You killed it, girl. Where'd you learn hip-hop?"

"Right here, tonight," I say. "This was my first class."

"Did you hear that?" he says to the dancers around us, drawing them into the conversation. "Curls here is a natural. It must have something to do with the hair." He points at my ringlets. "The girl's got more rhythm than I do."

I beam at the attention. It's like I'm fourteen again.

"Hey, Curls—"

"Mar. My name's Mar."

"OK, Curly Mar, listen up. After class, a bunch of us like to go over to Bobby G's for a drink," he says, naming a popular bar a few miles away. "Why don't you join us?"

"Sounds fun, but I don't have a car. I walked here from my apartment."

"You can ride with me."

Twenty minutes later, eight of us - five women and three men - gather around a long table in the dimly lit bar at Bobby G's. Jax takes the seat next to mine, which I believe is a deliberate move on his part to keep me in his sights. When it's time to order, a blond man at the far end of the table asks for a draft beer. Everyone else, including Jax, opts for mineral water or Coke. I expected them to be bigger partyers somehow. I don't trust the house wine at a joint like this, so I order a vodka and soda with a splash of cranberry juice. As the oldest one at the table, I worry whether I'll be able to hold my own in a group of hip-hoppers.

"How long have you been going to Seaside Fitness?" the beer-drinking man asks.

"About six months."

"Have you tried any of the other dance classes?"

"Just Zumba," I say, trying not to look nauseated.

"Whoa, I hope you don't make that face when you talk about hip-hop," says Jax.

"Your class is great. I mean it. I can't wait to come back."

"That's why we all followed Jax to Seaside from the dance studio where he used to teach," says a long-haired, pretty South Asian woman to my left.

"Is that what happened?" I ask. So, these are all new members.

"Yes. We've been dancing with Jax for a couple of years. The old studio closed. When he got the job teaching at Seaside, most of his students signed up for memberships."

"Except the ones that couldn't pay the freight," says a dark-skinned African American man with a shaved head seated across from me. "At the studio, we could pay by the class. The Seaside monthly dues . . . man, they are *high*."

"Yeah, I was lucky my parents bought me a membership to Seaside as a birthday present. I turned twenty-nine last week. Ugh," says one of the others, a heavy-set woman sporting a small nose ring and short, spiky hair dyed in multiple shades of electric purple and blue.

"Girl, you're a babe in diapers," says Jax. "Twenty-nine. Hah. I'ma turn forty-four next month."

Forty-four? It's hard to believe.

We talk for a while about Seaside Fitness. The rest of the conversation is benign chitchat on a range of topics. People discuss their jobs – the African American guy sells advertising for a local newspaper and shows interest in my editorial position. The South Asian woman has fraternal twins a year older than Benny, though I don't volunteer that I'm a grandmother. When the group discusses music videos and clubs, I'm out of the loop, but the rest of the time I'm comfortable with the conversation. These are nice young people.

When he drops me off in front of my apartment, Jax says, "Thursday night I'm going out to hear some friends of mine who play in a band. They do a mix of R&B and pop . . . great for dancing. Wanna come with me?"

Is this another group activity or a date? He's been flirting with me from the moment I walked into his class. With my own interest in sex so recently rekindled, I'm pleased by his attention. If Jax were as young as his students, I wouldn't be inclined to take up with him, but I'm only about six years older than him. Not enough to put me in cougar territory. Maybe he holds the potential to turn into a friend with benefits . . . the sort of relationship I'd hoped for with Charlie before things escalated out of control. Whatever happens, I won't make the same mistake I made the last time. Jax is a sweet guy, and his attitude seems very casual. Yes, things with Jax will be different. I hope.

Things are different, all right, but not in the way I imagined. Our first night out together, we are a party of two when we go to listen to Jax's friends, but he knows everyone in the place. Men and women stop by the table every few minutes to exchange greetings, though he doesn't invite any of them to join us. Nor does he ask me to dance. While he drinks Coke with lemon and I sip chardonnay, Jax informs me he's landed a gig dancing backup on a new music video involving J.Lo.

"You're going to dance with Jennifer Lopez?" I ask, impressed.

"She's not gonna be *in* the video herself, but she's one of the backers." He proceeds with a convoluted story. "I haven't met J.Lo yet, but my friend's kid goes to school with J.Lo's son, and she's trying to get me an introduction." The longer Jax goes on, the more confusing it gets. It gradually becomes clear that he hasn't landed the job yet, and that there may not even be a job at all, or a video. At this point, there's only an optimistic *plan* for a video project, more like a plan for a plan.

After half an hour of listening to Jax pontificate on his six degrees of separation from J.Lo, my mind is wandering. Meanwhile, the band sounds good, and I'm thinking it would be a lot more fun to get up and dance. But when I suggest that, he says, "I taught four classes today. I'm too beat to get outta this chair."

Wait, didn't he invite me here with the promise of dancing? At least I thought that was the plan. I guess it was more of a plan for a plan.

• • •

Same night, one week later, we return to the hotel bar for another evening of not-dancing. This time, he regales me—no, that's too flattering a word—he *subjects* me to a long discourse about a new opportunity to serve as a judge on a television dance competition. "The format will be a lot like *So You Think You Can Dance*," he explains, "except instead of a season-long competition, each show is a one-off. There are four new contestants every week and one grand prize winner."

"Are the judges one-offs as well? Would you be on the judging panel one time or for the whole season?"

He gives a garbled and long-winded response in which he avoids answering my question. When I make a polite inquiry about last week's big opportunity - "Anything new with the J.Lo video?" - he wrinkles his nose and waves me off with a dismissive gesture as if I'm annoying him with an irrelevant question. He also dismisses, once again, my suggestion that we hit the dance floor.

"Been breakin' in new shoes this week. My dogs are barking."

When he pulls his car up to my building this time, I debate whether to invite him into the apartment. Before I can say anything, he treats me to one of his winning smiles and says, "One of these days, I'm hoping you'll ask me up. But not tonight. Another time. Soon."

I'm fine with that. Though I'm attracted to Jax, I'm not at all obsessed with him. I continue to enjoy the hip-hop class - every time I go, I'm getting a little better. My life has fallen into a constant rhythm. I work, and I work out with classes and daily walks.

But today I'm limping around the apartment after stubbing my big toe. No beach walk for me. Restless and bored, I give Mum an impromptu call.

"Margy dear, hello. You're lucky to catch me when you did. I'm off to a birthday party in a few minutes."

"Sounds fun."

"Yes, my new friend Nina is turning fifty-eight. I met her in Zumba."

"I didn't realize you were doing Zumba. Your friend is in her fifties but she takes a Silver Sneakers class?"

"Why would you assume it's Silver Sneakers?"

"Uh, because you're seventy-seven?"

She lets out a snort. "You know me better than that. I still like to work out with the kids." The *kids*, I guess, are people who aren't yet Medicare-eligible. Given Mum's youthful appearance and attitude, I guess I shouldn't be surprised.

"Zumba is *so* fun, you must try it," she says.

"I have, but hip-hop is my thing. I'm taking an advanced class now. The moves are incredibly challenging. You should see me."

"I don't think your father would have cared for Zumba," she says, blowing right past my boastful statement. Daddy was sixteen years older than Mum, and he didn't live to see eighty. As his health failed, he acted like a tired old man. Had he doddered his way into extreme old age, he would have cramped my mother's style big-time. But while he lived, my father made enough money to fund an elegant lifestyle for both of them, and for Mum throughout the rest of her life. And for that, she always stayed loyal to him, and he to her.

Unlike Henry.

"Where's your party?" I ask.

"At Nina's condo. Darling, I've got to head over there now. Talk soon."

Next, I decide to try for one of my infrequent chats with Michael. We are still semi-estranged. He seldom picks up when I call his cell, but today he answers, sounding relatively cheerful for Michael. "Hi. What's up?" he says.

"Nothing much. Just checking in. How's the family?"

"We're good, business is good," he says. "I suppose you're busy with work too?"

"I am now. But actually, a couple of months ago, I quit my job for a while."

"You what?" He says this in a loud voice, which cracks in an upward inflection. I hadn't expected him to react to the news with such interest or emotion. "You quit after all this time? Why?"

"The publisher and I had an ethical disagreement about whether to publish an article. But we worked it out."

"So you're back together with the publisher guy? Robert?"

"That's a funny way of putting it, but yes, I'm back in my job as editor-in-chief. Robert pleaded with me to come back. He even gave me a nice raise."

"I didn't think it was about the money with you two," Michael says.

"What's that supposed to mean?"

A pause. "Nothing. It's supposed to mean nothing at all." I hear Benny's voice in the background, muffled but whiny. Then Michael says, "I can't talk now."

Boy, this sure has been fun. I must remember to call my family more often. I glance at the clock. It's nearly five. I'll pour a glass of vino and respond to a couple of emails from Robert. As I do this, my thoughts turn to Michael's puzzling comment.

I didn't think it was about the money with you two. What the hell is that supposed to mean?

20.

The following week, Jax and I go clubbing at a different place – this time, a bar up near LAX. "I gotta check this place out. A friend of mine is a silent partner, and he wants me to come in as an assistant manager," Jax says.

"I didn't realize you had club experience too."

"Oh yeah," Jax says, without elaborating.

We're both putting a positive spin on this, considering I've seen no evidence that Jax has any work experience outside of teaching hip-hop – although I've listened to extensive monologues in which he's described a good many things he's *not* doing. The silent partner is nowhere in evidence, nor does Jax know anyone else at the club. He slouches in a dejected pose, slurps down a super-sized Coke, and excuses himself to visit the men's room. While he's gone, a tall dark-haired man with the shoulders of a football player walks over from the bar and asks me to dance.

Why not? Hell could freeze over before Jax ever gives me a turn on the dance floor.

There's no band here, just a deejay who's playing a good dance track right now. We gyrate to the beat – and, having picked up some new moves after a few weeks of hip-hop instruction, I think I'm looking pretty fine. What would this guy do if he knew I was fifty? I'm guessing he's in his early thirties. As I ponder his age, the music changes to a slow track and he draws me into a classic couples' dance pose, one hand extended around my back, fingers spread, and the other holding my right hand. We haven't spoken since he asked me to dance, but now he smiles and says, "Hey, what's your name? I'm—"

"Curls here is with me," says Jax, all macho man now, cutting in on us. He pulls me close to him, caressing my back with his right hand as Football Player Guy retreats to his barstool. Jax is only a few inches taller than I am, so we can dance cheek to cheek without him bending down to me. His cheek is warm, dry, and smooth. "Hey, girl, you look good on a dance floor," he whispers in my ear.

"I've had expert instruction," I say, thinking about how Jax exhibited zero interest in escorting me to any dance floor until another man beat him to the punch. Now he's acting all proprietary as if we were fricking *engaged* or something. The dancing doesn't last long. At the end of the slow number, Jax leads me back to the table. The guy with the shoulders has found a new partner, and they're out there shimmying and shaking.

On the half-hour drive home, Jax describes yet another pipe dream that involves staging big dance parties after hours at Seaside Fitness and other health clubs. It's not a bad idea - but with Jax, I never know whether he's been engaged in serious discussions about this with club management or if he's coming up with the whole scheme right this moment, off the top of his head.

When Jax pulls into a parking spot by my apartment, he gives me a lingering kiss on the lips for the first time. Then - as if pre-empting a possible invitation from me - he says, "I dig you, Curls. I'm into you, for sure. But I can't come up to your place yet."

"Oh?"

"Yeah—but it's not you, it's me."

He really, truly says this.

"I gotta problem down in my junk."

"Excuse me?"

He points to his crotch. "An infection. Down there. The doc, he put me on an antibiotic, but it didn't work, so now I'm trying a new med."

Sweet Jesus—just when I think I've heard everything.

Jax promises that as soon as the infection clears up, it's *game on*. He's into me, as duly noted. But after I say goodnight and step out of the car, I know with absolute certainty that it's *game off* for me . . . even after such time that his pistol is firing again. It's not so much the sick dick as it is the motor mouth that has caused my disenchantment. I've grown weary of listening to Jax's long-winded and often incomprehensible rants about all the plans and schemes that will never materialize. He can't embrace a single idea for more than a day, sometimes not for more than an hour. All I can think about is how best to avoid any further tiresome one-on-one contact with him.

The next morning, I place a long overdue call to Mrs. Ostrowski. We've been trading emails for a couple of months now, and I've received a few more missed calls from her number, though she has stopped leaving voicemails. But since I have vague stirrings of guilt over my intention to blow off the friendship with Jax, I try to shake off that "you're-such-a-bad-person" flutter of self-loathing by making nice to my old neighbor.

"Hello?"

"Hello, Mrs. Ostrowski. This is Mar Meyer calling."

"Who?"

"Your former neighbor from the house next door."

"Oh, you mean *Margaret*. Hello there."

"Sorry I've been so impossible to reach."

"I'm sure you're awfully busy, dear. But I'm glad you called. I was hoping you might find a free hour to stop by."

I avert my head from the phone so she doesn't hear the sigh that involuntarily escapes my lips. "This week is crazy, but maybe we can figure out a good time in a week or two," I say.

"That would be wonderful."

"How are you doing? Like I said in my email, I'm so sorry about Mr. Ostrowski."

"Oh, no need to be sorry," she says, her tone breezy. "The man was a piece of shit."

Whoa. Meek, timid little Mrs. Ostrowski is using the "s" word to describe her dearly departed husband? This proves you can never know anyone. "I—I guess you're doing okay, then?"

"I'm fine, dear, thank you. The world is a better place without him."

I am speechless.

"How is a week from Friday?" she asks. "You could come by for tea—say, around three?"

I check my calendar. "Three o'clock, Friday, next week. Perfect." My voice is charged with newfound enthusiasm. What previously had all the earmarks of a bland condolence call has now acquired a much spicier flavor. I note the appointment on my cellphone calendar and find that I'm looking forward to paying a visit to my old neighbor.

• • •

I think it's wise to avoid Jax's class for a while. *Damn*, I'm going to miss hip-hop. Once again, I'm back to browsing the club exercise class schedule for a new alternative. I decide to investigate another dance class called *NIA*. The music resembles something you'd hear in a yoga class, and the teacher - a razor-thin man of indeterminate age with multiple tattoos, body piercings, and stringy dark hair tied back into a ponytail - leads the dancers in a series of long, fluid body motions. The ten or so people in the class, all women, are flapping their arms like swans preparing to take flight. Next, they sashay across the floor in long, twisty strides, and when they reach the far side of the room, they jump into a crouching position, arms extended and fists clenched as if poised for battle.

I've always considered it a serious breach of etiquette to walk out in the middle of a class, but no way can I tolerate an hour of this. I feign a gastric disturbance and run from the studio, clutching my stomach. Though I'm happy to have escaped, the relief is temporary. As I'm retreating from the gym, I run smack into Jax.

"Hey, Curls, you goin' the wrong way. Class starts in half an hour."

"I—I think I pulled something," I say, my faux ailment migrating from stomach to spine. I bend one elbow and reach back my hand as if to support myself, grimacing as I do so.

"Girl, that looks bad."

"Yep. Afraid I'll need to take a break from hip-hop." I back toward the exit with a little wave. "See you when I'm better."

In truth, I've burned so many bridges at this club, there may be no turning back. When I count all the classes I can no longer attend and the various instructors and members I mustn't cross paths with, I acknowledge that my once enjoyable health club experience has become an exercise in avoidance.

Effective today, there'll be no more hanging out in the women's locker room, no more group classes, no more dating. Definitely no more dating. Because, for all my bold talk about a sexual reawakening, was I really about to jump into the sack for a meaningless fling with a man I didn't respect? Superficial one-night stands might have been okay for Henry on his out-of-town trips, but they are not okay for me. Trouble is, I'm not sure what *is* okay for me anymore, not sure how to plot a safe course. With Jax, I was navigating in waters too shallow - with Charlie, in waters too deep.

PART EIGHT: AUGUST GRACE

21.

As I stir in the warmth of the early August morning, burrowing my face sleepily into the pillow, my first waking sensation is one of sensual pleasure. I've had a delightful dream about making slow, sweet love, and it's so real I think my partner is right here in the bed, holding me in a gentle embrace, kissing my face and neck.

Damn. I was certain the embers of my recent attraction to Jax had burned out along with his half-baked business schemes, but I guess I had that wrong. Alas, as I regain full consciousness and the dream returns to me in more detail, I realize it wasn't Jax making love to me. It was Charlie.

Double damn.

I jump out of bed, hurrying to escape the bedroom like a burglar fleeing a crime scene. I'd been successful at keeping Charlie out of my thoughts and fantasies ever since the breakup I instigated at the end of June . . . or at least I'd been successful until recently. One evening earlier this week, I went to a movie by myself. On the way out of the theater, I spotted Charlie walking several yards ahead of me with a petite, dark-haired woman. I ducked into the restroom to make sure he wouldn't glance back and see me, dateless, exiting the multiplex in his wake.

At first, I said to myself: Good for Charlie, I'm glad the poor man isn't nursing a broken heart. But I quickly buried this generous impulse and allowed pettier emotions to surface. Didn't take him long, did it? I guess his feelings for me weren't that deep after all. Son of a bitch. This brief flash of anger faded, leaving me with something even worse – a sensation of grief and sadness. My eyes filled with tears, and I was grateful to be seated in a locked toilet stall where nobody could witness the pitiful display. Was I mourning the loss of Charlie, or experiencing simple jealousy because I was alone and he was not? I tried to convince myself it was the latter.

But now, after this all too vivid dream, I'm not sure. I need to drive all thoughts of Charlie (and of sex in general) out of my head. I retreat to my office and the comfort zone of work. The morning air is heavy, and intense yellow sunlight streams through the blinds. The June gloom that lingered into July is gone now, superseded by one of LA's typical late summer heat waves. I turn on the air conditioning, grateful to have a luxury not available in most of the older apartment buildings along the coast.

As I scroll through my inbox and reply to the most time-sensitive messages, it occurs to me I haven't had a real conversation with another human being all week. Robert canceled the weekly Skype meeting because most of the staff is out on vacation, so all my business communication has been via email. Michael is traveling on holiday until the week after next. I only know this, I'm ashamed to say, because of the out-of-office automated response I received after emailing him a few days ago. I wrote to remind him it was time for a decision on whether to keep or discard the box of his mementos in my storage locker. Since I can't expect to hear from him anytime soon, I guess I'll have to extend the locker rental.

Adding to the sense of isolation is my self-imposed exile from Seaside Fitness. I've run into my beach-walking buddy Audrey and her dog, Petey, on my habitual esplanade stroll, but she has always been in a hurry, affording me only a quick smile and a brief hello as she and the terrier continue on their purposeful journey. And that's been the extent of my verbal interaction this week.

Today, however, I'm scheduled to have tea with Mrs. Ostrowski. I hope the tea will be iced, given the weather forecast for the afternoon. It's probably a good idea to call and reconfirm since several days have passed since her invitation. But when she picks up the phone and I ask if we are still on for three o'clock, she stutters with confusion.

"I—I thought—weren't we—wasn't it for tomorrow, dear?"

"No, you said Friday."

"Yes, that's what I mean," she says.

"Okay, but . . . today is Friday."

Silence. "Oh. I—I'm afraid that won't work. I'm sorry."

"How about tomorrow? I could come tomorrow." I don't need to consult my phone calendar to know there is only one appointment scheduled for the next two weeks, my semi-annual rendezvous with the dental hygienist.

But she demurs. "I've been a bit *off* the last few days. I think it's a summer cold, and I'd hate for you to catch it. Let's make it another time, dear," she says, without proffering an alternate date for the raincheck.

"Sure, that's fine. Feel better, Mrs. Ostrowski," I say with false cheer. It's disheartening to acknowledge how bummed I am that my old neighbor has canceled our afternoon date. Am I that starved for social contact? But I refuse to wallow in self-pity. Solitude is what I'd wanted, after all. I search the event calendar on a local entertainment website and purchase a single ticket to a concert up in Santa Monica the following week. Then I browse the movie listings and make notes on a couple of films I'd like to see.

But what if I run into Charlie again? Despite the low probability of another chance sighting, I resolve to attend a different theater farther from the beach area, where he is not likely to go. When Michael was a middle schooler, that was the only way he would let me take him to the movies. He didn't dare risk the embarrassment of being seen with his mother at the neighborhood cinema.

Now that today's schedule looms empty, I run through the possibilities. I could contact the free-lance writers who are scheduled to provide articles for upcoming issues, but it's past three o'clock on the East Coast, and nobody will want to hear from me on a Friday afternoon in August. I haven't been to Seaside Fitness since walking out on the NIA dance class last month, and I'm feeling indolent and flabby. I need *real* exercise—something more challenging than a three-mile beach stroll on a flat promenade.

I'll go for a hike.

It's mid-afternoon when I arrive at the same trail network Charlie and I had hiked on that June weekend, our last together. I find a parking spot close to the trailhead right away. The summer sun beats down with relentless power, and only the merest hint of a breeze stirs the air. My car thermometer read ninety-two degrees on the drive up the hill. Here in the coastal regions, it's unusual for the mercury to top ninety. No worries. My water bottle is full, I've applied high SPF sunscreen to every square inch of exposed skin, and I've remembered to wear my biggest visor. It can only do me good to work up a serious sweat. I've been entirely too lazy.

At the trailhead, I consult a detailed map of the intersecting trails, thinking I'll try to duplicate the route I traveled with Charlie. I'm not an ace map reader in the best of circumstances, and this one looks antiquated and hard to read, with its confusing network of loops and triangles. Still no worries. Wherever I walk on this hilly landscape, there will be a view of the sea below to help orient me. Posted beneath the map is an old sign that says, "Beware of rattlesnakes," with a faded yet scary picture of the fearsome viper.

I start down the main path at a brisk pace, but the intense heat soon causes me to slow down. I recall Charlie and I hiked for a couple of hours, but in today's conditions that target is too ambitious. I continue along the wide dirt path, sending billows of dust into the air as I hike. Before long, everything is covered in a thin film of brown dust: bare limbs, clothes, sunglasses, visor. I didn't expect it to be so damn dry up here. I take a liberal swig of the now-tepid water from my trusty BPA-free plastic bottle *(thank you, Judge Judy)* and soldier on.

Off in the distance, I see a familiar sight - the small grove of cypress trees that Charlie had pointed out. Good, I'm right on course. I remember he said to bear left at the fork in the trail near this grove . . . or perhaps he said bear right? On arriving at the fork, I hesitate before I hook a left, thinking of Robert Frost and pondering what sights would await me down the other unchosen path. Though I've exchanged greetings with a few other hikers along the main path, I am going it alone on this narrower ancillary trail. The brush stands much taller than it did in June, and it is substantially browner and drier.

The trail narrows further. That's when the first alarm bell sounds in my head. I don't remember the path being this tight and overgrown - in places, the branches are so thick I almost need a machete to hack my way through. And as I continue to fight through the thorny brush, raising little scratches all over my bared arms and shins, I notice something to do with the view.

There isn't any.

On the previous hike, we always had a glimpse of the Pacific below. But from my current vantage point, I can't see the water at all. I've hiked down into an area where two steep, rocky hills stand between me and any possible view that might help me calculate my position. Now that I've descended into this canyon, the last whisper of a breeze has disappeared. It's blazing hot here with no shade in sight. I drink a little more water.

Trying to fight the rising tide of panic, I tell myself I have an approximate idea where I am. With all these intersecting side trails, I'm not sure if I can retrace my steps back. But it isn't like I'm seriously lost; I just need to get back to one of the main paths. I pull out my cellphone to consult Google Maps, figuring GPS will guide me to the nearest road. I'm dismayed to find that I don't have a cell signal - not even one single puny bar. At the top left of my cellphone screen is a mocking "No Service" message.

I compose a mental list of all the calamities that might transpire on this journey. I could trip on a hidden root and fall, twisting my ankle, unable to walk or summon help. I could pass out from heatstroke. What are the symptoms? Consulting the dictionary app on my phone, which is still working, I find the definition:

HEATSTROKE: A life-threatening condition marked especially by cessation of sweating, extremely high body temperature, and collapse that results from prolonged exposure to high temperature.

Two of the three symptoms apply. My skin is sizzling hot to the touch . . . and though I haven't collapsed yet, I'm not sure how long I can hold out. *Cessation of sweating* is trickier to evaluate. My clothing is soaked with sweat. But how can I tell if I am still generating fresh, healthy perspiration or if I'm a desiccated hag on a collision course with heat-related cardiovascular collapse?

The term that troubles me the most in all of this is *life-threatening*.

I take another gulp from my water bottle. The liquid now tastes as if it's been heated over a Bunsen burner. I'll have to ration the few remaining ounces with restraint. I try to conjure up other hostile scenarios, as if by cataloging all the ills that might befall me, I'll strike a pre-emptive blow to ensure that I come to no real harm. There's *something* else I should worry about, but I can't think what it is.

That's when I hear the rattlesnake.

It sounds more like a buzz than a rattle. My first reaction—that is, after my heart completes its wild leap from my chest into my throat—is to freeze in my tracks. I should now back away from the snake with slow and deliberate steps, but I'm uncertain how to do that. The problem is, although I can discern even muted sounds from a long distance off, I have poor directional hearing. Judging from the volume of the rattle, he doesn't sound too close. But I don't dare take another step for fear I'll go the wrong way and find myself within striking range.

Not moving a muscle, I remain frozen in place as it rattles on. After waiting for what seems like two hours (but is probably more like sixty seconds), I see the snake slither across the narrow trail and disappear into the brush, headed in the direction from which I had come. I'd considered turning back and attempting to retrace my previous route back up to the main trail, but there's no way I can follow that strategy now and risk walking into a literal viper's nest. I continue the arduous trek forward, hoping the path will soon intersect with one of the main trail arteries.

The next forty-five minutes are mental and physical hell. Every little noise triggers another wave of anxiety. A rustling in the bushes turns out to be a squirrel jumping from one branch to another. A chirping sound, which I attribute to a baby rattler, turns out to be emanating from a cute little yellow bird. My throat is parched and my lips are cracking. My feet have swollen up after miles of walking, causing my toes and the tips of my heels to rub painfully against the hiking boots.

I ascend the path up a long and difficult hill, and at the top, I find the main trail. The vast ocean sparkles below me in the distance, blue and tranquil, oblivious to my agitation and discomfort. I turn left to hike back to the trailhead. It's a steady uphill path, with a few trees along the edge of the road to provide at least a smattering of shade, but it will not be an easy climb. I accentuate the positive. In another half an hour, tops, I'll be back at the parking area. The promise of a soft leather car seat and an efficient air conditioner keeps me motivated for the final leg of the journey.

When I stumble across the parking lot and half fall into the driver's seat, I buckle up, but I don't drive off at once. Sitting quietly, I take a series of deep breaths as I allow the cool air to wash over me. I should stop at a market to buy a big bottle of water, but I'm anxious to get home to my own place. It will only be another twenty minutes.

I take it slow and easy. As my body temperature continues to cool, I'm beginning to feel more like myself. I stop at a long traffic light, closing my eyes against the bright sunlight, and reflect how fortunate I was that nothing bad happened to me despite all my worrying. I blink my eyes open, watch the light change from red to green, and pull out into the intersection. By the time I see the big black SUV bearing down on me, it's too late.

22.

Impact occurs a split second later. The mammoth vehicle pushes my car across the intersection in what feels like slow motion. The faces of all the new people who've come and gone this year flash by in rapid sequence, their expressions solemn and detached. *Whitney. Judith. Sunny. Nic. Connor. Cheryl. Audrey. Jax. Charlie.*

Charlie. Charlie. Charlie.

The Prius doesn't stop spinning until I reach the other side of the intersection. My knees are knocking against each other with violent force - from the intensity of the collision or from pure terror? My back seizes in a painful spasm. Again, injury or fear - I can't tell.

A slender Asian woman with a round face and smoothly styled, chin-length hair appears at my car window, her dark eyes wide with concern. Her stricken expression alarms me nearly as much as the accident. "Are you all right?"

"I—I don't know. I think so." There's a distinct tremble in my voice. My hands on the steering wheel are shaking, too, and my knees still wobble, though at least they've stopped slamming together.

"I can't believe you're all right," she says, looking me up and down. "I watched the whole thing. The girl in that SUV ran the light."

"Thank you for—for stopping."

"My name is Grace, and I'm going to stay with you as long as you need me to," she says in a calm, reassuring voice. "I've already called 911. Do you think you can get out of the car?"

I groan and survey the damage around me. The windshield has shattered into a thousand tiny green pebbles that occupy my lap, the front seat, the floor, the pavement. Why didn't the airbag deploy? You count on something (or someone) to protect you, but then when you most need it, it's not there. Still, it seems I've escaped serious injury. I examine my arms and legs, which are speckled with a hundred tiny cuts and scratches, then realize I got those from hiking in the thorn-laden brush, not from the accident. I pause a moment to appreciate the engineering genius behind safety glass.

Sirens wail in the distance like screaming birds. When I'm reassured that I'm not merely alive but conscious, capable of speech, and able to move about, a surge of energy propels me out of the car. I'm good. In fact, I'm *great*. I must be invincible to sail through a crash like this unscathed, and in a modest little Prius, no less. I am . . . empowered. I jump out of the car. Okay, *jump* might be an exaggeration, but I'm moving more nimbly now than I have for the past couple of hours.

"What's your name?" Grace asks.

"Mar. Mar Meyer."

"Okay, Mar, if you'd like to hand me your phone, I can contact whoever you like."

"Whoever I like? On my phone?" I say, bewildered.

"Better that way. If I call your family from a cellphone they don't recognize, they're not likely to pick up. So, who can I call for you?"

Who can I call for you? Now there's a loaded question. Not Michael, who has flown out of state with his family to an undisclosed vacation spot. Not my mother, who lives thousands of miles away. Not any of the people who paraded through my consciousness at the moment of impact. And certainly not my ex-husband.

"No one. But thanks for asking," I say.

Grace encircles my wrist with one hand and lifts it in a gentle motion. At first, I think it's a gesture of friendship, or perhaps pity because I haven't been able to name a single loved one to summon. But no, she's taking my pulse. She glances into my eyes, then asks me if I can follow the movement of her finger from left to right and back again. I can.

"Are you a doctor or a nurse?" I ask.

"No, but I'm a home health care aide, so I've had some basic medical training."

"Ah. Lucky for me."

Within five minutes, the intersection is swarming with activity. The police have arrived, along with the paramedics and firemen in impressive red trucks that Benny would love. I'm also accosted by a man around my age who has arrived on the scene – his teenage daughter, he explains, is the one who hit me, and they are admitting fault. The girl stands on the curb several feet away, arms wrapped tightly around her torso as if to shield herself from a cold wind. She has waist-long hair the color of straw and a sharp, pointed chin that gives an edgy look to an otherwise pleasant countenance.

"While the paramedics check you out, is there anything I can get for you?" Grace asks.

"I could use some cold water."

"I'll be right back," she says.

A young EMT puts me through the paces. He begins by checking my vital signs and my responsiveness much the way Grace did a few minutes ago, although his exam is lengthier and more thorough. Every so often he nods or mumbles, "Good." I can tell from his reactions that I'm passing all my tests with flying colors, and I'm growing a little complacent.

"I'm *fine,*" I keep saying. "Considering my car resembles a twisted hunk of battered metal, I can't believe how good I am."

The EMT is having none of it. "Adrenaline," he says.

"Huh?"

"You're in shock from the accident, and your body is producing adrenaline, which gives you a kind of high."

"Is that good or bad?"

"Well, it's—it's what happens after a trauma. Your heart is speeding like a racehorse. But your blood pressure isn't bad, considering."

"I told you I'm fine."

He ignores this. "As soon as you're finished talking to the police, we'll strap you into that nice comfy stretcher for a joyride down to the ER."

"The ER? But that's completely unnecessary."

By this time Grace is back and is frowning at my response. I accept the water bottle from her and gulp down the full liter in a matter of seconds. "Wow," she says, watching me slake my thirst. "You know, Mar, the paramedics are right. You should go to emergency for a complete workup. They can do x-rays and other more comprehensive tests to make sure there's nothing funny going on."

"Oh, I can assure you there's nothing funny going on," I say, but she doesn't get the joke. "They can't *make* me go to the hospital, can they?"

"No, but I highly recommend it."

"I understand why you'd say that, but I'm fine, honestly," I say for the tenth time.

Grace lets out a big sigh, and I conclude she's given up the fight. But she stays by my side, guiding me through every step of the process. I realize I couldn't get through this without her. Because even though I think I'm alert and sharp, I have difficulty responding to simple commands, such as, "Show me your driver's license and registration." Grace helps me find things, she helps me communicate with the police, she helps me fill out the accident report and exchange information with the teenage girl's father, who holds the insurance in his name and will be the responsible party.

When the tow truck arrives, I ask if they are taking my car to the junkyard. "Oh no," says the policeman. "The insurance adjuster has to inspect it first to review the damage and determine whether it's a total wreck."

"Are you kidding me? Look up 'total wreck' in the dictionary and that's the car in the picture. My three-year-old grandson could tell you this vehicle is not fixable."

"Those are the rules, Ms. Meyer. That's how they do it."

He offers me a ride home, but Grace steps in and says she'll be glad to take me. The woman is a saint. I'm relieved and grateful to return to the apartment with her rather than in a police cruiser. As I'm hauling myself into the front seat of Grace's silver Honda, the young driver of the black SUV approaches me.

"I'm so, so sorry," she says in a squeaky little voice that's scarcely above a whisper. "I didn't mean to hit you."

A paragon of serenity and forgiveness, I say, "That's why they call it an accident."

She nods - grateful, I expect, that I've let her off so easy. I buckle myself into Grace's passenger seat and provide garbled directions to my place, causing her to make two wrong turns along the way. She wants to escort me upstairs to the apartment, but I decline the offer, thanking her and pronouncing myself "fine" for the eleventh time.

At home, I down another quart of water and turn up the A/C. Exhausted, I sink onto the soft couch. It then dawns on me that cocktail hour is almost over and I need to play catch-up. Is alcohol a good idea after I've been in a serious accident? Yes, it is, I conclude after deliberating for about six seconds. After all, I never lost consciousness and didn't suffer a head injury, though my neck is tightening up as if someone has stuck it in a metal vise. I pull a rosé out of the fridge, selecting a cork-free bottle. I doubt I could manipulate a corkscrew in my unhinged state. Maybe I'm not so fine after all. Food is of no interest, but wine will help me to de-stress. I remind myself to match every glass of wine with a tumbler of water to keep hydrated.

Around nine o'clock, my cellphone rings, and I literally jump out of my seat. That's how unusual it is for me to get a phone call these days.

"Hello, Mar? This is Grace. From the accident." She says it the same way a caller might identify herself as "so-and-so from the dentist's office," and somehow it tickles my funny-bone. I guess the three glasses of rosé have loosened me up.

"Grace, hi," I say with a giggle. "How did you get my number?"

"We exchanged contact information before I dropped you off, remember?"

"Oh, right." It all comes back to me. Grace was actually the one who entered the contact info into both cellphones. My quivering fingers and addled brain couldn't have executed such a demanding task.

"Are you doing all right?" she asks.

"I'm fine." I decide I should create a continuous loop recording of my voice saying, "I'm fine," and play it for anyone who inquires. I giggle again.

"I wanted to check on you and make sure."

"That's thoughtful of you. Listen, I can't thank you enough for helping me today. I don't know how I would have gotten through it without you."

"Don't be silly. Anybody would have done the same."

"No," I say, "they wouldn't have."

"Are you in much pain?"

"A little."

"You should get to the doctor tomorrow."

"Oh, I *will.*" But maybe not. It seems pointless to waste time on an unnecessary trip to the physician's office.

As I finish my final glass of wine, I alternate between elation over surviving the hiking-heatstroke-car-wreck fiasco nearly unscathed and post-traumatic shock over the frightening recognition that I faced multiple threats of injury or even death from many sources - solar, vehicular, and reptilian - in a single afternoon. Crawling into bed, I lie on my back, then roll to either side, but I can't get comfortable. Hours pass before I fall into a troubled sleep.

23.

Over the next couple of days, determined as I am to shake off the trauma of the accident, my aching body won't let me forget the physical punishment it's undergone. My neck is stiff and sore from whiplash, and I have three enormous and tender bruises: two on the inner sides of my knees from the violent knocking, the other along my left hip, which I must have banged against the car door from the impact of the collision. Two mornings after the crash, I break down and belatedly follow Grace's advice. I pay a visit to my doctor, who prescribes high doses of ibuprofen and a muscle relaxant at night.

Back home, my phone buzzes with a call from Grace. "Just wanted to ask how it went with the doctor yesterday."

"Good." I don't bother mentioning I waited until today to seek help. "I hope the meds will do the job."

"They will. You'll feel a little better each day," she assures me.

I'm touched by her continued attention and concern. "Thanks for checking in again. How are things with you?"

"Oh, I'm fine. I'm at work right now."

"I won't keep you, then."

"It's okay. The man I take care of is resting, so I have a few minutes."

"You said you're a home health aide, right?"

"Yes."

"Do you spend nights there too?"

"Oh no. My husband wouldn't care for that." We both laugh. "He retired a couple of years ago—my husband, I mean—so I've cut back to morning shifts so Mike and I can play golf in the afternoons."

"Sounds nice. Michael is my son's name too," I add. This leads to a discussion of children. Grace also has a grown son, just out of college. We talk about kids, and what we do in our leisure time, and how we feel about our jobs.

"The man I work for is such a sweetheart. He's widowed and has esophageal cancer."

"That's rough. How sick is he?"

"He's actually been doing pretty well the last few months since he stopped chemo, but I'm afraid the cancer will catch up with him before long. Hold on—he's calling for me."

I can hear Grace's footsteps as she walks away from the phone. In the background, I overhear her cheerful voice as she ministers to her patient. "You okay, Frank? Here, let me adjust those pillows. Better, right? I'm just going to hang up the phone and I'll fix you a nice snack. Then how about a foot massage?" I'm struck, once again, by her kindness and compassion. She comes back to the phone. "You heard that? I've gotta run."

"Of course. Thanks for checking in, Grace. I enjoyed talking with you."

• • •

There's endless busywork in the accident's aftermath: forms to be filled out, phone calls to the insurance companies, a trip to the car rental place to pick up the blue Camry that will serve as my transportation until the car issues are sorted out. I'm fortunate the cost of a loaner will be covered by the other driver's insurance. In a conversation with the woman at the rental counter, however, I learn I might've missed out on a bigger insurance windfall by refusing emergency medical treatment.

"When you have a report from the hospital documenting your injuries, you stand to collect more money," she informs me.

"Like, hundreds more?" I ask.

"Even thousands."

I guess I should've listened to Grace and the paramedics after all.

Once I've caught up on the accident follow-up and I've got wheels again, what to do? I'm too sore for any serious exercise. In more hospitable weather I could manage a stroll on the esplanade, but the record-breaking heat has persisted. Besides, the beach is packed with families trying to escape the even hotter inland temperatures, and I'm in no mood to fight the crowds and the noise. I call Mrs. Ostrowski. "How are you?" I ask.

"Not too good."

"Colds are the worst," I say.

"How did you know I had a cold?"

"We talked on Friday."

"We did?" She coughs like a maniac at the other end of the line before she's able to continue. "I think it's gone to my sinuses," she says. "I've got the worst post-nasal drip. It's annoying."

"You should get yourself to a doctor right away." Do as I say, not as I do.

"Oh, I will, hon, first thing tomorrow."

You can't bullshit a bullshitter. I know she's not seeing any doctor tomorrow morning. "Is there anything I can do?"

"Oh no, dear. Thank you for asking." She dissolves into another round of coughing, and we both sign off.

Twice rebuffed by Mrs. O., my next action reveals the full extent of my growing desperation. I call Mum and invite her to visit me in California.

"Visit you? In that terrible heat?"

"Not right now. In the fall—maybe October. When it gets chilly in New York."

"Oh, I don't know, Margy. I thought you lived in a small place. Where would I sleep?"

"You can have my bedroom. I'll use the futon in my office."

"Sounds like cramped quarters."

"I've told you, it's nice. You can watch the sailboats go by and smell the salt air. You can even hear the sea lions barking." It's pathetic how hard I'm selling it. There's a long pause during which I imagine she's framing the best way to make her excuses.

Sure enough, she says, "Could be tricky, darling. I've got a lot of plans with my friend Nina and tickets to several shows. Also, I'm helping the new crowd organize an end-of-summer party over Labor Day, and a wine-tasting event in the middle of October."

Parties, plays, wine tastings . . . Mum excels at living a carefree life. Why can't I be like that? "How are Mary and Jeanette?" I ask, referring to her two oldest friends. "You haven't mentioned them lately."

Mum sighs. "Those two are like a couple of miserable old crones. Mary's always begging off because of some imagined ailment or another. One day it's a sinus headache, the next day it's a touch of diarrhea. Jeanette is recovering from a hip replacement, and she's hired a caregiver to help her get around, so if I go anywhere with her, the aide has to tag along. It's dreadfully inconvenient."

That's my Mum. The soul of compassion.

"Anything else, honey? Because I'm running late."

"Well, I thought you'd want to know I was in a bad collision a couple of days ago. The other driver ran a red light."

"Oh no. You sound normal, so it couldn't have been too terrible."

"Actually, it was. The Prius was totaled."

"But you're okay? Did you go to hospital?"

"Well, no, but—"

"Oh good. I'm glad it wasn't anything serious."

I nearly break down and tell her how serious it really was, but I know this will trigger a "stiff upper lip, darling" lecture. So I just say, "Right."

"Thanks for calling, sweet pea. Talk soon."

"Sure, Mum." Her nonchalance burrows under my skin like a stinging insect bite. But everything has always been about her. God forbid she should waste any precious time on sympathy for another human soul. Then again, that's probably what Michael thinks about *me*.

Maybe the apple doesn't fall far from the tree after all.

• • •

A few nights later I drive up to Santa Monica for a concert. It's a musical revue with a small ensemble of performers doing numbers from shows by Sondheim, Kander and Ebb, and other Broadway luminaries. Instead of old chestnuts like "Send in the Clowns," the playlist features lesser-known titles, combined into clever thematic mashups. My enjoyment would be complete if it weren't for the nagging pain in the back of my neck. I forgot to take my anti-inflammatory before leaving home. Later, in the theater parking lot, I start the rental Camry and am about to put it in reverse when the whole car shakes with a loud *thud*. Someone has backed into me.

Seriously? Another accident? I would laugh if my neck didn't ache so much. I move stiffly out of the car to confront the other driver. She's a young woman, though not as young as the girl who piloted the black SUV.

"I'm so sorry. So sorry," she says.

I examine the rear of my loaner car. The right bumper has a bad dent and the plastic taillight cover is broken, but at least the car is drivable. Still, I'll have to contact the rental company right away, exchange the car, fill out another pile of paperwork, and lord knows what else.

"I'm sorry," she says again.

I turn to her. "You're sorry. Sure, you're sorry. *Everybody's* sorry. The teenager who ran a light and almost killed me last week, she's sorry. *Really*, really sorry. Her father, who's paying for the whole thing with his insurance, is sorry too, mostly because his rates will go up. Oh, and my ex-husband Henry, who fell in love with another woman . . . he decided he wanted a divorce, and he was really sorry about *that*." My voice is rising, and some of the other concert patrons have stopped to eavesdrop on my rant. I look around at the gathering crowd. "*Everybody is sorry*," I inform them, windmilling my arms in a fierce gesture. "Except my son Michael, who's never sorry because as far as he's concerned, everything that happens is *all my fault*!"

The woman who rear-ended my car is taking cautious steps backward in the same way I retreated from the dreaded rattlesnake on the hiking trail. Though I'm sure she regrets hitting me, I expect she's sorrier still to discover that she'll now be forced to engage with a lunatic.

Back at my place, I pop a much-needed ibuprofen, pour myself a glass of white wine, and discover—to my bewilderment—that I'm not in the mood to drink. I'm in the mood to cry.

Though I can tear up in a heartbeat watching some schlocky commercial for life insurance or animal shelters, *real* crying has never come readily to me. It's a product of my upbringing. While my friends' parents obliged them to stifle farts and belches, at our house Mum greeted tears with the same stern condemnation. A sobbing child was neither attractive nor genteel in her unsentimental world. So as I try to let go, the first sounds I produce emerge more like strangled hiccups than sobs. I scrunch up my face to summon emotion, but my eyes remain dry. And then, when I'm about to give up, the waterworks start. I cry and cry, and then cry some more, until I worry the tears will never cease.

I can't stop replaying Grace's question when she ran up to help me. *Who can I call for you?* Not having anyone else I dare to speak to, I'm tempted to phone Grace right now and tell her what happened tonight. But bothering her with this would be inappropriate. Besides, I doubt I could utter an intelligible sentence in my current state.

Who can I call for you?

Here's the thing. During happy times, it's all well and good to be fancy-free and independent. But when you're confronted with the tough stuff, when the bottomless well of tears leaves your eyes stinging and your head pounding, self-reliance loses its allure. When life surprises you with the collisions and the fender-benders and the near misses; with the heatstroke on a hike, or the aches and chills and flus of winter; with the friend who unexpectedly drops dead, or the parent who starts acting forgetful; with the biblical rainstorm that springs holes in your roof, or the earthquake that shatters every breakable item in your house; with your cousin's/sibling's/friend's kid who dies from a drug overdose/suicide/freak sports injury . . . when life deals you a shitty hand of any kind (and given the almost infinite combination of cards, there are many, many shitty hands to be dealt), you want to have someone to call.

Not a Good Samaritan like Grace, but someone you hold close to your heart. And suddenly, I have a realization that seems so important, so obvious, so *necessary*, I don't know how it eluded me until now. The next time a stranger asks, "Who can I call for you?" I want that name to be right on my lips, with no hesitation and no doubt that the person at the receiving end of the call will be there for me and will have my back.

PART NINE: SEPTEMBER
MRS. OSTROWSKI

24.

I ring the bell three times before she answers. When she finally opens the door, Mrs. Ostrowski squints up at me and blinks over and over, as if trying to decide whether I am a real woman or an apparition. "Margaret," she says. "What a nice surprise."

I'm surprised she's surprised. "Hi, Mrs. Ostrowski. We had a date for three o'clock. It's a few minutes past three right now."

"Oh—oh—yes," she stammers. "Sometimes I have trouble hearing that doorbell. I remember, of course. I was reading and I lost track of the time. Won't you come in, dear?"

I walk in from the bright sunlight and follow her into the kitchen. It's been years since I've seen the inside of this house, but nothing has changed. I remember the thick, grayish-green wall-to-wall carpeting in the living areas and matching linoleum in the kitchen, the furniture that looks like it came out of a Sears catalog, the old-fashioned seascape prints on the walls in ornate gilt-edged frames. I inhale the musty odor I've always associated with the house.

Mrs. O. ushers me into a chair at the round, Formica-top table in the kitchen alcove. There is no air conditioning, but an old ceiling fan above the table rotates lazily, stirring the warm air. With the blinds drawn and the fan operating, it's tolerable in the room.

"Is it hot outside?" she asks.

"Around eighty today. Not as bad as it was in August."

"Well, thank heavens for that. Sometimes we get our hottest weather in September."

I nod. Mrs. O. bustles around the kitchen and returns to the table with a tray bearing a plastic pitcher, two matching glasses filled with ice cubes, and a small plate of cookies. "What are we drinking?" I ask.

"It's—it's—you know, the drink named after that golfer. I forget what you call it—him. Iced tea and homemade lemonade."

"Arnold Palmer?"

"Yes, that sounds right," she says. "Good for you."

I take a tentative sip. It's delicious - lemony, aromatic, and refreshing, with a hint of sweetness. To my disappointment, the cookies are ginger snaps, which I've always regarded as more of a punishment than a treat, surpassed only by graham crackers in their lack of appeal. Not wishing to be impolite, however, I take one and nibble it around the edges. Before sitting down, Mrs. O. pulls a bottle out of the cupboard. Mount Gay rum. She adds a healthy pour to her own Arnold Palmer and poises the bottle above my glass.

"Join me?"

It unnerves me to discover that sweet little Mrs. O. is a tippler. Has she already been hitting the bottle? Maybe that would account for her confusion upon my arrival. "No, thanks." I reflexively hold a hand over the top of my glass. Three o'clock is a tad early, even for me.

She returns the rum to the cupboard, sits down at the table, and takes a large swig of her spiked tea. "Are you doing okay, dear?" she asks. "I mean, since the divorce and all."

"Yes, I'm fine. But how about you, Mrs. Ostrowski? You're the one who's had the real shock this year."

She sighs. "It was a shock, you're right. John wasn't sick for long. And I didn't expect him to die. I thought he was too mean to die."

What was it she said on the phone that day? "The man was a piece of shit." I say, "What happened to him . . . if you don't mind my asking?"

"He had bleeding on the brain. You know, from taking blood thinners. They drilled a hole to relieve the pressure."

"That sounds awful."

"Oh, it's no big deal; they do it all the time," she says. "Most people recover - that's another reason I thought he'd be okay. But John went downhill after the procedure, and he never came home again. They moved him from the hospital room into a hospice facility at the end. Do you know, he was yelling at me about something, and right in the middle of a sentence, he up and died? Just like that." She snaps her fingers.

"In the middle of a sentence? I didn't realize that was possible."

"With John, it was to be expected. He spent ninety percent of his time yelling about one thing or another. I've said it before, and I'll say it again - the world is a better place since he's gone."

"Mrs. Ostrowski, did he—"

"Nancy, dear. Call me Nancy."

"Did he—hit you or anything like that?"

"Not with fists. He never abused anyone in *that* way."

"He was verbally abusive?"

She nods. "Who said 'Sticks and stones may break my bones, but'—darn—how does it go?"

I complete the quote: "But words will never hurt me."

"Right. Well, whoever said that . . . he or she is a moron. John hurt me every day with his words, and I've got a million scars to prove it. Not here," she tells me, touching her cheek, "or here," she says, lifting an arm. "But *here*." She holds one hand to her heart. "It's better since he's been gone, but I can still feel the pain inside me. Sometimes I think it will never go away entirely."

"Oh, Mrs.—I mean, Nancy—I'm sorry."

"You must have known," she says, giving me a challenging gaze.

"That he was mean?"

"Yes."

"He always seemed . . . cranky. Never smiled, as far as I can remember," I say. "I thought maybe he just didn't like us. I hoped he was nicer to you."

"Well, he wasn't."

"Clearly."

"Your son sure was scared of him. And who could blame the boy after what happened with the bicycle."

At first, this statement makes no sense to me. Then, a shudder of apprehension. "What bicycle?"

"The red one. You don't know, do you?"

I shake my head, tense about where the conversation is going.

"You and Henry had given Michael that red bike for Christmas, I recall. Oh, how he loved that bike. But he was careless with it. That's how boys are, I suppose."

"Yes."

"One afternoon you were out somewhere - one of your business meetings, I think. And Michael was riding up and down your driveway, making figure eights with the bike. He was going too fast and he lost control and plowed right into the flowerbed in front of our house. John had planted some blooms there, and he'd been working hard on it all day. Well, it was about three-quarters ruined after Michael ran over it."

"Oh God." I raise my half-empty glass. "You know, Nancy, I think I'd like a little rum after all."

"Sure, honey." She stands and opens the refrigerator, peers in for a moment, and slams it shut. Then she opens cupboard doors, but not in the area where she stashed the rum. "This will sound silly," she says in an apologetic tone, "but did you ask me for something? I forget what I was looking for."

"Rum," I say, getting up and retrieving the bottle myself.

"Oh, of course. Help yourself," Mrs. O. says unnecessarily, since I'm already doing so. She sits back down at the table. "So, what are you up to these days?" she asks.

I steer her back to the story. "You were telling me about the bicycle. How Michael ran over your husband's flowerbed."

"Right, yes. John was outside when it happened, puttering with something or other, and he was *furious* with Michael. I don't think I've seen him angrier. And that's saying a lot."

"Did he—do something to the bike? Break it, or flatten the tires, or anything?"

"No, like I said before, John was never violent in the physical sense . . . not with people, not with things either. He confiscated the bike. Michael begged him not to, said he was sorry, it would never happen again. But John said, 'You're right it won't happen again because you've seen the last of that bicycle.'"

"Michael's version was different. He said he rode his bike to the park that day, and someone stole it when he left it unattended for a few minutes. I don't understand why he didn't tell me the truth."

"John made sure that wouldn't happen. He told Michael, 'If you dare tattle to your parents like a little crybaby, I'll plow my car into your father's precious BMW the same way you plowed your bike into my beautiful blooms. And I'll tell them the whole thing is your fault. You'll be in big trouble.'"

I top up my glass with a little more rum as I digest this news. In a quiet tone that I hope doesn't sound accusing, I ask her, "Why didn't *you* ever tell me?"

"Honey, when John was mad, you did *not* cross him. It's that simple. He stashed the bike in his workshop – the little shed behind the house. I waited a few days for him to calm down, and

I said to him, 'Why don't we return the bike now? Tell them how the boy ruined your garden, and we can say you took the bike away for a couple of days to teach him a lesson.' But John claimed it was too late. Said he already gave the bike away. Donated it to some kids' charity." Her shoulders sag in a posture of great weariness as she tells me this. "Margaret, I should've said something. But the man was such a bully. I was as scared of him as Michael was. I'm sorry. I'm sorry every day."

"You shouldn't be. It wasn't your fault."

"I mean I'm sorry every day that I wasted my life with that son of a bitch. Do you ever feel that way about Henry?"

I think about this before answering. "I can't say that I do. Our marriage wasn't wonderful, but it wasn't terrible either. In any case, it's better not to dwell on the past."

"That's good advice," she said, "except the past is all I have left to dwell on." After making this glum pronouncement, she shivers a little. I'm astonished at the way older people can be cold, even in the steamiest weather.

"Can I get you a sweater?" I ask.

"Oh, yes, please. I think there's one in the study."

She leads me down the hall to the study, where I hope to find a sweater draped over the desk chair. "I don't see it," I say. "Maybe the hall closet?"

"No, dear, I'm sure it's here." She searches up and down the floor-to-ceiling built-in shelves as she walks in distracted circles around the small room, which is cluttered with many years' accumulation of books, magazines, and paraphernalia. I wouldn't think she'd leave her sweater on a bookshelf, but I've seen odder things.

Then I notice something else that's accumulated on the walnut desk - bills. The desktop is a scene of chaos, scattered with a mound of papers that look as if they've been dumped out of a bag with no thought to organization. The invoices at the top of the mound bear prominent *Past Due* stamps. My heart sinks.

What a mess. Though I'm not shocked to discover that Nancy must have deferred to her husband about the finances.

She sees me frowning at the desk and says, "It's not a pretty sight, is it? I'll catch up on it next week. I must say, the one thing I miss about John is that he took care of all the bills."

I nod, grateful that I'm not part of that older generation of women who went through marriage depending on their husbands to handle all the business affairs and make the important decisions. Come to think of it, my resolutely independent Mum's never been that way either, even though she's not much younger than Nancy. "I could help you sort out the bills next week," I say. "If you like."

"Oh, that would be marvelous," she exclaims, looking relieved.

I feel a rush of pity for this poor woman who has lived such an unhappy life under the thumb of a man who treated her with cruelty. To be truthful, I'm also feeling guilty right now - guilty to learn that John terrorized not only his wife, but Michael as well, and right under my nose. And all the while, I dismissed the man as a crotchety old coot, unwilling or unable to recognize him as a treacherous bully.

I leave the Ostrowski home shaken by Mrs. O.'s revelation. After acquiring some distance from the event, however, I now question her reliability as a narrator. The woman is so muddled. Perhaps she's mixed up the details or fabricated the entire story. When I return the following week to help with the bills, I devise a sort of test. I ask Nancy to repeat the story and challenge her to add new information to check for consistency. "Do you remember what time of year your husband took the bike away from Michael?"

"It was in the winter, not long after Christmas," she replies. Whether or not she's correct about the circumstances of the bike's disappearance, she's nailed the timing.

"What color was it? I've forgotten," I say.

"Bright red, like a candy apple. And it had one of those little license plates with Michael's name on it." Right once more.

She tells me again about Michael doing figure eights around the driveway before skidding out of control, and about John donating the bike to charity before she could convince him to return it. Her story holds up. But she has zero recollection of why I've come today.

I apply myself to the task at hand in the study, knowing it may take hours to complete. Nancy settles into a chair on the opposite side of the desk, but whenever I ask her a question about anything, she grows befuddled. Fortunately, I discover John was a well-organized bully. There's a tall wood filing cabinet to the side of the desk where copies of older paid invoices have been filed in alphabetical sequence. The checkbook, check register, postage stamps, and envelopes are in the top drawer of the desk.

As I arrange the bills into neat piles, eliminating duplicate statements as I go, it occurs to me I may not be the appropriate person to delve into the Ostrowski finances. I know there are no offspring - Henry and I used to joke that any children in residence would've run away from home to escape Mr. O. as soon as they were capable of ambulation.

"Is there anyone who can help you pay bills, and run errands, and things?" I ask Nancy. "You know, like a close friend or relative I can contact?"

Who can I call for you?

Nancy sighs. "No one, dear. That's why I so appreciate you helping out."

Going through the files, I discover that most of the bills have been paid through May of this year, which was about three months after John died. It's only in the past few months that the task has been neglected. Perhaps Nancy understands how to manage household finances after all, or perhaps she had a previous helper who is now absent or forgotten. Either way, the situation points to recent memory loss as the culprit.

She's nodding off in her chair, and since she's no help to me anyway, I persuade her to lie down for a nap. While I put things in order and write checks, I notice a letter from a lawyer about matters concerning the estate. I make note of his name and phone number. I also find a pocket-sized address book, the old handwritten kind, and I flip through and find a couple of people named "Ostrowski." I note their names and numbers as well. I'm part busybody and part sleuth. Later, after Nancy signs the checks and I drop the payments in the mail, I'll make a few calls. Perhaps I can locate her next of kin and let them know she's struggling with memory issues. *Damn.* If only I hadn't ignored her messages for so long, perhaps I could've stepped in and helped her weeks before now.

25.

After more than a month's hiatus, I'm back at Seaside Fitness. The first time I walk into Jax's class, he greets me with a bear hug and a smile, but he doesn't ask me out or engage in conversation. I'm like yesterday's forgotten business idea. He's moved on to someone—or something—else without a backward glance. Perfect. Now I can enjoy hip-hop with no unwanted distractions or hidden agendas. In fact, I can enjoy all my favorite classes again. All except yoga. Because I am still compelled to avoid Charlie.

When I walk into the women's locker room for the first time since July, the girls welcome me back. They all exclaim at once, "Howdy, stranger. Haven't seen you in ages." "Hi there. Were you traveling?" "I hope you haven't been sick." "I've missed seeing you in power sculpt."

"Thanks, it's good to be back," I say, gratified by the warm greeting. "I was . . . taking a break. Wow, you got new hair," I say to Amazon Lady, who has abandoned her strawberry-blond tresses for a pixie cut.

"Yeah, I couldn't stand wearing it long during that heat wave," she says. "Now I'm not sure I made the right choice."

"I think it's cute. But it takes some getting used to."

"It sure does," she says with a sigh. "I think I'm experiencing cutter's remorse."

Some of the women are seated on benches, others are changing their clothes or stashing items in the lockers. "Ladies, I have a request," I say in a loud voice. The women stop what they're doing to give me their attention. "I'm embarrassed to admit this, but I am terrible with names. I *should* know you all by name, but I don't, so could everybody please say your names now, and I promise I'll try my best to remember?"

"I'm Susie," says Amazon Lady.

Patch's name is Carolyn. Dame Donut is Diane - at least that one should be easy to recall, given the alliteration. One by one, they recite their first names. "I think you all know *me,* but anyway, I'm Judith," says my former organizational consultant. "By the way, did you finish downsizing to a smaller mini-storage unit?" Leave it to Judge Judy to follow up with clocklike precision on the deadline she'd set for me.

"Yes, I did," I say, experiencing a flutter of guilt over this fib.

"I am so glad you asked us to do this," says Diane. "Susie, I've been chatting with you in this locker room for two years, and I never knew your name till now. I was too embarrassed to ask."

"Don't be. I didn't know your name either," Susie says.

"They ought to make us wear name tags in this place," says Jill.

"No kidding," says another woman whose name I'm already struggling to recall.

Then Amazon Lady—I mean, Susie—turns to me. "Wait—you haven't told us *your* name."

"My name is Mar . . . garet. Yes. Please call me Margaret." *Mar Meyer* never had a good ring to it, anyway. I'm not sure why I was so insistent on changing my name to something that sounded like barbwire. Margaret may be old-fashioned, but it's kind of pretty. Was it really necessary to make such a drastic break with everything that came before? Instead of throwing away my past, maybe this can be more of a winnowing process.

Maybe I can find a way to sift through the good and bad parts of my previous life and hold on to the things that are worth keeping.

• • •

Benny is turning four, and I receive an Evite to his birthday party from Michael and Heather. I RSVP online, declining the invitation as I did last year. It would be much too uncomfortable to spend two hours in the same room with Henry, Alice, and the kids, wearing a phony smile and feigning enjoyment in front of all the guests. Heather calls me after seeing my "No" response. This is unusual – she only initiates contact when I'm coming over to watch Benny, and when she does it's always via a text exchange. Perhaps she wants to chastise me for my continued boycott of Schuyler family celebrations?

But no.

"Margaret, I get why you don't want to be there. But Benny's your only grandchild. Why don't the three of us plan our own little celebration? I thought we might take him for lunch one day next week at the fish and chips place he likes down on the pier."

"That's a great idea, but it doesn't sound like much of a celebration. How about both of you come to my club before lunch and Benny can swim in the pool?"

"Perfect," she says. "He's started morning preschool now, but I can take him out early." We agree on the Wednesday after the birthday party. It occurs to me how lucky I am Robert doesn't care when I get my work done as long as I meet all my deadlines. I've been AWOL more than usual during business hours, what with the Mrs. Ostrowski business and my renewed enthusiasm for Seaside Fitness, but I shoot him an email every hour or two to reassure him I'm still plugged in, and I burn the midnight oil at my computer to make up for my daytime absences.

I expect a warm, sunny day for our birthday outing as is almost guaranteed in September, and I'm not disappointed. Heather and I take turns playing games in the adult pool with Benny, after which we watch him from our lounge chairs as he splashes around in the kiddie pool and makes tentative friends with a little blond girl around his age. Every five or ten minutes, Benny trots over to our chairs to assure himself we haven't forgotten him.

"Look at my hands," he says, showing me how his fingers have pruned up at the tips. He practically shoves them in my eyes, so close I can't focus. He does the same thing with his mother, then runs his hands through her short curls before hurrying back to the pool as Heather cautions him not to slip and fall.

Amazon Lady/Susie walks up to greet us. "Is this your daughter?" she asks.

"No, but everyone thinks so because of our curly hair," I say. "This is my daughter-in-law, Heather." They shake hands. Heather is several inches taller than me and more buxom, almost matching Susie in height. She is also attractive, though not in a conventional way, with high cheekbones and narrow but animated eyes.

Though I've belonged to this club for the better part of a year, it's Benny's first time in the pool. But I can't take all the blame for that, with Michael refusing to allow unsupervised visits. He continues to treat me like some paroled criminal who can't be trusted to interact with the child unless chaperoned by a social worker. Heather pulls out her phone and shows me pictures from last weekend's birthday party. Among the photos are several close-up shots of the cake, which is in the shape of a firetruck. It's covered in bright red icing, with windows, doors, and headlights outlined in white piping, and the cake is decorated with miniature plastic bells, ladders, and little firemen. It looks like a dessert you'd see featured on the cover of a cooking magazine.

"That's one helluva cake. Which bakery did it come from?" I ask.

"Alice made it."

I glance at the cake photo again, my eyes popping. "Well, fuck me." Damn. There I go again.

But Heather laughs - a deep, appreciative laugh. "I hear you," she says. "Alice can be kind of annoying."

I return the laugh.

"I mean, the woman never stops with the giving and the doing. She's just so *perfect* all the time. How can I keep up with that?" says Heather.

"My advice? Don't even try."

Heather nods.

"So, is she perfect?" Maybe I can coax a few more details out of my daughter-in-law.

Heather wrinkles her nose. "That's what we're expected to buy into. There's a widely circulated theory that everything Alice does is terrific."

"Who originated the theory?"

"Oh, that would be Alice herself . . . with a hefty assist from Henry." This mean-spirited discussion warms the cockles of my heart. Whatever that means.

It's time to lure Benny out of the pool and get him dressed for lunch, but he threatens a tantrum. "I'm big now. You can't tell me what to do anymore," he says to his mother.

I consider giving Heather a quick tour of the Seaside Kids area before we leave, but I think better of it since Michael made it clear he didn't like Benny going there. Anyway, if the child sees the bounce house, he'll demand to play there, potentially unleashing another tantrum. Instead, we entice him out with the promise of fish sticks, fries, and ice cream, after which he will open my birthday gifts. I'm kind of glad Heather isn't too into the health craze.

At lunch, Heather regales me with amusing stories about Benny's summer soccer camp and the antics of four-year-old boys. Halfway through lunch, my cheeks aching from all the grinning, I say, "I gotta tell you, I'm having such a fun time with you today."

In response, Heather reaches out to squeeze my hand, causing me to tear up a little to my surprise. I've always liked Heather, finding her even-tempered demeanor to be a good counterpoint to Michael's edginess. Caught up in my own turmoil, I lost sight of my affection for this young woman. Now I see in her a friend and a possible ally. And I see Benny continues to love me, even though I am a non-baker of firetruck cakes who does not spend as much time with the boy as I should.

If I've caused any damage with that, at least I'm confident it's reversible.

26.

In the quest to develop my softer side, I abandon my usual political tomes and biographies in favor of novel reading. My inspiration: the study finding that literary fiction fans possess higher levels of empathy. What better place to start than the collected works of Sexy Eyes, better known to readers as Charles Kittredge?

Though I'm tempted to begin with *Bicoastal,* Charlie's biggest bestseller and box office smash, I approach his books in chronological order. His first novel is *Change/Of Course,* the title being a double entendre that alludes both to a change of navigational direction and the certainty that change is inevitable. This book is unique among Charlie's works in its use of magical realism. Set in the Northeast over a ten-year span ending with 2001 - or to be more specific, with the events of 9/11 - the world it portrays is familiar and realistic but for one thing; the protagonists, a brother and sister growing up in rural Pennsylvania, possess powers that enable them to change events. Such a rare gift is no guarantee of omnipotence, however. Whenever they experience negative emotions such as jealousy, rage, or a lust for revenge, the boy and girl lose their powers, like Superman weakening under exposure to kryptonite. The siblings cannot perform good deeds in a vacuum. Positive change can only be achieved through inner purity of thought and conscience.

Though it is on one level a morality tale, *Change/Of Course* has a fast-paced plot and characters I fall in love with, adding up to an intoxicating read, even for a rookie like me. Major book reviewers praised it as a "stunning debut" and "a richly textured examination of motivation, self-control, and the sometimes blurry distinction that exists between good and evil." I'm not sure what I expected Charlie's books to be like, but this isn't it. However, I'm not disappointed. And from what I've been reading about Charlie's career, I can anticipate a different experience reading his next novel and his next one after that.

Though I did my research on Charlie back when we first dated, this time my information source is not some scholarly essay but the Charles Kittredge entry in *Wikipedia.* One characteristic that makes Charlie popular with critics, I read, is his successful experimentation with different themes, genres, and literary styles. While perusing the *Wikipedia* to refresh my memory on Charlie's accomplishments as a novelist and review his book list, I jump down to the section on "Personal Life." It mentions his late wife, Elizabeth, and says only that she "died suddenly," along with the month and year of her death – but no further details. No other wives, no other partners, no children.

I traverse *Change/Of Course* from cover to cover in two days, and when I put it down, I float around my living room, giddy with exhilaration. To think that I had intimate knowledge of the author! I remember how it began as an idle infatuation with those sultry gray eyes and later blossomed into a deeper admiration of his fun spirit and – let's be honest, the *real* draw up till now – his delightful physicality. Now, I'm no longer enchanted by the body as much as the body of work. Now, I'm captivated by those "richly textured" sentences that grace every page, and by the imaginative mind that has created them. Now,

I'm—but wait. There is no more *now* for us as a couple. The exhilaration vanishes as I crash back down to reality.

How did I fail to appreciate Charlie's exceptional qualities? What a catch! I could've had all of him to myself - body, mind, and soul. Instead, I wantonly discarded his affections like an angler tossing an undersized game fish back into the water. I remember he once told me, "There are little pieces of me in everything I write." Having let him go, now I will troll through the pages of his novels, casting my net to try to capture some of those little pieces of Charlie for myself.

Now, that's all of him that is left to me.

Though I'm tempted to dive right into Charlie's second novel, the much-lauded *Bicoastal,* I tear myself away to devote a little time to the Nancy Ostrowski situation. I leave a phone message for her lawyer, who returns my call within a couple of hours. It's clear from our conversation that the lawyer has great fondness for Nancy and is distressed at the news of her mental decline - which, as I'd surmised, must be a recent development. "I haven't spoken to Nancy in a few months," he says, "but last time I called her, she sounded coherent. She told me she was paying all the bills and that she'd begun sorting through John's belongings to donate to charities."

"That may be true, but she's done nothing in the study except make a mess," I say. "I wonder what else she might be forgetting, like important medications." I ask him about close relatives, including the Ostrowski names I copied from the address book I found in the desk.

"Those are both nephews of John's from the Midwest," says the lawyer, "but Nancy's closest living blood relation is a niece who lives north of Santa Barbara. Her mother was Nancy's older sister, who I believe died several years ago."

"How can I reach her?"

"I'm not permitted to give out contact information, but I'll call her right away and ask her to get in touch with you. If you haven't heard from her in a day or two, let me know and I'll make sure you two connect." The lawyer also promises to call Nancy's financial advisor to make sure there are sufficient funds in the checking account to cover the bills. Before hanging up, he says, "Thank you for alerting me to the situation and for looking after Nancy so well. She's lucky to have you."

That evening I get a call from the niece, who had been waiting to return home from her job as a schoolteacher before phoning me. Her voice trembles with worry. "Is Aunt Nancy all right? I was so alarmed when the lawyer called me at school today."

"She's all right—I mean, apart from the memory issues."

"Do you think she's frightened or upset?"

"Not that I can tell. She seems to be in good spirits. Not exactly the grieving widow. She keeps saying the world is a better place without John."

"Amen to that," says the niece. "My mother couldn't stand that man. She used to beg Nancy to leave him. They didn't have to stay together for the children, since they never had any. But Aunt Nancy was always meek and retiring. I don't think she had the courage to stand up to him."

"I know, and she regrets it now."

"Do you think she needs to be in a home or something?"

"Oh no, she isn't that bad. If you catch her on a good day, you might not even suspect anything is wrong. But I think she could use a part-time caregiver. Someone to help with errands and make sure she's getting proper meals, taking her meds, that sort of thing."

"Makes sense, though I'll still need to find a way to pay her bills."

"I can help with that until you find a more permanent solution," I say.

"That's kind of you, but I don't want to impose on you for long. Once I get down there and make copies of all her invoices,

I can set up online bill pay for her and manage it from my computer." She sighs. "But with the new school year, things are so busy I don't think I can make it down to LA for a week or ten days. Unless it's absolutely urgent . . . is it?" she asks.

"No. I don't think she's in any danger. And I promise to check on her again in the next day or two."

"Oh, she's lucky to have you as a friend." This is the second time in a day I've been rewarded with this unaccustomed compliment. "Any idea how I might find a caregiver in the area?"

"That isn't my field of expertise," I say, "but I promise to put out feelers."

The first call is to my formerly homeless friend Sunny. "How's life in Northern California?" I ask.

"It's good. My job at the day spa is going well. And living in my cousin's guesthouse has given me a chance to pay down my debts."

We spend a few minutes catching up on recent events, and I tell her about Nancy. "I remember you said your mother suffered from Alzheimer's, so I thought you might know of a caregiver."

She sighs into the phone. "Sorry, but no one I can recommend. The woman who took care of Mother turned kind of nasty when I cut her hours back to save money, and things between us didn't end on a good note. I was partly to blame, but still . . ."

"I understand. Figured it wouldn't hurt to ask." We chat for a few minutes longer before I wish her well, and we both promise to do a better job of keeping in touch. Then I place another call.

"Mar—it's good to hear from you."

"Hello, Grace. You can call me Margaret."

"Oh, I thought—never mind. How's everything going with you?"

"Much better, thanks for asking. No more aches and pains. And you?"

"I'm fine. Did you get your new car?"

"I did. I'm the proud owner of a shiny new Prius, and it has a few bells and whistles that the old model didn't have."

"Thank you again for the flowers," she says, referring to a bouquet of summer blooms I sent her in thanks for her help after the accident. "It was unnecessary, but much appreciated."

"Glad you liked them. I'm calling for a professional reason as well." I tell her about Mrs. Ostrowski and my discussion with the niece. "She doesn't know how to go about finding a reliable home health aide, and I'm in no position to advise her, but I thought you might have some ideas."

"I can't believe you're asking me about this," she says.

For a moment I think she's rebuking me. "Sorry - I didn't mean to impose."

"Oh, you're not imposing at all. I meant I can't believe the timing. Last week, the man I'd been working for took a turn for the worse. He had to go into a nursing home. It happens I'm available. If Nancy and her niece approve, I'd be interested in applying for the job."

I pour myself a glass of chilled Sancerre to celebrate the hope that Nancy Ostrowski will receive the care she needs and deserves. I'll call the niece back and connect her with Grace, then I'll make a date with Nancy. When I visit, I'll sit her down and explain what a nice woman Grace is and how much help she can provide. I don't think Nancy will resent the interference, but I'll have to be careful how I position it. I make a mental note to discuss all this with the niece to be certain we're on the same page.

I've had a few sips of my wine when my cellphone rings and Nancy's name comes up on the caller ID. "Nancy, hi. Is everything okay?"

"Everything is fine, dear. But can you come over?"

"You mean—now?"

"Oh, I think it's a bit late for that, but how about tomorrow? There's something important I need you to see."

• • •

When I knock on her front door the following afternoon, Nancy is not the least bit baffled by my arrival this time. "I've been waiting for you," she says, ushering me in. "Can I get you an Arnold Palmer? I polished off the rum, but I could mix it with vodka for you. Or maybe plain iced tea?"

The lemonade, tea, and rum cocktail she served up on my previous visit was delectable, but I don't want to be distracted from my purpose. "Plain tea is fine," I say.

"I'll get it in a bit. But *first* . . ." She digs an ancient, tarnished key out of her pocket and thrusts it in front of my face, so close to my eyes that it's a blur, like Benny's wrinkled fingertips at the pool. "Look what I found."

"A key to . . . what?"

"John's workshop, in the shed behind the house. He didn't allow me to go in there. He called it his private man space or something like that."

"Man cave?"

"Yes, maybe that was it. Anyway, after he passed, I tried to go back there to clean it out, but the door was padlocked. I forgot all about it until yesterday, when I found a few loose keys in the desk drawer. I tried them on the lock to the workshop door, and *voila.* This one opened it right up." She flashes a satisfied smile. "Follow me," she says, and we walk around back. When we reach the shed, she turns the key in the padlock and opens the door with a dramatic flourish, like a magician showing her most impressive trick. "*Tada,*" she says, observing my reaction.

I always thought the term "jaw-dropping" was a figurative expression, but I think my jaw literally falls a few inches upon seeing what Mrs. O. has revealed. I stand there agape as I stare in disbelief at . . .

. . . Michael's bicycle. The notorious red bike from sixteen years ago. It's still red and—impossible as it seems—still shiny. In case there was any doubt about its identity, the little personalized license plate hangs from the back. "It isn't even dusty," I say. "How is that possible?"

"I cleaned it and polished it all up for you." Her entire face glows with pride. "But I'm afraid I couldn't fix the tires," she says, pointing to the two flats.

"I thought your husband gave the bike away."

"I thought so too. That's what he told me."

"I don't understand. Why would he keep it hidden here all these years? Doesn't that seem strange to you?"

"Oh, Margaret," she says, shaking her head, "you have no idea."

"I think I can squeeze it into my Prius if I put the back seat down. You meant for me to take it, right?"

"Oh yes, and give it to Michael, of course. Imagine how surprised he'll be."

He will be, indeed. But it won't be the reaction of a gleeful child celebrating the return of his most prized possession. It's many years too late for that. What *will* Michael's reaction be? Knowing him, he might be chagrined or even embarrassed to be caught out in the lie he told us long ago when he pretended the bike was stolen. But this time, I won't let the negative thoughts take over. Somehow, I must show him that the recovery of his old bike can serve as a bridge between us, a way to heal old wounds and allow us to behave in a kinder fashion toward one another going forward.

I can't expect Nancy to understand all this, but now that I've gotten over the initial shock, I share her enthusiasm over finding the bike. "Thank you, Nancy. This means a lot."

She beams back at me. "I know you didn't believe my story the other day," she says with a wink. "You thought I had it all mixed up about John taking the bike. I don't blame you for thinking that. I get confused about little things sometimes. But my recall is good."

I nod. I have to concede, she *is* much brighter and sharper today.

"I remember meals I ate forty years ago. In 1980, John took me to New York City for our anniversary. Have I told you this?"

I shake my head no.

"We went to a Belgian restaurant in the east fifties. We both ordered the house special for lunch – rotisserie chicken, which they served with a big pewter bucket of *frites*. The potatoes were the crispy, shoestring kind." She smiles at the recollection. "Those were the best fries I ever ate in my life."

Smiling back at her, I wonder if I've overreacted about her memory issues. "Speaking of lunch, are you hungry?" I say. "Or have you already eaten?"

"Yes. I ate . . . I ate . . ." The happy expression fades and her jaw trembles a little. "I'm not sure I even ate lunch at all." She rushes toward the kitchen, flitting around the room and peeking here and there as if on a treasure hunt. In the kitchen sink, she finds an empty can of chicken noodle soup, a bowl, and a spoon. "I must have had this soup," she says. "The evidence is right in front of me. But I can't remember it." Her face falls. "I can't remember it at all."

Poor Nancy. I walk over and fold my arms around her. "It's okay. We're gonna get you some help so you don't have to worry about these things."

"Promise?" Her voice is soft and childlike.

"I promise." And though I know it's a lie, I say, "Everything is going to be all right."

PART TEN: OCTOBER
AUDREY

27.

Petey the Wheatie has finished a long drink from the communal doggie bowl at the little beachside park. He nuzzles his long, wet beard against my legs, dripping cool water down my shins. I find the sweet spot behind his ears and give him an enthusiastic scratch. "How have you been?" I ask Audrey. "Lately when we cross paths, you seem a little distracted."

"Is it that obvious?" she says. "Sorry—I hope I wasn't rude."

"No, it's okay."

"You're right, I *have* been distracted. Too much going on in my life these days."

"I can relate."

"Do you want to walk with Petey and me to the pier and back?" she says. "Maybe we can yak a little."

"That sounds good." The two of us start at a brisk pace with the Wheaten between us.

"I think I told you I work for a pharmaceutical company? Well, they're getting ready to reorganize the sales team, and I don't know how it's gonna impact me."

"Are you worried you might be laid off?"

"Oh no. If anything, I expect to be promoted."

"But that's great, isn't it?"

"It depends," she says. "They might just give me more responsibility, but there's a chance they'll relocate me. If it's relocation, I'm not sure where they'll want me to move."

"I had a bumpy few months with my own job," I say. "But it all worked out."

"Oh good - but the job isn't the only issue," says Audrey. Her cheeks are flushed, wet strands of hair cling to her neck and forehead, and her breathing is labored. A hefty woman, she appears to be overheated from the exertion of our fast walk. "My boyfriend, Nathan, is pressuring me to live with him."

"How can you do that when you might have to move for work?"

"That's what I keep telling him. But then he says he'll move wherever I go. He wants a commitment."

"And you're not ready?"

She shrugs. "I waver. Hell, I don't know why I unloaded all this on you. Actually . . . I do know why."

"Oh?" Now I am curious.

"You see, my friends and family adore Nathan. He's kind, he's considerate, he's good-looking. They think I'm crazy not to jump at the chance to settle down with him. If I try to discuss this with them, they'll take Nathan's side."

"But you figure I'll take *your* side?"

"I figure you'll at least be neutral. You won't try to push me in one direction or another like everyone else is doing."

"True. Audrey, have you noticed some of the words you're using?"

"Which words?"

"*Pressure, push,* like Nathan and your friends are forcing you to do something against your will."

"Wow. I didn't realize I was doing that. Now that you bring it up, I think they are pressuring me. I can't decide when there's so much uncertainty with the job."

We walk in silence for a few minutes. Then I say, "Uncertainty is the worst." And suddenly, out of nowhere, I'm telling Audrey the whole sad story of the breakup with Henry – the abandonment, the fear, the isolation. I surprise myself with this disclosure. Until now, I hadn't shared the story with any of my new acquaintances inside or outside the gym – not even Sunny, with whom I'd had many deep conversations.

Not even Charlie.

"The hardest period was when I accepted that our marriage was over, but I didn't know what would happen to me," I tell Audrey. "Where would I live? How would I cope with being single after so many years? Everything felt scary. I can't say I'm happy now, but at least I'm less panicked. More settled."

"Jeez," says Audrey, "I'm such a jerk, crying on your shoulder when you're the one who's been through the real crisis. My troubles seem small by comparison."

I shake my head. "Not at all. Your worries about your boyfriend and your career – that's your future. I wouldn't call that small."

She smiles. "I suppose not. What about you, Petey? What d'ya think?" She says this in an excited voice that causes the dog to bark and jump up, pounding his front paws against her chest. She gives him an affectionate hug. "Thanks for listening," she says to me.

"Any time." Before we go our separate ways, Audrey asks if I like jazz. Though I could take it or leave it, I don't want to sound disparaging. "Sometimes. Why do you ask?"

"There's a bar down near the Manhattan Beach pier where they have a live jazz combo every Wednesday night at happy hour. They play outdoors, so I can take Petey there. It's really nice hanging out on the heated patio with a drink. If that sounds good to you."

"That sounds great."

"I'll drive. Parking is so bad over there, it's crazy to take separate cars." We agree on a pickup time the following Wednesday.

• • •

Michael's old bike is at a repair shop where I dropped it off a few days ago for a complete reconditioning. I thought it would only take a day or two but was disappointed when the proprietor handed me a job ticket and said, "About two weeks, ma'am."

My face falls. "That long?"

"It's our busy time of year," he says.

Who knew? Well, it's been sixteen years since Michael last laid eyes on that bike, so I suppose another couple of weeks won't matter. When it's ready, I'll arrange a meeting date to present it to him.

I stop by the Ostrowski place to visit Nancy and Grace, who is now on board as part-time caregiver. Nancy's niece came down for several days to sort out her aunt's affairs. She and I met twice during that time to review what I'd done, and I also introduced her to Grace, who was hired on the spot to work six mornings a week. Grace comes in time to get Nancy up, assist her with washing or showering, and feed her a hot breakfast.

Sipping a glass of ginger ale, Nancy inquires, "How is your son doing? Did you give him the bike yet?" She's forgotten Michael's name, but she remembers the notorious bicycle incident and seems determined to set things right after all this time.

"I've taken it to a bike shop to get new tires and whatever else they do to refurbish an old bicycle," I say. "I think it's going to cost a lot more than we paid for that bike in the first place. But it's worth it."

"Oh, let me pay for that, dear. It's the least I can do."

"That's sweet, but not necessary. Thank you though."

She stands slowly, holding both palms flat on the tabletop to support her as she rises from the chair. Grace puts a hand around the older woman's upper arm to help steady her. "All of a sudden, I'm so sleepy," Nancy says. "I think I'll lie down for a bit. Thanks for stopping in, dear."

When Grace returns after settling Nancy down for a nap, I ask how it's going.

"Better."

"That's great news."

"Don't get me wrong - I'm not saying her memory is improving or anything like that. But she's not as confused now that I'm here to help keep her on track. She likes to run errands with me after breakfast, or sometimes we go for a short walk instead, and she dozes afterward. Lunch is her big meal of the day and it's when she takes most of the meds. After I clean up from the midday meal and put her down for the afternoon nap, I fix a sandwich and leave it on the table for her supper with a cookie, packed in a little cooler with a reminder note on top. When I come back the next morning, most of the sandwich is gone, if not all. At least she's remembering to eat."

"What will happen on Sunday—your day off?"

"Well, her niece plans to drive down every other week to spend the day with her aunt. The alternate weeks, I understand you've volunteered to stop by and make sure Nancy is doing the important stuff."

"Right—like eating, and taking her meds, and not setting the house on fire."

Grace laughs. "We can add *not drinking* to that list," she says. "Turns out she was hitting the bottle with considerable gusto. Alcohol and dementia don't mix well. The good news is, she's forgotten that she likes to drink."

"Ah. The silver lining of memory loss," I say. "But will she be okay without you here on Sundays?"

"She'll be fine," Grace assures me. "If you fix her lunch, give her the pills, and put out her supper the way I described, she can manage. I'll leave extra sandwiches and snacks in the fridge that you can take out at your discretion. And I'll write you notes on what to do."

"Sounds good. What happened when she went to the doctor for tests?" I ask.

"They did some cognitive testing, and they've ordered an MRI," says Grace. "Nothing definitive yet, but the doctor thinks this is most likely Alzheimer's."

I shake my head and sigh. "Poor woman. She finally gets out from under the thumb of that awful husband after all these years, and now this."

"Yeah. It sucks."

"What happens when morning care isn't enough?"

"When it gets to the stage where Nancy needs a second caregiver, I know people who can pitch in."

"Glad to hear that. How—how long do you think it will be before that happens?"

"Your guess is as good as mine. Years? Months? Days? Everyone is different with this illness."

• • •

I devour Charlie's blockbuster novel, *Bicoastal.* As with *Change/Of Course,* he employs a double entendre in the title. This time, Anthony (the protagonist) is a man leading a double life, supporting a spouse on either coast; but his California partner (Evan) is male, while the New York partner (Nomi) is female. With my editor's eye, I can see that his writing is more mature and self-confident than in the first novel. It's a compelling story and a total page-turner. But as before, the dazzling prose elevates it to the lofty realm of literary fiction.

Halfway through the book is a yoga bondage scene, the details of which resonate with a clarion ring of familiarity. I'm not offended to discover that my memorable moment with Charlie on the yoga mat turned out to be a reboot rather than original material. It's flattering to have been part of the creative process, though I'd love to know where the idea started. Is this art imitating life, or life imitating art?

After finishing the book, I view the film adaptation on Netflix, pleased with myself for not cheating and watching the movie first. The film has a star-studded cast, from the bisexual two-timer and his partners down to the many cameo roles. I somehow missed the movie when it first played in theaters. I investigate the film's approval rating on *Rotten Tomatoes:* ninety-two percent positive reviews from critics, eighty-four percent from audiences. Not too shabby. If people were rated using the same system as films, I might rack up a ninety percent popularity score from my superficial acquaintances at the gym, but only thirty or forty percent from close relatives - maybe even lower from my sternest critics. Like Michael, to pick a name out of a hat.

Next, I dive into *Newlyn Nights,* Charlie's sole foray into historical fiction. It's the story of a World War I veteran who returns to his hometown in Cornwall and reconnects with a young woman with whom he had a brief affair ten years ago, before going to war in France. He now suffers from PTSD - or shell shock, as they called it back then - and he finds it painful to interact with this gentle young lady and her close, cheerful, boisterous family. Though he keeps trying to withdraw from them, they gradually win him over with their compassion and generosity. By the time I finish the last chapter, I am warm, wistful, and teary from reading this testament to the redemptive power of love. I want to be part of a family like this. A group of good, simple, loving people who don't play mind games with each other. Do families like this even exist in the real world?

Newlyn Nights wasn't a smash hit, either with critics or with readers. I remember Charlie telling me a producer optioned it for a TV movie, hoping to coast on the laurels of the previous bestseller, but the project never got off the ground. Successful or not, the book has a powerful effect on me. I decide on impulse to write Charlie and tell him this. Before I lose my nerve, I send him a text.

Margaret: I've been reading your books. I found Newlyn Nights so moving. It's been days since I finished, and it's still on my mind.

Hours go by with no response, and I think he's blown me off. But then he writes back:

Charlie: I hope you know you're an outlier. That book was never a popular favorite.

Margaret: Well, it's a favorite with me. Can I look forward to more historical fiction from you?

Charlie: Doubtful. After that novel, I decided to stick with the old "write what you know" dictum.

Now I'm emboldened by the fact that he's engaging with me.

Margaret: Maybe I could buy you a cup of coffee sometime to discuss?

A few minutes elapse before his response pops up on my screen:

Charlie: Probably not a good idea.

Oh. Is he avoiding me because he's involved with that woman I saw him with at the movie theater? Or does he simply want nothing to do with me? But I continue to read his books, and I text him with a comment and a question about his fourth novel, *The Chandler* – the story of an overaged hippie whose modest candle-making business grows into an empire, causing him to become a greedy capitalist and reverse roles with his once ambitious wife. Charlie replies to my question, and I text him back one more time:

Margaret: Thanks for the info. My offer of coffee still stands if you ever change your mind.

But he doesn't respond.

28.

On the morning of my Wednesday happy hour date with Audrey, she calls to tell me there's a problem. "Sorry to do this, but on Wednesday afternoons I take Petey on therapy dog rounds. We go to a board and care home in the area," she says. "Anyway, I'm running way behind schedule with work. The board and care is halfway between here and Manhattan Beach. The only way I can fit everything in is to visit the patients on the way to happy hour. Can I pick you up early? You'll need to come with us on the rounds."

"That's like an assisted living place, right?"

"Yeah, but much smaller. Only ten patients. I know it may sound depressing, but it's fun. Petey's in his element, and most of the residents love visitors."

Hmm. Though this isn't what I signed up for, I don't see how I can refuse. Besides, there will be a glass of chilled wine at the end of the tunnel. I silently hope the musical entertainment will be something improvisational—maybe classic jazz or blues. Please, God, anything but smooth jazz, which grates on me like elevator music.

• • •

The board and care home is on a quiet residential street. I knew it would be small, but I find it more homelike and comforting than I expected. I follow along as Audrey checks in at the front entrance and leads Petey around first to the communal lounge, and then on to some of the individual guestrooms, where he meets and greets the senior residents and entertains them with a few tricks. It's not a complicated drill.

"This is a kinder, gentler Petey than the dog I've gotten to know on the esplanade," I say to Audrey as we make the rounds.

"For sure. When he's on duty, there's no jumping up allowed, no aggressive behavior, no loud barking." As Audrey says this, Petey nuzzles one of the patients with his soft snout as he stands still and strong, allowing the man to pet him. Another patient, a woman, walks over to them and starts smacking the dog's back and pulling his tail with child-like excitement. Petey remains stoic and unthreatening throughout. Most of the patients smile and even applaud when Petey approaches them, engaging happily with the dog. On the far side of the room, though, a couple of women hang back, regarding us warily. We keep our distance so as not to frighten them.

Of all the residents we see, a charming gentleman named Vincent is the self-appointed ringleader. Though confined to a wheelchair, he's devoted to his fellow patients, wheeling around to check on them and informing the staff if someone needs a drink of water or toileting help. Petey and Audrey are both smitten with the old man, and I soon follow suit.

Intelligent and cheerful, Vincent sports a headful of wavy white hair and a flowing beard that makes him resemble old Saint Nick, albeit a thinner version with a California tan. I wonder if Nancy Ostrowski would be happy in a place like this, surrounded by activities and people her age, with this man as an amiable housemate. Vincent clearly enjoys our visit and seems to view us as his connection to the outside world. "What movies have you seen? Any good restaurants open up lately? They could use some decent Chinese food in this town," he says.

Another thing that endears Vincent to me - in his room, on the bookshelf, are four of Charlie's novels. Gesturing toward the books, I maneuver the conversation around to Charlie like a tween girl nursing a crush. "Did you know Charles Kittredge lives in the area?"

"I heard he's a local boy," says Vincent. "Love his books. Ever meet him?"

Not only have I met him, but remember that bondage scene in Bicoastal? This is what I don't say. What I do say is, "Yes, we've met. He goes to my health club."

Impressed, Vincent raises his bushy white eyebrows as he caresses Petey around the head and neck. "What d'ya think about that, old boy?"

Petey responds with a subdued woof - a breathy noise that sounds more like *fff*. Audrey has trained him not to engage in full-out barking when wearing his therapy dog harness. The dog is a professional through and through.

When we take our leave, Vincent smiles at me and says, "See you again next week, I hope."

Audrey gives me a hesitant look. How can I disappoint such a thoroughly pleasant man?

I say, "Sure—if it's okay with Audrey."

"You bet," she says, beaming at each of us.

Later, I have an idea. I send a text message to Charlie:

Margaret: I'm volunteering at a local board and care place where I've met a delightful patient named Vincent. Big fan of yours. Would you be willing to stop by and meet him sometime? He'd be thrilled.

He replies a couple of hours later:

Charlie: Yes, but not until the week after next. New book coming out for the holidays and I'm up against some tight deadlines with the publisher.

I recall reading that the much-anticipated sequel to *Bicoastal* is coming out soon.

Margaret: Can I circle back with you in a couple of weeks?

He texts back with a thumbs-up emoji.

I smile, anticipating how excited Vincent will be to receive a visit from the great Charles Kittredge. But there goes that old flutter in my gut, followed by the familiar flush of heat - my conscience signaling that I'm not arranging this meeting as an act of kindness to the old gentleman, but to further my own agenda with Charlie. Not fair, I argue to my conscience. This is for Vincent. Kind of.

• • •

On a walk the following day, I ask for Audrey's advice on how to talk to Michael when I bring him the red bike. "I want to take the responsibility off his shoulders for the whole incident," I say. "He needs to understand that he wasn't the one who messed up."

"I dunno. I'm not sure this is really about a bike. I'm not even sure it's about you neglecting Michael when he was a kid, although you seem to carry a helluva lot of guilt about that."

"Then what is it about?"

She pauses. "I think it's about basic communication. This may seem harsh, but it sounds like nobody in your family ever communicates about the important stuff."

"Michael complained earlier this year that I never listen."

"That cuts two ways. If you want someone to listen to you, first you have to speak."

"Wow. When you put it like that, it sounds obvious . . . but I never thought of it that way before."

She grins. "It's always easier to analyze someone else's problems. Like when you made me see how everyone's been putting pressure on me about Nathan. That should be obvious too, but I was clueless."

"Maybe this is something we can continue to help each other with," I say. "It's cheaper than paying a couple of shrinks."

She laughs at this remark. "That's a deal. Hey—I may need your help with something else."

"What's that?"

"Two weeks from now, my company has a full week of planning meetings scheduled. I don't think I'll have time for the board and care visit. Would you be able to take Petey on the rounds by yourself? I hate to disappoint those nice old people."

"Sure, I can do that," I say. "As long as the director is okay with it."

"Oh, he won't mind," she says with a wave of the hand. "I'll call first to explain the plan, but by next week everyone at the place will know you. Besides, walking Petey around the facility isn't exactly rocket science."

Petey rakes a paw against Audrey's leg. *Don't insult me,* he seems to say.

29.

Swamped with work throughout the following week, Audrey squeezes in the therapy dog appointment with me, but she has no time for the daily beach walks. "Poor Petey. I'm lucky Nathan can walk him most days, but it's not easy for him either," she says during my second week of therapy rounds with her and the dog.

"Still no news about the reorganization?"

Audrey groans. "I wish they'd get it over with. I should find out more after the next two rounds of meetings."

Ordinarily she devotes weekends to Nathan, but on Saturday morning she texts and asks if I'm free to join her for breakfast and to walk Petey on the esplanade afterward. Audrey picks me up and we share an order of blueberry pancakes with our coffee on the dog-friendly patio, where Petey is content to stretch out next to Audrey and people-watch. "Nathan and I had a big fight last night. Huge," she says.

"What about?"

"The usual. He wants to move the relationship ahead, and I'm not ready."

"Did you ask him to be patient?"

"I did." She shrugs. "But I dunno. Last night was . . . different. Usually Nathan acts sad when we have these talks, but this time, he was frustrated with me. Super pissed, in fact."

"Any more news on your job?"

"No, but it's getting close. You wouldn't believe how long it takes a big pharmaceutical company to move ahead on *anything*."

"I guess I'm lucky to work for a small firm where one guy makes all the decisions."

"Yeah, if they're good decisions," Audrey says as a sigh escapes. "I keep thinking Nathan might've waited till after my meetings to bring this up. He knows I'm on pins and needles."

"The stress must be taking a toll on him too."

"I suppose you're right," she says.

As we're driving to the beach after breakfast, I receive a text from the bicycle shop. "Michael's bike is ready. Oh jeez."

"Why *oh jeez*?"

"I was excited about bringing Michael his old bike. But now that the time has come, I think I'm getting cold feet."

Audrey gives me a stern look. "What are you scared of?"

"Uh . . . everything?"

Her expression grows sterner. "Margaret. You need to face your damn family."

"I *know*, but I also need to prepare for this."

"You already told me you've been rehearsing what you'll say to Michael."

"Right, but I'm not sure I've rehearsed *enough* yet."

"You're not starring in a Broadway musical. You're just gonna have a talk with your son."

"Okay, okay. I'll bring him the bike," I say, eager to end the conversation.

"When?"

"Soon. Maybe tomorrow. Or . . . soon."

Audrey shakes her head at me. "I've got a better idea," she says. "Why don't you bring him the bike now? We can pick it up and I'll drive you over. No time like the present." Audrey drives a company car, a large SUV with plenty of room for her cartons of pharmaceutical samples. Right now, the back is empty, and it would be a breeze to throw the bicycle in. I recall how I struggled to cram the bike into my Prius when I collected it from Nancy's place.

"What about our walk?" I say.

"I'll walk Petey in the neighborhood while you two talk. You can text me when you're done. No hurry. You know Petey . . . he'll walk all day if we give him the chance." Audrey sees my reluctance and adds, "You could text Michael first and make sure it's okay to drop by."

But she's already won me over. Saturday is Michael's day to putter around the house and yard, so he's almost certain to be home. If I text him for permission, he may respond with some excuse, which will only cause me to lose my nerve again. The element of surprise might be exactly the right strategy. Then I remind myself, this is the delivery of a bicycle, not the invasion of Normandy. "Never mind the text. Let's just do it," I say.

I direct her to the bike shop, and twenty minutes later, red bicycle in tow, we pull up to the curb in front of Michael's place. I don't see his car, but it might still be in the garage. Audrey and I agree to monitor our cellphones. "If you haven't heard from me in half an hour, it's okay to text or call me," I say. "I left the ringer on with the volume up. Make sure yours is the same way, in case I need to make a quick getaway."

"Will do," she says. She strides off with an enthusiastic Petey, who is surely excited at the prospect of peeing on new hydrants and sniffing undiscovered lawns.

I wheel the bike down the sidewalk, engage the kickstand to park it near the front entrance, and ring the doorbell. Heather cracks the door open in a hesitant manner, a puzzled look in her eyes.

"Surprise!" I shout, pushing the door wide open.

"Aren't *we* supposed to say that?" says a tall, jowly man. It's Steve Schuyler, Henry's older brother.

I encounter a sea of faces - maybe a couple of dozen, to put a more accurate number on it. About half of them I recognize as family, friends, or long-time Schuyler employees. The other half are unfamiliar to me. Friends of Alice's, perhaps? And—oh yes—Alice herself is there too, in a multi-colored broom skirt and peasant blouse that are holdovers from a distant era. If a photographer wanted to capture the many faces of perplexity and discomfiture, he would find the perfect shot right now, right here, in this room.

Heather starts talking so fast I can barely follow her. "Margaret. Gee, this is unexpected. I thought you were Michael arriving with Henry. They're due here any minute now—for the surprise."

Shit. Now I understand what's going on. I've totally forgotten that it's Henry's birthday this weekend. He's turning fifty, and from all appearances, Heather has arranged a surprise brunch at their home. I suppose Michael has been tasked with luring his father to the house on some pretext. No doubt Alice has been cooking for days in preparation. I'm guessing she's even baked a cake in the shape of a fricking golf club.

Gazing across the room, I see that I'm right. A chocolate golf club birthday cake, adorned with rainbow-colored candles, is displayed on a small round table in the middle of the room. Next to it is a big vanilla-iced golf ball, a considerate alternative for the non-chocolate-eating guests.

"Oh, Heather, I think I picked the wrong time to make a delivery," I say. "Maybe I should come back another day."

But it's too late. Michael and Henry are coming up the front sidewalk and staring, mystified, at the red bike. At first, they don't understand what's happening, and who can blame them?

"Mom? What's going on?" Michael says.

"You found a red bike like the one Michael used to have - and brought it here on my birthday? Margaret, why would you do that?" says Henry.

Their voices are raised in annoyance and disbelief. They think this is a deliberate attempt to sabotage Henry's surprise party - which he doesn't seem all that surprised about, I'm noticing. (I will later learn that Benny blew the secret earlier that day, announcing to his grandfather that "Nana Alice roasted a chocolate golf club for your party.") No, as it turns out, the big surprise of the hour is me. Me and the mysterious bicycle, which they believe to be an impostor.

Eager to save the day, the ever-conciliatory Alice opens her arms towards Henry, Michael, and me in a sweeping gesture and says, "Why don't you come inside and celebrate Henry's birthday? Let's all be happy together on this special day."

But Heather steps between Alice and the three of us, addressing Henry's girlfriend in a cordial but firm tone. "Alice—these three have something to discuss, and they need to do it in private."

"Oh, but, what about the party—"

"The party will take care of itself," says Heather. "We've got appetizers and big pitchers of bloody marys and mimosas. Michael, why don't you and your parents talk outside? We'll be fine in here until you're ready to come in."

Brava, Heather.

Alone outdoors with my son and ex-husband, I'm uncertain how to begin. My prepared script has been rendered useless by this unexpected turn of events, and I'm not a master of improvisation. But I need to set the record straight. "Henry, I did not go out and find a bike 'like the one Michael used to have.' This is the original bicycle from his childhood."

"But I thought it was stolen," he says, turning to Michael, whose gaze remains fixed on the bike as if he can't believe his own eyes.

"It happened such a long time ago. I—I don't remember now," Michael says, the classic reluctant witness. Then again, maybe the incident with Mr. O. was so traumatic, he blocked it from memory.

"I can understand that," I say, sympathetic. "But when I visited Mrs. Ostrowski next door, she reconstructed the whole story for me about how her husband took away the bike to punish you for crashing it into his garden. I didn't believe her until she found the bike a couple of weeks ago, locked away in his old workshop."

"She just now found it after all these years? That makes no sense," says Henry.

I walk them through the sequence of events, explaining how John lied to Nancy about donating the bike to charity.

"Why didn't you just tell us the truth?" Henry says to Michael. "I would've made sure the bastard returned your bike that same day."

"I don't know, Dad. I guess I was afraid." His voice small and whiny, Michael sounds as though he's regressed to the actual time of the incident. Prepared for this response, I leap to his defense.

"It's okay. It's not your fault. You were a little kid, and Mr. O. was bullying you. He was a terrible man, Michael. His own wife referred to him as a piece of shit."

Both Henry and Michael look astonished by this revelation. Or *gobsmacked*, as Mum might put it. "Mrs. Ostrowski said that?" Michael asks.

"I know, it's a shocker. Anyway, this is my fault too."

"How so?"

"I should have been there for you. I should've paid more attention. Maybe I would've figured out something else was going on—that you were hiding the truth from us."

"How could you know that?" Michael says.

"What I mean is, I was too impatient with you, too absorbed in my work all the time. I see that now. Sometimes when you were upset, I didn't take the time to figure out what the real problem was. I was too quick to jump to conclusions. Now I understand why you disliked being left alone. I'll bet this wasn't the only time Mr. O. bullied you."

"No, it wasn't."

"Bullying is no joke. Maybe the boy should have seen a therapist," says Henry unexpectedly. My ex is not big on therapy. He casts an accusing glance at me, suggesting it is indeed all my fault for failing to act on this. It would've been my job to do so. Henry's job was to travel around the country raking in truckloads of money, which he would then spend on extravagant gifts and ski weekends with Michael. That's what the *fun* parent gets to do.

"A therapist, great idea," says Michael, scowling. "Maybe it's not too late. I'm sure I must still need professional help to get over some asshole taking away my bike a million years ago." He walks around the bicycle, examining it. "It's true. This is my old bike, isn't it? Unbelievable."

"I had it refurbished at the best repair shop in town. It will be a great bike for Benny when he's older," I say. But not wanting to glom all the credit, I add, "Mrs. Ostrowski helped clean it up too."

"It looks like new," he agrees.

My hands are twitching nervously, so I walk over to the bicycle and grip the handlebars to steady myself. Then I address Michael with my prepared remarks. Afraid to meet his eyes right now, I stare down at the bike instead as I speak. "I'm not sure how to say this, but it's no secret you and I have trouble getting along sometimes, trouble communicating. At the risk of sounding like a therapist myself, we have some unresolved issues. Getting this old bike back resolves *one* of those issues, at least. Maybe we could regard it as a positive sign - a step forward on the right foot. A way to mend things between us. Know what I mean?"

He doesn't answer right away, but when he does, his tone is sharp. "No, not really. I don't see how finding an old bicycle is gonna fix everything that's fucked up about this family."

Now I look up from the bike to gaze at him. "Are we so very fucked up?" I ask, hoping the tremble in my voice isn't too pronounced.

"Oh no, we're all supernormal here," says Michael.

This isn't how the discussion was supposed to go. I vaguely remember Audrey saying something impressive-sounding about the need for basic communication, and how first you need to speak if you want the other person to listen, but I can't figure out how to work this into my argument. "I'm not saying this will fix *everything*. It's going to take time, and—"

"I don't get how this has anything at all to do with the bad shit between you and Dad."

"Which bad shit do you mean, specifically? Dad divorcing me for Alice?"

"Well, yeah, *that* . . . but also what led up to it."

"I'm not sure what you're referring to. I already told you, I blame myself for not paying enough attention when you were younger, for being too caught up in my work."

"I used to think it was your work that bothered me all those years. But it was the secret life that went along with the work."

I think of the main character in *Bicoastal*, who really did have a secret life. But I say to Michael, "Again, I don't know what you're talking about."

"You don't? Think hard, Mom." He casts a meaningful glance at his father.

"What secret life? What did you tell him, Henry?"

I think my ex-husband would rather be on a holiday in hell than participating in this conversation. "This isn't the time or place, Margaret," he says, pivoting on one heel to go indoors. "There's a roomful of guests inside, waiting to celebrate my birthday."

"You're not getting off that easy," I say, grabbing him by the arm to stop him from leaving. "Somebody needs to tell me what is going on." I turn to face Michael. "What did your father say about me? Tell me what the hell he said."

Michael squirms with discomfort. "He told me you'd been having a long-standing affair with your boss, and that's why you acted so distant and so obsessed with your job all the time. He said it made life very lonely for him."

"Wait, back up. He told you I was having an affair? *With Robert*?" I am incredulous.

"He didn't use the word 'affair.' It's more like he implied it."

"And how exactly did your father *imply* this?"

"He said the two of you had a—I think he called it an 'unholy alliance.' He said Robert was more than just a boss to you."

"*An unholy alliance*? Oh, that's good," I say with a sardonic laugh. "Did you believe this, Henry? Did you think I was having a years-long affair, or was it a convenient way to justify your own behavior?"

"I suspected it might be true."

"You suspected. Did it never occur to you to ask me?"

"Since when do we ask each other things in this family? That one time I told you about what happened on the road—"

"That *one* time? Meaning there was only one time you strayed, or only one time you confessed to it?"

"—I felt like you would have preferred not to know."

Well, he's right about that. "Since we've chosen this occasion to air the family's dirty laundry," I say, "why don't we ask each other now? *Did* you have other affairs when you were traveling on business?"

"Dad, you had affairs on your business trips?" says Michael, wide-eyed.

"Again, I don't think this is the right time—"

"Why not? Because it's your birthday?" My voice grows louder with every sentence. "Or because you don't want to disclose something you'd prefer to keep swept under the rug? Because I'm happy to disclose what happened between Robert and me. Nothing! Absolutely nothing!"

"Omigod," Michael says.

I shove my hands into my pockets to hide the resumed twitching. "How can I make you believe me?" I ask, blinking away tears. "I wish there was some way to prove what I'm saying."

"I do believe you."

"You do?"

"I can see you're telling the truth. You've always been a shitty liar. You tell it like it is, even when you *should* use a little tact."

I can't help smiling at this, grateful that he's finally willing to give me a fair shake. "When did Dad tell you—oh, I mean, when did he *imply*—that I was having this alleged affair?"

Michael and Henry exchange uncomfortable glances. "The day I found out he was seeing Alice."

Of course. A light bulb illuminates inside my brain. I was bewildered by Henry's bizarre, unjust accusation - but now that I understand it, I'm downright furious. "Son of a *bitch*!" I say to Henry, shoving him in the chest with both hands. "I can't believe you would stoop to this! Is it so important for you to be the popular parent every time?"

"Hey, watch it!" Henry says, raising his arms in self-defense. "I don't see what popularity has to do with anything."

"Oh, I think you do. *Poor put-upon Henry*, so lonesome and abandoned. If you made Michael believe *I* was the one to turn my back on our marriage, then you couldn't be faulted for finding someone else. You didn't hesitate to throw me under the bus, just so you could look like the good guy." I glare at him with disgust. "Honestly, Henry."

He must recognize there's no acceptable answer because he doesn't even try to cobble together a defense. He throws a questioning glance at Michael, who says, "Jesus, Dad," and turns away, scowling.

Knowing Henry, he will later try to entice our son back to his corner with some form of bribe. But for now, Henry is in retreat, Michael is in shock, and I'm still in attack mode. As Henry hurries back into the house, I follow close on his heels, still ranting. "We are not finished talking about this, Henry Schuyler! You owe me and Michael an apology. This lie has been poisoning our relationship while you've been getting off scot-free."

Once inside the house, I'm startled to remember that twenty-five partygoers are now witnesses to our family feud. I study the sea of faces again. With all the murmurs and side conversations, I'm not sure how much they've heard. Most of the guests wear dopey grins, suggesting they're pleasantly hammered with the lovely buzz that comes from day-drinking on an empty stomach. Their expressions are more curious than uncomfortable, more amused than embarrassed. My confrontation with Henry has reached a dead end. I'm deciding what to do next when I feel a tap on my left shoulder. I turn around to face Audrey and Petey. The dog is wagging his tail, always happy to work a crowd . . . but Audrey has tears streaming down her face.

"Nathan broke up with me. He called while Petey and I were on our walk."

"Oh, sweetie."

"He stayed up all night thinking about it. He decided if I loved him enough, I wouldn't put him off this way. He said it had to be an *emotional* decision, not a *rational* one, and if I couldn't summon up that kind of emotion for him, it wasn't meant to be."

"And what do you think?"

"I—I think he's right. But it's still sad." She swipes one palm across her cheek to wipe the tears away. Petey cocks his head and emits his polite little *fff* sound, as if trying to reassure her that everything will be okay.

"I'm sorry."

She looks around the room, bewildered. "There's a potty here?" It seems odd that Audrey should use the toddler term for bathroom until it sinks in that she is referring to the birthday celebration – Henry's surprise *potty,* as they would call it in New *Yawk.* I nod in response.

"I texted to say I was coming back. I need to pee wicked bad. That second cuppa coffee was a big mistake."

"End of the hall." I point her in the right direction as I extract Petey's leash from her hand. I lean in towards her to say, "Go pee, and then let's get the hell out of here."

I note Alice is also leaning in, trying to eavesdrop on our conversation. Now she's taking big strides in our direction, arms outstretched, broom skirt swaying. "You and your friend should stay for the party," she says in her treacly radio commentator voice. "We're all a family here."

You are not my fucking family.

The words reverberate with such volume inside my head, I think I've shouted them to the group. But looking around at the complacent faces of the half-stewed guests, I realize I must not have spoken. I'm sure nothing would make Alice happier than for me to leave – but what did Heather once say about her? "She never stops with the giving." I suppose this is Alice being selfless and compassionate. But is that what's really going on here? It dawns on me – if I stomp out, Alice will be the hero to everyone in this room. She'll come off as the warm, inclusive one, and I'll be the shrill harridan. Alice will be Portugal, I'll be North Korea.

No. I will not let her play me like that. I am going to out-Alice Alice.

I turn to her and smile. "What a lovely idea; of course we'll stay." I raise my voice to make sure the group can hear me. "Alice, could you get a bowl of water for Petey? And mimosas for me and my friend." I throw my arms around Alice's neck and reward her with a big hug as I say, "You're a lamb." And as I glance over her shoulder, I see my daughter-in-law Heather - facing Audrey and me with a shit-eating grin on her face, her two hands raised, giving me a double thumbs-up.

PART ELEVEN: NOVEMBER
VINCENT

30.

Vincent's weather-beaten face crinkles into a broad smile when I give him the news. "Charles Kittredge? Coming to see *me*?" he says, incredulous.

"That's right. He texted to say he'll be here in ten minutes." Charlie is running early. I had suggested two-thirty, and it's not yet two o'clock. I want to give his visit my full attention, so Petey and I will have to push back our rounds with the other patients.

"Now, isn't that something? That is *really* something," Vincent says with a chuckle. "What will I say to him?"

"Oh, I wouldn't worry. He's friendly. And you're not the type to be at a loss for words."

"I guess not, but I've never had a celebrity visit me before. Maybe I'll get tongue-tied. I wish—I wish I'd had more time to prepare."

"I didn't know until a little while ago if he'd be coming." I'd considered giving Vincent advance notice, but I decided against it on the off-chance that Charlie might have to cancel and disappoint him. Charlie took a day and a half to respond to my reminder text, and when he wrote back this morning to confirm the address, he reiterated how busy he was and cautioned me that his visit would be brief.

"Why don't we have him autograph your books while he's here?" I say.

"Now, that's an excellent idea. Would you grab them from the shelf for me? You can put them right on the table there." I do as he asks while Petey sits next to the old gentleman's wheelchair and sniffs his arm. The paperback copies of Charlie's novels are almost as weathered as Vincent himself, causing me to wonder how many times he's read them. More than once, according to a lengthy conversation we had during last week's visit.

"Is there anything in particular you'd like to ask?" I say. "Like how he became a writer, or which book is his favorite?"

"Hmm . . ." Vincent scratches Petey around the ears as he ponders this. "Sometimes I wish I could find out what happens to the characters *after* the story ends. Should I ask him, do you think?"

"That's a terrific question," I say, smiling.

When Charlie arrives a few minutes later, I show him into the room and make the introductions. Being in close quarters with him after all these months has an unnerving effect on me. A powerful force tugs at every fiber, as if a magnetic field is pulling me into his orbit. It takes all my strength to resist this force, to keep myself from running to him and flinging my arms around him. Instead, I busy myself moving chairs around for our visit. I arrange the seating into a kind of triangle, placing my chair close to Vincent's wheelchair and leaving enough space for Petey to settle on the floor between us. For Charlie, I place a large armchair facing the two of us.

Charlie takes off his fleece hoodie and drapes it meticulously across the back of the chair, smoothing out every wrinkle as if he were fussing over an Armani suit jacket. Anything to postpone looking at me, I suspect. When he finally takes his seat, an awkward silence follows. Glancing back and forth between Charlie and me, Vincent raises one bushy eyebrow and then comes to the rescue, assuming his favorite role as master of ceremonies. The old man leans in toward my chair as he addresses Charlie. "I thought I knew your books better than anyone, Mr. Kittredge, but this gal has me beat. We had a lively discussion about your work last week."

"I'm flattered she's become a fan of my work," Charlie says to Vincent, as though I were not in the room with them. "And please, call me Charlie."

I search his face for some kind of clue, but he is a closed book. *I'm more than just a fan of your work,* I want to tell him. But of course, I can't say that—especially not here, not now. "I pulled out Vincent's copies of your novels to sign," I say, gesturing toward the stack of paperbacks on the bedside table. "He's been following your career from the time *Change/Of Course* was published."

Charlie takes the books without looking at me. Now Vincent promotes me shamelessly. "She gave me insights I never had about that book, even after all the times I've read it. We're sure lucky to have your friend as a volunteer."

Charlie hesitates before saying, "Yes—you are." I wait, hoping he will look at me and smile or let his guard down, but when he pivots in my direction, he still avoids eye contact. "I thought you didn't read much fiction."

"That used to be true. But lately I'm consuming it nonstop, trying to make up for lost time. I—I hope it isn't too late." I'm uncertain whether Charlie grasps the hidden undercurrent of meaning in my words, but we finally lock eyes and I see a look of—what? Hurt? Sadness? Longing? As diverse as those emotions may be, I think I find all three in his gray gaze. For a hopeful but fleeting moment, I detect a chink in the armor, a tiny opening through which Charlie might start letting me in again.

But he turns back to Vincent, who jumps in once more to fill the cavernous silence. "Never too late, is it?" says Vincent, winking.

"To read? I should say not," Charlie says. "Tell me what it's like, living here. Are you able to get your hands on new books? Is there any sort of discussion group?"

"Oh, things are pretty informal at this place, but a few of us exchange books, and sometimes I still—"

Vincent's response is interrupted when an aide knocks on the door and opens it partway, sticking her head into the room. "Sorry to barge in, but we need you to bring Petey out to the back patio," she says to me. "A patient's grandkids are visiting out there. They have to leave in a few minutes, and I promised they could meet the dog."

"I—I—of course." I give a light tug on Petey's leash and he jumps up, rubbing his head against my leg to signal cooperation. As we pass Charlie on our way to the door, he reaches out to pet Petey on the head.

"Handsome dog. How long have you had him?"

"Oh—Petey's not mine; he belongs to a friend. We volunteer together here." As I walk Petey out, I turn to the two men and say, "I'll be back as soon as I can. Maybe you'll still be here." Charlie gives me that same brief but complicated look again, the look that reignites a few embers of hope. I check the time on the wall clock, making a note to return in around ten minutes.

It's chaos at the board and care today. The family visit on the patio takes longer than expected. Then, I cross paths with a visiting nurse who's come to administer flu shots. I wait for her to finish before letting Petey interact with the other residents. I try to lead the dog away, promising to return soon, but one of the more cantankerous patients clucks her tongue and says, "Stay right here. I refuse to miss out on my time with Mister Petey."

When I'm at last able to break away from this madness, I hurry back to Vincent's room, hoping to escort Charlie out to his car and have a private moment with him. But he's already gone. *Dammit.* The big opportunity for us to reconnect has evaporated, and I bleakly acknowledge there's no telling when or where we might cross paths again.

Vincent, at least, is pumped up from the visit. "You were right. He's a helluva nice guy. I thought he'd be more serious, you know? Like his books. But he's easy to talk to."

"Yes—yes, he is." I force a smile, but I guess an involuntary grimace of pain must cross my face.

"Are you okay?" Vincent asks, and I can tell he understands my disappointment.

"Yes. No. Sort of."

"I picked up on a little, uh, tension between the two of you? You're welcome to tell me it's none of my beeswax, but maybe it'll help to talk about what's going on."

"We were seeing each other for a while, but things didn't work out."

"I figured it was something like that."

"By the way we were acting today?"

"Last week. Your face lit up when you talked about his books."

I sigh. "It was my fault. I got divorced the year before, and I wasn't ready for a serious involvement. Charlie and I didn't want the same thing at the same time."

"Bad timing is never anyone's fault."

I shrug.

"How long did your marriage last?" he asks.

"Twenty-eight years."

"My goodness, I wouldn't have guessed from looking at you."

"Thanks." I smile at him.

"Do you ever miss it? Marriage, I mean."

I think about this. "I miss the safeness of it, the feeling of security. But I don't particularly miss *Henry*."

A bushy eyebrow shoots up again in that perceptive way of his. "I see."

"Anyway . . . I ended it with Charlie because I felt like I needed time alone. Time to sort myself out."

"Sometimes you can sort things out more readily with the right person by your side."

I stop to digest his comment. "That may be true. But six months ago, I didn't see it that way."

Vincent nods, then sighs and leans his head back. "I feel a catnap coming on. The excitement must have worn me out." He holds his arms up to me, and as we hug he says, "Thank you for today. It meant the world to me, meeting my favorite author."

"I'm glad it worked out for you." But sadly, not for me. I tell myself it's ridiculous to feel wounded over Charlie leaving without saying goodbye. He's under tremendous work pressure, and I knew he might have to take off in a hurry. With all he has going on, I'm sure he wasn't even thinking about me.

And that's what hurts the most.

31.

Michael is manning the grill while Heather stir-fries vegetables in her copper wok. Knowing I'm next to useless in the kitchen, she puts me in charge of entertaining Benny during the dinner preparations. The two of us are working on a farm animal jigsaw puzzle. Though I'm a whiz at word games, my jigsaw skills are about on par with my culinary abilities, and Benny has figured this out.

"GrandMar, why are you so slow?"

"I'm not a visual person. I'm verbal."

"Fur ball? Like kitty cats get?"

I laugh. "No, VER-bal. A verbal person is someone who talks a lot or writes a lot."

"Which do you do?"

"Both, I guess."

"All done," he says, dropping the last piece of the puzzle into place. "I want to do another one."

"How about this jungle puzzle? It looks fun." I reach for the box.

Benny grabs the box from me and clutches it with both arms. "By myself," he says.

"Self" has always been one of Benny's favorite words. As a toddler, he'd point to his own chest and say "self" whether I was trying to feed him, guide the water bottle into his mouth, or fasten the Velcro strip on his shoe. It's not a term of selfishness with him; it's a declaration of independence. "You can play by yourself, but put away the farm puzzle first," I tell him.

I walk over to the kitchen island to find some way to be useful to my daughter-in-law.

"Can I top off your wine? *That* I know how to do." Heather laughs and nods in the direction of her stemless glass, which I refill along with my own. "This is a pleasant way to begin the weekend," I say. "Was dinner tonight your idea?"

"Yes. Michael's been perfecting his grilled salmon recipe for a couple of months now, and I told him I thought you'd enjoy it."

"And he was okay with that?"

"He—Michael is still struggling with what happened the day of Henry's surprise party. But he wants to get back on a better footing with you."

"That's good."

"Why don't you bring him a glass of wine and keep him company while he's grilling?" says Heather. "Oh, and you can take this serving platter out for the salmon." She hands me a clean glass and I pour some chardonnay before placing the wine bottle back in its snug collar. Slipping my jacket on, I balance both glasses on the platter and head out to join Michael.

"Mmm. That smells great," I say, inhaling the aroma of the thick-cut salmon steaks on the barbecue. "What's your recipe?"

"I start with a sweet bourbon sauce I buy from the fish market, then I add fresh lemon juice, soy sauce, and crushed garlic."

"Sounds yummy." We stand in silence for a couple of minutes as I watch him turn the salmon on the grill. "How've you been doing?" I ask.

"Oh . . ." He sighs. "For a while, my main emotion was shock. Then anger. Then confusion. Now, though, it's . . . relief."

"Relief? How so?"

He hesitates. "I was really shaken when you and Dad separated and then divorced. It felt like the whole foundation of my family had—I don't know—crumbled, or something like that. The two of you split up, then my childhood home was sold—"

"The foundation of your childhood family *did* crumble. But you have a wonderful home with Heather and Benny now," I say gently.

"Of course, I know that. But the whole thing was still traumatic."

"So, in what way do you now feel relieved?"

"When Dad took up with Alice - and led me to believe you'd been in another relationship for years as well - I felt like both my parents were serial adulterers. This may sound stupid, but . . . ever since the divorce, I've been worrying that some infidelity gene was passed down to me. That I would eventually cheat on Heather and ruin our marriage. I love her so much, but I felt like it was out of my control. Like—like I felt guilty of a crime I hadn't committed yet. So it was reassuring to me when I found out you were innocent in all this."

"I'm glad we set the record straight. But you learned something pretty upsetting about your father at the same time."

His expression darkens. "I'm still pissed at how Dad misrepresented the situation. What he did makes me sick. But when I think about Heather, I can't imagine being unfaithful like he was. So that's reassuring too."

"Have you discussed this with him?"

"I've tried. But Alice always seems to get in the middle, and it's not helpful. She wants to minimize the problems by talking about how wonderful everything is. She's a lot like Dad that way."

"How do you mean?"

"They're all about appearances. Better to avoid the truth than face conflict or unpleasantness."

I give him an understanding nod. "I'm sorry you've had to go through all this. But I'm also relieved that we can work on restoring your trust in me."

"I feel guilty about being mean to you, taking Dad's side the way I did."

"You and Dad have always been close. And he's your boss. You see the man every day. It's not surprising you would line up on his side."

Michael shrugs.

"I won't deny you were mean to me at times, but I haven't been a perfect angel this past year either," I say. "I made some dumb mistakes about Benny's care that eroded your trust in me. So you're not the only one who feels guilty. But you know what? I am sick and tired of guilt. It's such a useless, exhausting emotion."

"Heather keeps telling me to put aside guilt *and* blame."

"Your Heather is a wise lady. You know, it's easy for me to blame Dad for everything too. But I'll tell you something that's going to sound weird – I honestly think he couldn't help himself, spinning that yarn about me and my boss." I've been wondering how many other yarns Henry has spun over the years. Like the time he confessed about his one-night stand at the hotel. Did he really sleep with that woman to comfort her as she grieved over losing her parents, or did he concoct that story to make his own behavior less despicable?

Michael says, "It *does* sound weird for you to be defending Dad. Heather says you and Dad are such different people, she's convinced in the long run you'll both be happier apart than together."

"She said that?"

"Yes, and not just recently. Long before you and Dad split up, she talked about your differences."

I nod. "Hmm. My friend Audrey says it's easier to figure out other people's problems than your own. I guess Heather is proving the theory. She saw what I couldn't see myself for twenty-eight years."

Seconds later, I receive a text from Audrey.

Audrey: Thanks again for covering on Wednesday. Did everything go OK? I've been in endless meetings.

It's true Audrey hasn't had time to come up for air. When she picked up Petey Wednesday afternoon from my place, she was on a business call the whole time and couldn't do anything other than wave to me and mouth "thanks" as she guided the dog into the car.

Margaret: Petey and I had a great time. Everything went fine.

Well, everything except my brief and unresolved contact with Charlie, which has left an even bigger ache than before.

Audrey: More meetings next week. Hate to ask, but can you take him again next Wed?

I check my calendar before replying.

Margaret: Yes, I'll do it.

She also asks if I can walk Petey on Monday and Friday. I agree.

Audrey: You da best, Margaret. I promise to make it up to you.

• • •

I'm on my hands and knees on the side lawn of Seaside Fitness, a grassy area where they hold yoga classes in good weather, and a forty-pound goat is balancing on my back. Heather and Benny stand on the sidelines holding hands, and the little boy bounces up and down on his feet. His grin is so wide it nearly bisects his face.

When I learned the club was offering a special first-come, first-served goat yoga class, I figured, why not? Yoga, hiking, and even partying with goats are the hot new trends in

California, and I wanted to see what all the fuss was about. I'll admit, I've also been trying to find an excuse to lure Benny and Heather back to Seaside Fitness, and I figured this was a great way to accomplish my goal.

Besides, maybe Charlie will attend.

He doesn't. Surveying the vast group, I see one or two familiar faces, and I now understand this event has not attracted the serious yogis. But it's a sell-out crowd of fifty participants, with only two trained goats. I'd hoped for a more favorable goat-to-human ratio, but the handlers do an efficient job of leading Goldie and Sparky around with enough speed that nobody is neglected.

As thrilling as it all is, an hour of yoga cannot hold a small boy's attention, even when it involves goats standing on his grandmother's back. Heather gestures to let me know she's taking Benny to explore the area, and she'll bring him back by the end of class when there will be an opportunity to take photos and pet the young animals. Once they're gone, I focus on the breathing and the various positions – it *is* a real yoga class, after all. Though it's shocking at first to have goat hooves teetering on top of me, I get used to it in time. I can't honestly claim, however, that the goats are *helping* me with my yoga as they are purported to do in the promotional literature. They're more of a novelty. But they bring smiles to everyone's faces and a palpable spirit of joy and energy to the group.

At the end of class, Goldie hops up on me one last time. I glance over at Sparky, the black-and-white goat, who is perched on the back of another woman two rows down. There's something familiar about her profile, and when she turns her head in my direction, the big green eyes are unmistakable.

Sunny.

She runs in my direction and I meet her halfway, closing in for a strong hug. "I can't believe you're here," I say. "Why didn't you tell me you were in town?"

"I didn't think I'd have time to see anyone. Then I decided to stay longer."

"It's great to see you."

As I say this, Heather walks up with Benny. "Sunny, this is my daughter-in-law, Heather. Heather—my friend Sunny." Benny hides behind his mother's legs during the introductions.

Sunny and I exchange hesitant glances. I have no idea what Michael told his wife about that day, months ago, when he rebuked me for leaving their child in the care of "a homeless woman." Has Heather identified Sunny as the notorious babysitter? And if that's the case, are we all in for an awkward scene right now? No doubt, Sunny is asking herself the same questions. But Heather steps forward to give Sunny a firm handshake and a warm smile.

"Nice to meet you," she says. "Benny spoke to me about you."

"He did?" says Sunny, her eyes darting back and forth between Heather and me.

"He told me you made a happy face out of banana slices and gave it to him on a plate. It made a big impression."

"Oh, I'm glad. It's always been one of my go-to strategies to get kids to eat."

"Worked like a charm with Benny."

Sunny grins, then crouches down. "Nice to see you, Benny. Do you remember me?"

He sticks his head out from behind his mother's legs long enough to give Sunny a shy nod.

"Sunny lives and works in Northern California now." I want to make sure Heather knows my friend is no longer homeless - if she even knew in the first place.

"I manage a day spa up in Mill Valley. The owners are thinking about opening a second spa in this area, and they sent me down here to scout locations."

"I didn't know you were promoted to manager," I say. "Congratulations."

"Thanks."

"Do you like it up there?" Heather asks Sunny.

"Mill Valley's a great little town, and I love San Francisco, but I'm a Southern California girl at heart. I have to admit I miss the beach, not to mention all my favorite haunts in the South Bay."

"Will you have any free time while you're here?" I ask.

"Absolutely. Text me."

After Benny pets Goldie and Sparky and we snap a few selfies with the goats, the three of us head to the car. We walk past the Seaside Kids building. "Benny and I came over here during your class, and he showed me the bounce house and some of the play equipment," says Heather. "What a great kids' club. We'll have to bring him back here sometime soon."

"I'm not sure that's a good idea."

Heather tosses her head and says, "Don't worry; I'll handle Michael. I can't fathom why he got so freaked out about Benny going there in the first place." As we get into the car, she says, "By the way, your friend Sunny seems lovely. I like her. Again, I don't understand why Michael had a meltdown over her babysitting." She sighs. "Actually, I *do* understand."

"Because that's our Michael?"

"That's our Michael."

"But we love him just the same?"

"We love him just the same."

• • •

"I hate it when we go off daylight savings time for the winter. It's five o'clock. and we're already losing the light," I say. It's the following evening, and Sunny and I are relaxing on my balcony, observing the post-sunset skyline.

"I know." She shivers and yanks the zipper up on her fleece hoodie. "I'm getting a little chilled."

"Me too. Let's go inside." I open the sliding door and we carry our wine into the living room.

After I've replenished the wine and brought out pâté and crackers, and we're seated on the couch, Sunny says, "I had a long chat with Charlie Kittredge yesterday."

I try to act nonchalant. "That's nice. I'd forgotten you two were friends. How's he doing?"

"Busy. His new book is coming out next week."

"That soon?"

"Yep, it's a sequel to *Bicoastal.* It's called *Second Chance,*" she says. "He told me the main character is Nomi, the New York wife in *Bicoastal,* and the story is about her new relationship after the divorce. Oh, wait—you haven't read his books, have you?"

"I read them a few months ago. They're brilliant." I bury my face in both hands.

"What's wrong?"

"Charlie and I were seeing each other back in June. It didn't go on for long, but it was intense while it lasted. I broke it off because I wasn't ready for a relationship like that at the time."

She looks surprised by this revelation and pauses, as if trying to regain her composure. "Understandable so soon after becoming single."

"Right, but now I regret what I did. The problem is, Charlie's made it clear he's not interested anymore—and besides, I think he's seeing someone else."

"Why do you think that?"

I tell her about spotting him with the little dark-haired woman at the movie theater.

"He isn't seeing anyone," she says.

My heart rate accelerates. "How do you know?"

"He said so himself. Listen, I'm gonna repeat what he told me about the two of you."

"He told you about us?" I take a couple of deep breaths.

"Charlie said he was seeing a woman last June, someone he had deep feelings for. He told me, 'I fell pretty hard, pretty fast.' But he said it didn't work out with her. He didn't name names. I had no idea it was you."

"Maybe it wasn't."

Sunny gives me a *get real* look. "Margaret, come on. He told me the woman ended the relationship because she didn't want to get involved. You think he had *two* serious affairs in the same month?"

"I suppose not."

"He also said he's dated a couple of other women since then, but nobody who meant anything to him. He's decided to go it alone and focus on the new book launch."

"Oh." The "go it alone" part fills me with despair.

I tell Sunny about my recent efforts to reach out to Charlie: the inquisitive text messages about his novels, the invitations for coffee, and how I arranged for him to meet with Vincent at the board and care. "He's never outright rude to me, but he's chilly," I say. "I've tried acting friendly and flirty with him, but I don't think he wants anything to do with me." I lean towards her, my eyes pleading. "I don't know what to do next. Do you have any ideas at all? *Please*?"

Sunny clutches her wine goblet in both hands and stares into it as if consulting a crystal ball for the answer to a burning question. "The thing is . . . you really hurt the guy. So if all you want to do is act friendly and flirty, Charlie's gonna run away from that. It only spells more trouble for him going forward."

"That's not what I want."

"Then what *do* you want? Because he's been through a lot and he doesn't deserve more heartache. Charlie is one of the rare good men out there, Margaret." Sunny's voice shakes a little and her mouth twists into an odd expression, as if we were discussing her problem instead of mine. "Be sure you know what you want from him before you go ahead with this. Don't mess with him to satisfy your own vanity or maybe just to get laid."

I nod as I mull over her advice. "But how do I make him believe I'm serious when he won't even agree to see me? Send him a snail-mail letter? Hire a sky-writing plane?"

"I can't answer that for you. You'll have to find a way."

"But what if Charlie agrees to see me only to tell me he's not interested?"

"Then you won't be any worse off than you are now, will you?" says Sunny. "And at least you'll know the score, and you'll move on once and for all."

"I guess. Oh God, it's so hard to figure this whole thing out. Are you headed back north soon?"

"Two more days. But I'm always reachable. You know me - my phone is attached to me like another limb." She gives her phone an affectionate pat.

"Will you be coming back?"

Sunny shrugs. "It depends on whether my cousin goes ahead with this expansion plan. If she opens a spa in the South Bay, she might send me back to run it."

"Wow. That would be fantastic," I say.

"But don't count on it."

"I don't count on anything these days. Believe me."

32.

Vincent is in the hospital. When Petey and I make our board and care rounds, I ask why he's not there and learn he was rushed to South Bay Medical Center's cardiac care unit following a heart attack four days ago. The other patients are sad and subdued without their ringleader to watch out for them. Even Petey can't perk them up today.

"How's he doing? Can I visit him there?" I ask.

"They moved him from the ICU to a patient room yesterday, so you should be able to visit," says the director. "Vincent DiLorenzo, room 334, East Wing."

I drive straight over to the hospital and lead the terrier into the East Wing lobby. At the front desk, I show the receptionist Petey's therapy dog certification. "The patient loves Petey, and I think a visit from the dog would be beneficial," I say. "Maybe I should have called first? I just found out about Mister DiLorenzo and hurried over."

She studies the papers and says, "Okay, and where are your credentials?"

"*My* credentials?"

"Yes, both the handler and the dog have to be certified for patient visitation. Hospital rules."

I escort Petey back to the car. "Sorry, buddy, but you'll have to wait out here while I check on our friend Vincent. I won't be long." He hops into the back seat and cocks his head at me as I crack the windows to let the cool breeze flow through the car. *Have I been a bad dog?* he appears to say, ears twitching.

"Petey, it's not you, it's me." This has become an all too familiar catchphrase during the past year. But I never expected to utter these words to a dog.

Vincent is awake and sitting up in his hospital bed when I enter the room. He looks comfortable, and his mouth curves into a grateful smile upon seeing me. The one shocking aspect of his appearance is his pallor. I'd thought his dark suntan was permanently baked in, but his skin has faded to a pasty grayish hue in a week's time. "How are you doing?" I administer a gentle hug and pull up a chair next to his bedside.

"Tired. Weak. But better today than I've been since the heart attack." His voice is thick with fatigue.

"I rushed over right away when I heard you were here. I tried to bring Petey in to visit, but it wasn't allowed."

"Now that's a shame."

"I apologize for showing up empty-handed. Let me swing by again tomorrow with some books for you."

"Oh, no need, Margaret. The volunteers bring me reading materials—when I'm not snoozing, that is. I don't think I could focus on a novel right now. Or anything much deeper than *People* magazine. Too drowsy from the medication, you know?"

"I can imagine. Everyone misses you back at your place. Petey and I could both sense it today."

"I miss them too. I never thought I'd miss an assisted living home, but it's the Garden of Eden compared to the ICU. And to think I even got a visit from my favorite novelist. That would've never happened if I were still living in my old apartment. Thank you again." Vincent's eyes flutter closed and we sit together, silent, for a couple of minutes. "Have you seen him again?" he asks.

"Charlie? No."

His eyes still closed, he says, "You know, lying in this hospital room has made me think about the past. I had a woman in my life for over thirty years. We were friends and companions, we traveled together, but we never married. I think that was deeply disappointing to her. But I never had a passion for her." Vincent's breathing deepens, and for a moment I think he's dozed off. But then he says, "That husband of yours—the one you don't miss—I'm guessing he wasn't exactly the love of *your* life either."

"True enough."

"Maybe it could be a different story with Kittredge?"

"Oh, I think that ship has sailed."

"I wouldn't be so sure. Any man who acts that nervous around a woman must have powerful feelings for her."

"Well, Vincent, you finally got a smile out of me."

Without opening his eyes, Vincent smiles back and says, "There was someone else in my life. When I was a young man in college, I fell in love with a girl named Amelia."

"Such a pretty name."

"Such a pretty girl. When we both finished UCLA, she wanted to move in together."

"And did you?"

"I wasn't ready, so we went our separate ways. Then a couple of years later, we started seeing each other again." Vincent's voice is so low, I have to lean in to hear him.

"I remember thinking, 'Now. Now I want to see this woman's face every day when I wake up.' But Amelia had other ideas," he continues. "She'd been accepted into a graduate program at Boston University, and that was the end of it. The timing never worked for us."

Same as Charlie and me. Then my thoughts turn to Audrey and Nathan. They broke up for the same reason.

"Some people like to say the devil's in the details. But I say the devil's in the timing," Vincent adds, his breathing growing labored.

"I'm afraid all this talk is exhausting you."

He opens his eyes and gives me a piercing gaze. "Let me finish. Then I'll rest. It doesn't have to end the same way for you."

"How can I change the ending?"

"You can try fighting for it. I didn't do that. When Amelia got into that program at BU, I let her go. I could've tried to talk her out of it. Hell, I could've gone *with* her."

"Sorry to say, I don't have much of a fighting spirit."

"Neither did I. That's why I'm telling you, don't do what I did. Don't give up that easily."

"I—I'll think about what you said."

"Good."

His eyes close again. I hesitate, trying to decide whether to stay with him a while longer, but his breathing has deepened into a soft, rhythmic snore. I return to the car, and I don't realize I'm crying until I hug Petey and all he wants to do is lick the briny tears off my cheeks. I tighten my hold on him. Suddenly, I wish I possessed the power to keep them both safe and well. Petey . . . and Vincent.

Later, at home, I see an announcement online: *Second Chance: A Novel. A woman's marriage falters when she finds she is still haunted by her troubled past in a stunning sequel to* Bicoastal *by* New York Times *bestselling author Charles Kittredge. This title will be released on November 20.*

I pre-order two hardcover copies from Amazon - one for myself, the other for Vincent. Before I settle into an evening of work, I take care of one more item of business online. I set up a Google Alert on my computer for Charles Kittredge. Now I'll be able to keep tabs on the *Second Chance* book launch, critical reviews, and live appearances.

It's official. I've degenerated from dewy-eyed fan to creepy cyber stalker.

As I open up the Word document for the *Powder World* cover article I'll be editing tonight, I take a long sip of chamomile tea. Last week, for our annual plant safety issue, I wrote a column on the topic of how safety can impact workers' rights. The column focused on a Copenhagen food processing plant that gave their workers free beer all day long as a perk. Management rescinded the privilege over concerns about personnel safety, and the workers went out on strike. Despite the protest, the unpopular new policy remained in force, though the workers received one concession – free beers in the cafeteria after work. I've decided it might not be such a terrific habit to nurse a glass of wine during every working moment, so I've substituted herbal tea for my own safety. But like those Danish workers, I'm not embracing abstinence. I reward myself with a glass of something nice when I shut down my computer at the end of the day.

• • •

Audrey, Petey, and I are at the halfway point in our beach walk, and she asks if we can sit down on a bench and take a break. Her cheeks are flushed and she is more out of breath than usual. "This work schedule is wrecking my health," she says. "I need to get back to my walks."

"Are the planning meetings over?"

"For now."

"And have they determined your fate at the company?"

"I was about to update you on that." She takes a swig of water, looks down at Petey, then over at me. "I'm being promoted – but not to southwestern regional sales manager, which I thought might be the next move. They offered me a staff position instead."

"Congratulations. Where?"

"Well, that's the thing. Corporate headquarters. New Jersey."

"Oh my. How do you feel about that?"

"Excited. Nervous. Freaked out. I'm eating too much and running on no sleep."

"When will you have to move?"

"January fifteenth is the official date. But I'll need to spend a lot of time back there between now and then for end-of-year meetings and apartment hunting. I can't believe I'm moving back to New York after all these years. Well, Jersey . . . close enough. I guess they figured I'd fit right in with this accent of mine."

"What about Petey?"

She sighs. "That's the hardest part." She pronounces it *hoddest pot.* "Petey can't go with me, but my parents will give him a home."

"They live someplace east of LA, don't they?"

"Yeah, about ninety minutes from here, on the road to Palm Springs. They love Petey, but it's not ideal. For one thing, it's wicked hot out there in the summer, and Petey hates the heat."

"Must be that Irish blood." I learned from Audrey that the soft-coated Wheaten terrier breed originated in Ireland.

"Yeah, no kidding. And my folks are only in their sixties, but they're both couch potatoes, ya know? I worry they won't be able to give him enough exercise."

"He'll miss the board and care visits too. It seems like Petey needs stimulation and a sense of purpose."

Audrey nods and wipes away tears. "Shit. I'm crying like a baby these days. Sometimes I don't even know if I'm sad about Nathan, or Petey, or leaving this beautiful place."

"Probably all the above." Petey's radar homes in on a golden retriever walking by, and the terrier emits a low growl. Though goldens are the most happy-go-lucky dogs in the world, Petey is unimpressed by their good nature and treats them with suspicion and even hostility. A bit like me with Alice.

Audrey leans in to give the dog's neck a comforting massage. "Take it easy, pal."

"Petey could come live with me." My words tumble out so fast, I'm not sure how it happens. I hadn't consciously planned this . . . it's as if my mouth became an independent instrument with a mind of its own.

Audrey's eyes are wide with surprise. "But you're in a small apartment with no yard. Can you keep him at your place?"

"Dogs are allowed in the terms of my lease. Besides, this is Petey's home turf. He'd have his regular walks on the beach and his therapy dog routine. And he's already familiar with my place from the afternoons he's spent with me when you've been working late. I honestly think this could work."

I watch Audrey's excitement build as she thinks it through aloud. "If you need to travel for business or go away on vacation, my parents could take the dog. And they'd drive in to pick him up and deliver him back to you—I'm sure they'd do that. Like I said, they're both crazy about Petey. Nathan misses him too. He can walk him sometimes if you're too busy."

"You see? I told you this could work."

"You're a doll to offer, but we don't need to decide anything today. It's a big decision. Take your time and think about it."

"I don't need to think about it."

Mum will disapprove, for sure. Though she adores animals and makes a great fuss over other people's dogs and cats, she believes pet ownership interferes with one's own self-centered pursuits. "It's better not to have a dog," she's often cautioned me. Petey will be a big responsibility, and there'll be a learning curve involved, thanks to Mum's strict policy of pet-free living while I grew up. But I want this. I'm not sure why I want it so much. I only know that I do.

• • •

"What is that ingredient in turkey that makes you sleepy?" says Heather. "Because I'm drowsy as hell right now."

I Google it on my cellphone. "Tryptophan. But wait . . ." I scroll down. "It says that's a myth. The tryptophan in turkey doesn't make you any sleepier than a lot of other foods."

"If that's true, it's got a pretty strong placebo effect. I think I could sleep for the next twelve hours," says Michael.

It's Thanksgiving, around seven-thirty in the evening - though it feels more like midnight. The room is so quiet, the only sound is the crackling of logs in the fireplace. Benny is dozing face-down on the family room rug, and the adults are comatose with food. We're gathered around the fire as we finish our last crumbs of dessert - the four of us, Michael's next-door neighbors, and a single friend of Heather's, a young woman from Manhattan Beach. Henry and Alice are out of the picture, as they've gone to spend Thanksgiving with her sister in Scottsdale. Thank God. On their way to the airport this morning, Alice had reportedly swung by to drop off a centerpiece of fall flowers she'd arranged in a turkey-shaped vase, and a pumpkin cake she'd baked in the shape of an actual pumpkin. As I bite into the cake, I comment, "Alice is four hundred miles away, but she still manages to steal the show." I say this in a joking way, and even Michael is amused.

My contributions were two top-notch bottles of vino and a store-bought apple pie. "The pie was out of this world," says Heather. "I liked it better than the pumpkin cake."

I blow her a kiss and say to Michael, "You married well, I hope you know."

"I do." Michael is nursing an after-dinner scotch and acting unusually mellow.

"This has been delightful, but I'm going to head out now," I say, rising to indulge in a luxurious stretch in front of the warm fire. I turn to Heather. "Can I take a small packet of dark meat for Petey?"

"It's already wrapped in foil. And I packed some other leftovers for you in sandwich bags. Everything's on the counter, to the right of the fridge," she says.

"Thanks."

"I still can't believe you're about to become a dog owner," says Michael. "It's nuts."

"You sound like your grandmother. Mum's been trying to talk me out of it all week."

"No, no, I meant nuts in a *good* way. I think it'll be fun for Benny. This dog is okay around kids, right?"

"Better than okay. Don't forget, Petey's a trained therapy dog."

"Right."

"Also, don't forget my offer to babysit this weekend. Unless you have plans with Dad and Alice when they get back from Scottsdale?"

His upper lip curls into a little snarl. "No plans. And to be honest, I don't give a sh—" He looks down at Benny on the floor. "I don't care to see them."

I recognize all too well the bitter, antagonistic tone that has now pivoted from me to his father. "We talked about this before. It doesn't help, carrying this kind of resentment around. Let it go. *I* have." And though I didn't know it till now, I truly have.

I've given the matter a lot of thought, ever since the big blow-up on the day of Henry's birthday party. That day, I got on his case for sweeping his infidelities under the rug. But all those years ago, when he made his tearful confession about that first one-night stand, I see now that I was complicit in the sweeping. Perhaps if I hadn't let it go so readily, if I'd shown passionate outrage, if I'd pushed back and insisted on family counseling, the long-term outcome might have been different. But I didn't put up a fight. Call it acceptance, call it indifference - whatever it was, I handed Henry a free pass to continue the unfaithful behavior. I say to Michael, "Your father and I were both so young and naive when we got married, we were clueless about the effort that goes into a successful marriage. Instead of confronting our problems and working them out, we ignored them and hoped they'd resolve on their own."

Michael says, "That doesn't bode well for Heather and me."

"Because you married young too?"

"Yes."

"Michael, trust me - there's no gene for infidelity, or for cluelessness. Your relationship isn't doomed just because your parents screwed up. Learn from our mistakes. Talk with Heather about your differences. Work together to keep the marriage strong."

He nods, and I enfold him in a hug. He stands stiffly at first but then wraps his arms around me so tightly it hurts, though just a little. He walks me outside, and we hug again before I slide into the driver's seat. I'm chilled to the bone with that sensation you get after a large meal, when all the blood rushes to the stomach, leaving the extremities brittle and exposed. I had planned to visit Vincent in the hospital tonight and surprise him with the newly published copy of *Second Chance,* which arrived yesterday, but I think the hour is too late. Besides, I'm wiped out. I did some editorial work in the morning, worked out at the gym, and took Petey on our therapy rounds for a special holiday visit before going to Michael's for the Thanksgiving feast. I'll bring the book to Vincent tomorrow, right after my power sculpt class.

When I go to the hospital around midday on Friday, I bypass the reception desk and ride the elevator up to room 334. The room is empty. Maybe they've taken Vincent out for a walk or to a therapy session. I stop at the nursing station to inquire. "I'm here to visit Vincent DiLorenzo. Can you tell me where I'll find him?"

"Are you a relative?"

"No, a close friend." That's a bit of a stretch, but I figure it's the only way I'll get any information out of her.

"I'm sorry to tell you, Mister DiLorenzo passed away."

I reel back as if punched in the face. "When?"

"Early this morning."

I stand there rigid, absorbing the news. I look down at the jacket of Charlie's book with the sorrowful realization that Vincent will never see it now. I had rehearsed what I was going to say on this visit. *I've given a lot of thought to your advice, and I'm determined to go for it. I promise I'll try my hardest to find a way back to Charlie if he'll have me.* Vincent would've loved this pledge, as he would've loved receiving his favorite author's new book. If I'd stuck with my original plan and gone to the hospital on Thanksgiving, maybe both the gift and the promise might have brightened Vincent's final night on earth. But I waited until today, and now it's too late. It wasn't meant to be. Is this an omen that Charlie and I are not meant to be, either? Or a sign that I should honor Vincent's memory by following through on my undelivered pledge?

I'm not sure, but I know that fine old gentleman was right about one thing. The devil is indeed in the timing.

PART TWELVE: DECEMBER
PETEY

33.

Margaret: WTF? I fixed his dinner the way you told me to, but he won't touch it. I hope he's not sick.

This is the text I send to Audrey, the latest of several panic-stricken communiqués today. She's gone to Jersey on business until Friday night, and this is my first lengthy stretch of time alone with Petey. Our shared custody arrangement will continue until Audrey's permanent move to the East Coast in the middle of January. I'm excited to have him with me - but nervous, as any new mom would be.

The evening meal I've prepared for the Wheaten incorporates dry kibble, canned dog food, warm broth, grated raw carrots, pre-cooked brown rice, and liquid vitamins and supplements mixed into an aromatic stew far more elaborate than the frozen dinner I'll be microwaving for myself. When I set the bowl down on the kitchen floor, the dog walked over, gave it an apathetic sniff, and sauntered off to the living room to lie down.

Audrey texts me back.

Audrey: When did you give him the food?

Margaret: Half an hour ago.

Audrey: Is that all? I told you, Petey eats like a terrier.

Margaret: And that means what?

Audrey: He doesn't chow down, he grazes. Like a cat. Don't worry, I promise you he won't starve.

A little later, I grow alarmed again when Petey goes out to the balcony and runs in frantic circles, barking, growling, and whining as if fending off a fearsome predator. After this behavior continues for several minutes, I wonder about his sanity. I make a short video of the dog's run-bark-whine circuit around the balcony and text it to Audrey. Her reply comes within seconds.

Audrey: LOLOL. Totally normal.

Margaret: Are you serious?

Audrey: It's his active time of day. I call it Wheaten Witching Hour.

Margaret: OMG. He's going to continue this for a whole hour?

Audrey: Yes, but no longer than that if you're lucky.

Though Petey has a few quirky traits, in other ways he's easier than I expected. When I settle in at the computer after my evening meal (Petey remains uninterested in his, even after I toss in a few scraps of chicken from my own plate), I worry he'll distract me from my work with more whining or some new attention grab. But he doesn't pester me at all. He lies down close to my chair, head resting on his forepaws, a comforting and undemanding presence.

When I finish my editorial work for the evening, I print out a series of online forms to start the process of getting myself certified as a therapy dog handler. It's an elaborate undertaking. There's a comprehensive exam in which I will administer basic commands to Petey in thirteen different test situations. Petey can ace all of this, I'm confident, but I still have a lot to learn. Once certified, the fees I pay to the therapy dog association will include liability insurance coverage. I'll also be responsible for the dog's annual health care record and proof of inoculations. I'm supposed to trim his nails and keep him clean, well-groomed, and brushed for our visits. Petey's long, silky coat can develop invisible clumps and mats below the surface. Unless I'm diligent about brushing, the mats will become so hopelessly tangled, the only remedy will be a buzz cut. I can't subject this beautiful dog to such a fate. Once I earn my certification, I can escort Petey to hospitals and nursing care facilities as well as the residential board and care home. Yes, it'll be a lot of work, but . . .

"I think it's worth it, don't you, Petey?" I say aloud to the dog.

He opens one eye and emits a low *fff* sound in agreement before returning to his nap.

When I crawl into bed later to read a book, I pat the covers and he jumps up next to me, then he lies down and curls himself against my legs. I like the warmth his small body gives off and the reassuring sound of his soft breathing. I hope he'll sleep on the bed with me all night, but after about fifteen minutes, he slinks down and pads over to the doggie bed that Audrey has placed in the far corner of the room. Maybe Petey prefers the familiar scent and softness of his old bed.

Or maybe he's just not that into me.

Audrey and I have agreed that Petey will continue to receive one long daily exercise walk along the beach as he's accustomed to, along with two or three short walks, as time permits, to allow him to take care of business. After the first walk of the morning, I check my phone calendar and marvel over how packed my schedule has become. Work continues as before, but now there are many other agenda items. Petey's daily care and feeding. Practicing for my certification. Therapy dog rounds, which I hope to expand on after I'm certified. Helping with the holiday toy drive at Seaside Fitness – I promised Susie I'd lend a hand. Christmas shopping – so many more people on my list this year. My workout program at the gym. My activities with Benny, Heather, and Michael, which are taking up more and more of my time these days. The online book club I joined, where we discuss a work of classic fiction every month. And of course, there's Mission Kittredge, my quest to see Charlie again.

I decide it's time to make some changes in my work life. Assuming my boss cooperates, that is.

Robert answers my call right away, knowing I rarely use the telephone unless it's something important. "Morning, Margaret. Everything okay?"

"Fine."

"How's the new supplement coming along?"

I fill him in on a special trade show supplement we plan to insert in the March issue, a new offering for next year. Then I say, "I've got something important to discuss with you. Is this a good time?"

"Go for it."

"I'd like to cut back to a reduced work schedule after the holidays."

"When do you propose *not* to work?"

"All day Wednesdays, and Friday afternoons. I understand you might need to give me a pay cut since I'd only be available three and a half days. Though I think I can still get the job done on the reduced schedule."

"I think you could get the job done in your *sleep,* Margaret. You know I don't care that you keep odd hours. I've always given you a lot of rope."

"And I'm grateful for that, believe me, but now we're not talking *odd* hours, we're talking *fewer* hours."

"Makes no difference to me as long as the work doesn't suffer."

"That's great. And what do you think would be fair in the way of a pay adjustment?"

"Let's give it a trial run for three months with no change to your salary. We can reevaluate after first quarter and agree on how to continue."

"Wow. That seems more than fair. Very generous, in fact. You sound so serene about the whole idea."

"Not serene—relieved. I was scared to death you were going to resign again." He chuckles.

"No, I love my job. But I'm loving my life a little more these days too. Okay, *love* is too strong a word, but at least I don't hate it any longer. And I want to make time for some new activities."

"I'm happy to hear that. It's been a rough couple of years for you."

"Yes, it has. One other thing. You've always let me moonlight on the side, but that's all going to stop. I don't want you to think I'm giving you short shrift in favor of other work."

"Good. I appreciate you telling me."

True to my promise, right after hanging up I email my freelance clients, informing them I won't be accepting any more projects after year-end. Then I text Heather and Michael and offer to sign up for more frequent childcare duties.

Margaret: I can pick up Benny from pre-school after my volunteer work and keep him with me through dinnertime on Wednesday afternoons. And I should be able to take him for a couple of hours on Friday afternoons too.

Heather: That would be fantastic!

Her reply ends with that prayer-hands emoji people use to mean *thank you,* even though it looks more like *please.*

Though all else is going well, I'm fresh out of ideas on what to do about Charlie. The obvious strategy would be to track him down at the club. I've resumed yoga classes, but there's been no sign of him. The launch of *Second Chance* must be occupying all his time. The two copies of the book I purchased before Thanksgiving are sitting on my coffee table, untouched, so I embark on a weekend reading marathon. *Second Chance* is a worthy sequel to *Bicoastal.* It picks up the story five years later, focusing on Nomi, Anthony's New York spouse. Remarried to a kind and trustworthy man named George, Nomi is so damaged by her first husband's treacherous betrayal that she propels the new relationship into a downward spiral. Gentle George becomes the punching bag on whom she unleashes all her frustration and fury, though not in the physical sense. It's much more subtle than that.

There's a scene one of the reviewers has labeled "the dishwasher diatribe." It begins with Nomi leading George into the kitchen by the hand, like a parent about to scold a wayward child. She berates him for his ineptitude in loading the dishwasher. In a voice oozing venom, she picks apart every aspect of his incompetence. He's failed to stack the plates symmetrically, leaving large gaping holes. He has loaded forks and knives with the handles facing down, but the spoons with handles up. He's even committed the egregious *faux pas* of putting wooden-handled utensils in the machine as only an imbecile would do. She attacks him in this fashion over other mundane tasks. When poor George can no longer stand the constant verbal abuse, the harping over every detail, he moves out. The final third of the novel tells the story of Nomi's atonement as she confronts her own cruelty and tries to work her way back into George's good graces. In the end, after Nomi's concerted efforts to undo previous wrongs, the couple reconcile.

I call Sunny to share my reactions. "That dishwasher thing . . ." I say. "Charlie takes the most trivial domestic scenario and charges it full of dramatic tension. I stayed up late reading it."

"Yeah, me too. He's writing about a kitchen appliance, for God's sake, but it's like reading a Stephen King story."

"This got me thinking about how much Charlie's writing has changed since his first novel."

"The one about the brother and sister who have superpowers?"

"Yes. It's like Charlie has pivoted a hundred and eighty degrees since that book from magical realism to this kind of gritty, ultra-realistic style where the characters' flaws are exposed under a microscope." Hah. A year ago, I didn't even *like* fiction, and here I am commenting with authority on the various fictional sub-genres.

"It's powerful," Sunny says.

"Changing the subject, how's it going with the plan to open a new spa down in this neck of the woods?"

"I'm working on it," she says. "How's it going with the plan to reconnect with Charlie?"

"I'm working on it."

Google Alert messages are dribbling in as more of the leading literary critics publish their reviews of the book – most of them positive, I'm happy to note. I also see alerts on book signings and appearances in Northern California. This explains why Charlie hasn't been to yoga class. Then, a few days later:

Book signing event, December 10th, 7:00 p.m. Meet bestselling author Charles Kittredge, who will read excerpts from his new novel, Second Chance.

The notice cites a venue in Culver City, about thirty minutes away. Bingo. This is the opportunity I've been waiting for.

The announcement includes a link that I use to purchase a ticket online. The admission fee is steep, but what do I know about author events? I click on a second link that takes me to a page on the publisher's website, where I find a full list of Charlie's book launch activities. How did I not see this before? He is scheduled for another appearance closer to home, but I prefer to go to a more remote location where I won't run into a roomful of familiar faces. Anyway, I've already bought this expensive ticket for Culver City.

• • •

Petey and I are settling into our new arrangement. He is a good boy most of the time, except for one problem – the incessant barking on the balcony during Wheaten witching hour each night. The next-door neighbor leaves me a snarky note, and I'm worried he'll complain to my landlord if I don't control the situation. I come up with an ingenious solution. As the witching hour approaches, I strap Petey into his therapy dog harness. Sure enough, now that he's put on his work uniform, the training kicks in. He knows he isn't supposed to bark and dials back the volume to subtle "woofing" mode.

Good dog parenting, Margaret. My stratagem works brilliantly—for three days. On day four, as I'm strapping him into the harness, Petey gives me a look that says, *I'm on to your tricks, lady.* Harness or no, he reverts to full-throated barking.

"Petey, stop. Please. Be a good boy. Here's a treat." But my pleas and bribes have no effect, and I'm forced to lock the dog inside. He paces back and forth by the balcony door, whining and panting, while I try without success to focus on my editing work. My one-year lease runs out at the end of December. When I signed it last year, the property manager told me I could go month to month when the initial lease ran out. She remarked at the time on how easy it is for them to rent out waterfront apartments in the current real estate market.

I shoot out a quick email to her: *Effective January 1st, I wish to rent on a monthly basis as you said I might do. I understand you require thirty days' notice to vacate the unit.* After the holidays are over, I'll start the search for a small house to buy or rent in the area. I'll lose my beautiful view, but I'll gain a little yard for Petey and Benny, and a real home for us to share. Hopefully one with tolerant, dog-loving neighbors. When I imagine us together in that cozy little house, with a fenced-in yard lined with tall hedges, my insides tingle with warmth and pleasure. I'm optimistic that whatever happens, I will be all right.

34.

The night of the book signing, I allow an hour and a half for the twenty-mile drive north. When I reach Culver City and park in a municipal garage, it's much too early to go into the lecture hall. Calculating it will be at least forty minutes before they open the doors, I duck into an Italian restaurant across the street and find a counter seat at the cozy bar next to the dining room.

The bar menu includes several popular Italian dishes in appetizer portions, including white lasagna. I remember that's a favorite of Charlie's, and I'm tempted for a moment. But that's a heavy dish, and even a small serving might leave me droopy-eyed. Falling asleep during the reading is not the ideal path to Charlie's heart. Instead, I order a *tricolore* salad and a three-ounce pour of a Sangiovese red blend – enough to take the edge off, but not enough to induce sleep.

The auditorium is packed by the time I go in. There's a long table in the back of the room where two women are handing out copies of *Second Chance*, and now I understand why the ticket price is hefty – it includes a hardcover copy of the novel. I already have my two Amazon copies in the bag I'm carrying, and I worry whether that's bad form, like bringing your own entrée into a restaurant. Well, too late now. At least they're tucked away where no one can see them.

"Did you want a blank copy, or pre-signed?" The woman behind the table points to two stacks of books. "The blank copy is for Mr. Kittredge to personalize after the reading. You might prefer a pre-signed copy if you don't want to wait in line after the discussion."

"I'll take a pre-signed one, please." I add it to my book bag, which weighs me down like a sack full of boulders. I will donate the pre-signed copy to my local library and ask Charlie to sign the others. Most of the remaining empty seats are toward the front of the room. Why is it nobody ever wants to sit in front? I grab a seat around six rows back, but I'm not sure if Charlie will notice because the man sitting in front of me is quite tall.

When Charlie is introduced, he walks out wearing a geometric print silk tie, slim-fit jeans, and a gray sports jacket the color of his eyes. I've never seen him dressed like this before. Muffled gasps escape from some of the women in the audience. The sight of him - combined with the crowd's reaction - makes me wonder if my quest is hopeless. This man is a celebrity, and right now he could pass for a movie star.

Charlie is a relaxed and confident speaker. He pays his respects to the moderator and the staff, he thanks the audience for coming out during the busy holiday season, and he warms up the crowd with a few humorous stories - one of them using his Cary Grant voice - before reading excerpts from the novel. After Charlie finishes, the moderator opens the event up to questions and instructs the audience, "Please raise your hand if you have a question, and I'll bring you the microphone. One other ground rule: If you've already read the book, please - no questions or comments that contain spoilers. We don't want to ruin anyone else's reading experience."

The first question is an old chestnut that Charlie must've answered a thousand times, delivered by an elderly man in the back of the hall. "How do you get your ideas?"

I remember Charlie telling me how he likes to make up little stories about observations in day-to-day life . . . like the time he mistook an Irish setter for a woman breaking up with her boyfriend at a traffic intersection. But he doesn't tell this story tonight.

"I don't find the ideas as much as they find me," says Charlie to the attentive crowd. "It happens first thing in the morning, right after I wake up. Random thoughts, fragments of ideas literally pop into my head. I can't tell you where they come from, but I write them down as fast as I can. I revisit the notes later, over and over, to see which ideas are the ones that stick."

I like this response. The next question comes from a youngish woman two rows back from me, who wants to know whether we can expect to see *Second Chance* on the big screen as we did with *Bicoastal.*

"I certainly hope so," says Charlie, "although you might see it on a *small* screen instead." A soft ripple of laughter follows this comment. "With all the different paid TV channels and various streaming services, it's become more difficult to get a film adaptation into theatrical distribution. But on the bright side, an author today has many more options than a couple of decades ago, when we only had the movies and a handful of television networks. So far I've had a few nibbles, but nothing I can announce to you yet."

I've been trying to catch the moderator's eye, and finally I succeed. I stand to accept the portable mic from him, and as I do, Charlie reacts with a startled double-take. He recovers his composure so quickly, I doubt anyone has noticed but me. "First, I'd like to tell you how much I enjoyed *Second Chance,*" I say.

"Thank you. So you've read the book?"

"I have. And the title intrigues me because I think it refers not only to Nomi's second marriage but also to whether people deserve multiple chances to correct their behavior."

"You remember the caveat about no spoilers?" he says.

"I do—don't worry. Let me phrase it this way. Regardless of what happens to the characters in this book, is it fair to say that you yourself believe someone deserves a second chance to shape and redefine a relationship? Especially after that relationship has faltered?"

"Yes . . . but only under the right circumstances."

"And what are those circumstances?" There are maybe two hundred people in the hall, but Charlie and I are having a private conversation.

"For a second chance to succeed, the person needs to have changed. And it's not enough to express the *intent* to change. The actual *accomplishment* of change is much harder to achieve. People sometimes confuse the two."

"How do you know if someone has truly changed?"

"It has to be shown through actions. Not words. Take old Ebenezer Scrooge - he transformed himself from a heartless miser to a kind, sentimental, and generous benefactor. Now there's a guy who knew how to change." I hear soft laughter from the group.

Following the Q&A, I wait in line for him to autograph my two copies of the novel. When it's my turn, I step forward and say, "Please sign this first one to Heather." He flips to the title page and signs it. "And this one is for me," I say as we exchange copies.

"Should I make it out 'To Mar,' then?"

"'To Margaret,' please. And I'd appreciate if you would also write, 'To better times—and better timing.'"

Charlie gives me a curious look, but he does as I ask . . . and when he hands the book back to me, I detect a smile playing at the corners of his mouth.

• • •

When I wake the next morning, Charlie is sitting up on the other side of my bed, jotting notes on a little yellow pad. "Did an inspired idea pop into your head?" I ask.

"Oh yes, a very inspired idea." He puts the pad and pen down and turns to me, enveloping me in his arms and flinging one warm bare leg over mine.

"I think I'm going to like your idea," I say in a whisper, and he rewards me with a slow, deep kiss.

Okay, this isn't happening in real life, only inside my head. I've been indulging in elaborate fantasies since my conversation with Charlie at last night's book signing. I know this is pathetic. I'm acting like some loser kid with an imaginary friend. I've taken the first step, connecting with him at the author event. The challenge now is to keep up the momentum.

I attend a yoga class, one that used to be on Charlie's regular rotation at the club. He's not traveling on the book tour - I've practically memorized his schedule for the next ten days - so I'm hopeful he might make a rare appearance in class. But it's a no-go. This is disappointing because one of our talks over coffee on the poolside deck would be an ideal way to continue the conversation from last night. I will have to come up with a Plan B.

Much later, after Petey's beach walk, I pull up Charlie's book launch schedule online and compare it with my own Outlook calendar. His professional commitments appear to be tapering off next week, probably given the proximity to Christmas. My own calendar is chockablock with entries, and there's no sign of it lightening up. Next Friday is good for me, though, and Petey will be with Audrey that weekend. Better not to have that complicating factor in the picture.

Next comes the difficult part - composing a text to Charlie. My years of professional writing experience are no help to me now. I spend a full hour drafting and re-drafting the text message on my computer since I'm more articulate typing on a keyboard than I am punching my fingers into a phone. I experiment with a dozen different versions, and each time I picture Charlie reading and rejecting it. When I'm on the verge of ditching the entire plan, I think of Vincent and my unfulfilled promise to him. I copy the final message into my phone and hit the send button before I have time to lose my nerve.

Margaret: You gave Nomi a second chance. Now, how about me? One chance, please, to show you how things have changed. How I have changed. Dinner at my place next Friday, 7 p.m.? I make a wicked good white lasagna.

Nothing to do now but worry.

Time slows as I await Charlie's reply. After ten minutes - more like ten hours in my tortured imagination - my cellphone rings. The sound sends an electrical charge through my nervous system. He's calling instead of texting. That has to be good, right? But when I grab the phone, I see it's only Susie from the gym.

"Hey, Margaret. I'm calling to remind you that tomorrow is the gift-wrapping party. Four o'clock, in the first-floor studio."

"I'll be there." This literal "wrap party" is the final step in the club's holiday gift drive I've been helping with since the beginning of December.

"Oh, and I need a favor. Judith was supposed to bring an appetizer, but now she can't make it. Can you take care of that?"

"Sure, Susie. No problem."

"Great. See you then."

I make a note on my calendar to pick up cheese and crackers for tomorrow afternoon. Another ten minutes pass before that tinkling glass chime signals the arrival of a new text message.

Heather: Michael and I talked, and he agreed it's okay for you to take Benny to Seaside Kids next week when he's on winter break from pre-school.

The message is followed by an emoji of clapping hands. I respond:

Margaret: Good work convincing him.

Benny will be thrilled to get back to the bounce house. I text her another idea.

Margaret: If the weather warms up, maybe we can take him to the pool too.

Heather replies with a thumbs-up. I pour a small glass of wine to steady my nerves while I wait to hear from Charlie. Then it occurs to me it could be hours before he responds, or – oh God, what if he doesn't answer me at all? I need to stop obsessing over this. I kick off my shoes, plunk myself down on the couch, and turn on the news.

A few minutes later, the text chime pings again. This time (hallelujah) it's Charlie.

Charlie: White lasagna? I thought you hated to cook.

Margaret: That's changing. Lots of things about my life are changing.

Charlie: Tell me.

Margaret: But Charlie, you said change must be shown through actions. Not words. That's why we need to see each other.

The phone goes silent for a few more minutes, then rings again. This time it's the director at the board and care residence where Vincent used to live. "Can you bring Petey a little earlier next week? To coincide with our holiday luncheon."

"What time?"

"Noon."

I check my calendar. "Yes, we'll be there."

After noting the time change, I open the Amazon app on my phone and search for reindeer antlers for dogs. I find a cute little number that combines bright red antlers with a Santa hat, and I order it for Petey. Given his proud terrier temperament, I hope he won't find it demeaning to wear. Impossibly, the phone rings *again,* and I pick up to say hello to Grace. "Hi there. Everything okay with you and Nancy?"

"Yes, she's having a good week. I'm calling to see when you want to get together."

I've bought Christmas presents for both women, and we've agreed I'll join them at Nancy's house one day next week for lunch and a gift exchange. "How about Tuesday?"

"Tuesday's fine. We don't have a lot on the schedule here." She laughs. "See you around noon."

Another text arrives. This time it's a group message from some of Jax's students who are trying to arrange a get-together after hip-hop class. As if I had room on my calendar for another holiday party. To complicate my life further, Mum has finally decided to come from New York over Christmas week. In her usual inconsiderate fashion, she hasn't informed me when or for how long.

Yet another text. Whenever my phone emits a sound, it shaves a year off my life expectancy. But this time it's Charlie again.

Charlie: The lasagna. Do you actually layer it yourself?

He's referring to the day in his kitchen when I asked that same question about the dish he served me. I try to duplicate his response as well as I can remember it.

Margaret: I layer it, I sauce it. All the required steps.

Please, Charlie, can you just say yes or no to the goddamn invitation and put me out of my misery?

And then I wait some more. I walk barefoot into the kitchen to fix Petey's dinner, placing my phone on the counter. Assembling, warming, and mixing the numerous ingredients will distract me for a few minutes at least. Petey joins me in the kitchen to supervise my work. I've known dogs that leap about with wild enthusiasm as they await their dinners, but Petey observes the preparations with blasé indifference.

The millionth text of the hour comes in, and I snatch up the cellphone to read the newest message. I drop the phone back onto the counter, bounce up and down on my toes, and say,

"Petey—he said yes. He said yes!" Petey barks and jumps up on me, feeding off my enthusiasm. His entire backside wiggling with unbridled joy, he plants sloppy kisses on my nose as I throw my arms around him and bury my face in his soft, clean-smelling coat. "He said yes."

I peel myself off the ceiling long enough to finish preparing Petey's dinner, but I can't think about food myself. The torturous series of texts from Charlie has left me excited but overwrought. Then, self-doubt creeps in as disturbing questions percolate in my head. My breath quickens. I've promised this man a new and improved Margaret, but can I deliver on that? What if I've made the classic mistake Charlie warned about at the book signing, that of confusing the intent to change with the actual accomplishment of it? *Have* I changed - and will the change be enough for Charlie to begin to trust and care for me again?

As if sensing my nervous excitement, Petey pads over, his tail trembling in a tentative wag. He rests his head on my lap and gazes up at me with devotion and concern. If dogs could talk, I think he'd say, *Margaret. Don't worry about whether you can change. You've been changing all along.*

And so I have. As I gaze into Petey's warm and trusting brown eyes, I think about what's been happening in my life - not only with the dog, but with all the people and activities that now pleasurably fill my once empty calendar. My transformation may not be as dazzling as Scrooge's, but I've safely crossed some major hurdles. I stroke Petey's head while thinking about next Friday's dinner. I promised Charlie homemade white lasagna, which poses a different type of hurdle for a blundering cook like me. I've already downloaded an astonishingly complex recipe I'll have to make from scratch, an expression that doesn't even make sense to me. But after the more challenging tests I've faced this year, creating a casserole of lovingly layered noodles, meat, cheese, and sauce should be within my grasp.

• • •

The big day arrives, and seven o'clock is fast approaching. I've been hard at work since morning, and everything is ready. Well, nearly. I step into the overheated kitchen, where rich cooking odors envelop me, to check on dinner again. Earlier this week, I had the brilliant idea to bake a test lasagna and deliver it to Nancy's house for my visit with her and Grace. The trial run didn't go so well. Distracted by re-reading *Second Chance,* I detected a faint odor of smoke and raced to the oven, dismayed to find the cheese starting to burn. I cut the crusty blackened edges off and salvaged the rest, but Nancy and Grace appeared to struggle with it at lunch.

It's a good thing I've got a second chance with the lasagna. This time I'm determined it will be perfect. As I spoon a little homemade béchamel sauce on to moisten the dish, breathing in its intoxicating aroma, I spill some on my white silk blouse. Cursing myself for not wearing—or even owning—an apron, I hurry to the bedroom to change my top. I slip on a form-fitting red cashmere sweater with a plunging neckline I'd previously dismissed as too seductive. Maybe a sexier look isn't a bad idea for tonight, though, and at least the sweater's more tasteful than, say, a tight leather miniskirt and fuck-me boots.

I'd envisioned Charlie and me starting the evening on the balcony, sipping champagne, enjoying the effervescence that feels so impossibly wet and dry all at once. But the crisp December air stings my cheeks. It's too chilly to sit outdoors. Still, we might step out to listen to carolers and admire the holiday lights that twinkle along the harbor, so I want everything to look inviting. Toweling dried leaves off the balcony furniture, I give an involuntary shiver. I allow myself a brief fantasy of Charlie catching me in his arms and covering my mouth with a kiss so scorching, I no longer feel the cold.

Back indoors, I glance at the clock. It's time! I'm so on edge, I pace the room and wonder how I'll get through the evening. A few minutes later, a knock. My heart is galloping. I open the front door and there stands Charlie, handsome as ever, clutching a festive wine gift bag. He looks anxious, but then I remember something Vincent said about him that day in the hospital: *Any man who acts that nervous around a woman must have powerful feelings for her.*

Heartened by those wise words, I trust that Charlie and I will be all right. I utter silent thanks to Vincent for helping us find our way, thinking how delighted he would have been to witness this moment. Then I greet Charlie with a warm smile as he crosses the threshold back into my life.

THE END

Don't miss the sequel to My Year of Casual Acquaintances:

The Unexpected Guests
– available late 2024

When a renowned author becomes the reluctant host to a misbehaving widow and a woman with a troubled past, he and his two guests struggle to conquer their demons . . . or lose the person closest to their hearts.

Visit https://ruthfstevens.com to sign up to receive publishing updates.

Excerpt: Chapter 1

Have a drink. Eat dinner. Break up with her.

As Margaret opened the door, Charlie reminded himself to stay on track with his game plan. She'd told him she was serving lasagna, and mouth-watering aromas enveloped him as he entered the cozy, waterfront apartment. On the coffee table, a bottle of champagne nestled in an ice bucket, its stainless steel surface glistening with beads of condensation. The eating and drinking portions of the evening were already a fait accompli.

Margaret looked good – *too* good – in jeans and a clingy red cashmere V-neck sweater, her soft brown curls falling to her shoulders. The breaking up part of the agenda might not be so easy. "Break up" was probably the wrong term, considering they'd barely seen each other during the past six months. Their relationship had been a whirlwind affair – only one short, passionate month. Charlie had fallen for Margaret – fallen hard; but she'd broken things off without warning last June, and the rejection wounded him to the core. But now she'd asked him to dinner, making no secret of the fact that reconciliation was her goal.

"Charlie. I'm glad you came." Her face lit up with a welcoming smile.

"Hi, Margaret. I thought you might like to serve this with dinner." He thrust a package toward her – a bottle of wine inside a knitted Christmas gift bag with candy cane striping, tied at the top with a red ribbon from which a pair of jingle bells dangled. All at once the bag appeared silly, embarrassing even. But he was glad he'd brought it. If nothing else, it created a physical wedge between them, a barrier that kept them from touching or kissing.

"Thank you," she said. "Do I need to chill this?"

"No, it's a red. Sangiovese." He had to stop himself from adding *your favorite*. He mustn't sound nostalgic. It might encourage her. She motioned for him to sit on the couch as she popped the cork on the champagne bottle and picked up a pair of crystal flutes, filling each glass with the bubbly liquid. Champagne seemed inappropriate, yet he couldn't accuse Margaret of a social faux pas in choosing it. She had no way of knowing he'd come on a mission of closure, not celebration.

In the December darkness, Margaret's place felt warmer and more intimate than he'd remembered. The recessed lights were dimmed. Candles flickered on the dining table. In the distance, looking out beyond the sliding door that led to the balcony, he could see Christmas lights twinkling from the masts of sailboats docked in King Harbor in Los Angeles's South Bay area. The effect was charming. Margaret had set the stage for a romantic evening. Her texted invitation was clear on that point.

Margaret: You gave Nomi a second chance. Now, how about me? One chance, please, to show you how things have changed. How I have changed. Dinner at my place next Friday, 7 p.m.?

Though Margaret was not a writer of fiction like Charlie, she edited a technical journal, and the woman knew how to turn a phrase. The words *second chance* echoed the title of Charlie's newest novel, about a woman named Nomi who sought forgiveness after cruelly driving away her husband. In the end, the husband took her back. Margaret (who had never been cruel, merely honest) wanted from Charlie the same consideration he'd granted his own protagonist - another chance to make things right. But it was too late for that.

This wasn't the first time in the past few months that Margaret had been in contact. In early November, she'd recruited him to visit a fan named Vincent at a senior home where she volunteered. Then she'd turned up at one of Charlie's book signing events. The dinner invitation soon followed. Perhaps he should have turned her down, but he'd decided to meet face-to-face and explain why he couldn't pick up where they left off six months ago. That was the plan - to let her down gently but firmly and close the door on their relationship once and for all.

• • •

"That was scrumptious," he said, laying his fork across the empty plate.

"Beginner's luck. I've never made it before." Margaret laughed softly, her dark gaze warm and inviting. The delicious white lasagna - his favorite - told Charlie how much effort she'd made to please him.

He was struck, as always, by how young she seemed for a woman of fifty. It wasn't just the candlelight working in her favor; her skin was smooth, her cheekbones pronounced, her hair natural, her expression animated. No one would ever call Margaret gorgeous, but she had an aura about her that Charlie found more alluring than any classic expression of feminine beauty.

Dammit. He shouldn't have come.

"I can't pretend cooking has become a new passion. But I've been changing a lot of things about my life."

Here we go. Over champagne and dinner, they'd confined their conversation to safe topics. They spoke at length about the early success of *Second Chance,* published the week prior to Thanksgiving. They discussed their friend Sunny Ericsson; he learned from Margaret that she was planning to move back from the San Francisco area. And they lamented that the holiday season was always so hectic.

But Margaret was pivoting to a more serious subject. This would be the perfect time for him to segue into his rehearsed remarks. *I'm glad you've made positive changes, Margaret, but I can't be part of your life going forward. When you broke things off, I had an extremely tough time.*

Perhaps the worst part had been the effect on his writing. *Second Chance* was already being prepared for publication when Margaret gave him the bad news. Charlie was trying to build momentum on a new manuscript back then, but after their breakup he had frozen in his tracks – unable to write, unable to focus. This had never happened to him before, not even when Bet died of a stroke more than four years earlier. Back then, work had been a soothing balm, a way to escape the traumatic shock of his wife's unexpected death.

After enduring a much graver loss, why did he fall apart over Margaret? It made no sense. He'd given up trying to puzzle it out, concluding only that he was better off staying unattached. He couldn't risk letting another romantic rejection disrupt his success as an author after so many years of disciplined work. But he didn't share this with Margaret. Instead, he said, "Why don't we step outside for some fresh air?"

"Great idea. It's stuffy in here."

Out on the balcony, they gazed down at the distant marina. "Do you hear that?" Margaret asked, cupping one hand to her ear.

"Carolers," said Charlie. "I hear them, but I don't see them."

"They're way down on the docks, but the wind is blowing the sound toward us." It was a chilly evening by California standards, cold enough for them to see their breath. Margaret shivered. If Charlie was being a gentleman, he'd offer his jacket or put an arm around her. But no. There'd be none of that.

"It's colder than I realized," Charlie said. "Maybe we should go back indoors."

"Listen to us—it's too hot, it's too cold," she said, lightly diffusing the awkwardness.

On the way in from the balcony, Charlie stumbled lightly over a rawhide dog bone. "You have a dog?" he asked as they took their seats back at the dining table.

"Petey. Do you remember him? He's the Wheaten terrier who was with me at the senior home."

Charlie thought back on his meeting with Vincent, a kindly old gentleman who knew all of Charlie's novels. How nervous Charlie had been that day, seeing Margaret for the first time in months. She'd seemed tongue-tied as well, and he recalled the way Vincent tried to build them both up, singing each one's praises to the other. Charlie suspected Margaret had an ulterior motive in inviting him. But he only saw her for a few minutes during his hurried visit. He also recalled the handsome terrier lying by Vincent's wheelchair, doing his job as a therapy dog. "I remember Petey. But I didn't know he lived with you."

"Long story, but I have him on a sort of shared custody basis with his original owner. She's moving to New Jersey sometime in January, and then Petey will be with me full-time."

"Ah. And how is Vincent doing?"

"He—Vincent died," she said, looking down at her uncleared dinner plate and tracing the rim with one finger.

"Oh, no."

"He had a serious heart attack a couple of weeks after you met him. When I visited him at the hospital, they'd moved him out of the ICU, and he seemed to be recovering. But he didn't make it."

"I'm sorry to hear that. I could see you two were good friends."

"At the hospital that day, he talked about you."

"He did?"

"Yes. He told me how much it meant for him to meet you." Margaret glanced up, tears filling her eyes. She looked so vulnerable, he half-wanted to slip his arms around her. Why did he feel this confusing urge to hold her when he'd come to push her away?

Acknowledgements

Whipping a manuscript into shape is a bit like conditioning one's body at the gym. A solo endeavor doesn't achieve the best results. It takes the time and expertise of a dedicated team.

In thanking my own unofficial team, deepest appreciation goes to my dear friend and personal editor, Mary Todd. She continues to dazzle me with her delivery of profound insights, combined with uncanny attention to miniscule details. And through it all, Mary never grows tired of (or bored *with*) correcting my prepositions!

I'm also grateful to my three critique group colleagues – Julie Mayerson Brown, Mary Jo Hazard, and Tricia Hopper Zacher – for their invaluable feedback. They are skillful writers and kind but honest critics. The four of us started the journey through this manuscript with weekly live meetings, and we then learned how to navigate Zoom together when the pandemic changed everything.

A big thank you as well to Amy Gordon and Erica Karlin. Their thoughtful notes led to important improvements as I continued to revise this work.

Heartfelt thanks to my other early readers for their comments and enthusiasm: Tish Andrewartha, Katherine Bradford, Donna Israel, Mary McKinney, Lisa Moeller, Winifred Morice, and Ritas Smith.

To Debbi Gelbart, thank you for briefing me on therapy dog training and certification.

To my former client Camfil APC, and two trade publications – *Powder & Bulk Engineering* and *Powder/Bulk Solids* – thank you for instilling in me a knowledge of the dry processing industries.

To Becky Marietta, huge thanks for your insightful editorial feedback and for listening as well as critiquing. My gratitude, as well, to Julee Balko, Andrea Couture, Joani Elliott, Marsha

Jacobson, Susan Paxton, Leslie A. Rasmussen, and S.M. Stevens, fellow authors whose work I highly respect.

To my fellow AlzAuthors and Renegades, thank you for supporting me through the trials and tribulations of this book's publishing journey.

To Reagan Rothe and the team at Black Rose Writing, I am indebted to you for turning my dream of being traditionally published into a reality.

To my family and friends, I applaud you for supporting and encouraging my insane efforts to launch a creative writing career late in life. True, I've always been a writer. But after all these years, it's fun to focus on topics more glamorous than industrial dust collection and metal building construction.

Seaside Fitness, the health club where much of the action is centered, is a fictitious place; but those familiar with the South Bay of Los Angeles will see similarities to The Bay Club Redondo Beach. For years, as a work-from-home P.R. professional and then playwright and novelist, my fitness club memberships have been a valued part of my daily routine. Not only do I go for the workout – I go for the people. Though admittedly, like the narrator of my story, I don't know everybody's names.

So, thank you to The Bay Club and the other fitness organizations I've frequented over the years . . . for offering me social interaction with like-minded people; for stimulating me to try everything from hip-hop to goat yoga; and, of course, for inspiring this novel.

Finally, without an audience, my story would have no more resonance than that tree falling in the middle of the forest. So I'll end by thanking my readers.

See you at the gym.

About the Author

Photograph courtesy of Richard Ruthsatz

Ruth F. Stevens likes to create stories that will make readers laugh and cry. A former public relations executive in New York and Los Angeles, she is a produced playwright and author of a previous novel, *Stage Seven*, which was a featured selection of national online book club and Alzheimer's awareness organizations. Ruth is a proud member of the Women's Fiction Writers Association and the Dramatists Guild of America and serves as a volunteer and acquisitions editor for AlzAuthors.

Ruth lives in Torrance, California with her husband. In her spare time, she enjoys travel, hiking, hip-hop and fitness classes, yoga, Broadway musicals, wine tasting, leading a book club, and visiting her grandsons in NYC.

Visit Ruth at: https://ruthfstevens.com/ and consider signing up for her monthly newsletter to receive publishing updates, book reviews, and special offers.

Note from Ruth F. Stevens

Word-of-mouth is crucial for any author to succeed. If you enjoyed *My Year of Casual Acquaintances,* please leave a review online—anywhere you are able. Even if it's just a sentence or two. It would make all the difference and would be very much appreciated.

Thanks!
Ruth F. Stevens

Printed in the USA
CPSIA information can be obtained
at www.ICGtesting.com
JSHW022046021024
70975JS00001B/5